S0-BZA-558

THREE AT THE DOOR

ALSO BY NANCY PRICE

NOVELS

A NATURAL DEATH
AN ACCOMPLISHED WOMAN
SLEEPING WITH THE ENEMY
NIGHT WOMAN
NO ONE KNOWS
L'INCENDIAIRE
(Published in French)
UN ÉCART DE JEUNESSE
(Published in French)
L'ENFANT DU MENSONGE
(Published in French)
200 MEN, ONE WOMAN
STOLEN AWAY
PLAYING WITH FIRE
NEVER BEFORE

POETRY

TWO VOICES AND A MOON

THREE AT THE DOOR

A novel by
NANCY PRICE

A Malmarie Press Book
Malmarie, Inc.
Windermere, Florida

Copyright © 2018 by Nancy Price

All rights reserved. No part of this book may be reproduced in any form or by any electronic or mechanical means including information storage and retrieval systems without permission in writing from the publisher, except by a reviewer who may quote brief passages in a review.

The names, incidents, places and characters in this book are the product of the author's imagination. Any resemblance to actual events, locales, or persons alive or dead, is completely coincidental.

First Printing

Malmarie Press and colophon are registered trademarks of Malmarie, Inc.

ISBN-10: 0-9744818-7-4
ISBN-13: 978-0-9744818-7-6
Library of Congress Control Number: 2018937247
First Malmarie Press hardcover printing 2018
Illustrated by the author

Poems by Nancy Price in this novel previously appeared in the following publications:
    "Hackberry" in THE NATION, 11-10-'69
    "Trick or Treat" in THE ATLANTIC, 11-'67
    "Childbirth" in CHILDREN OF THE MOON, 1973
    "Cassandra and the Double-decked Doom" in THE ATLANTIC, 5-'63

Malmarie, Inc., 11915 Cave Run Avenue, Windermere, FL 34786

E-mail: nancypricebooks@aol.com   Website: nancypricebooks.com

ACKNOWLEDGEMENTS

My son, David Thompson, and my good friends, Barbara Lounsberry and Amy Lockard, have read *Three At the Door* in manuscript, and have offered many helpful suggestions. Charlotte Thompson, my son John's widow, and her family help send my books around the world. I thank them all.

I am grateful to Cedar Falls, Iowa, my home. Cedar Falls celebrated my novels and book of poetry in 2017 with a stone erected in Seerley Park (one of the settings used in *Three At the Door*). The film of my novel, *Sleeping with the Enemy*, was shown in that park, and tours brought visitors to the Cedar Falls homes I have lived in or used in my writing.

My work was also honored by The Hearst Center for the Arts in Cedar Falls: they hosted a discussion of my third novel and its film, held a book signing, and mounted displays of my book illustrations.

Such relatives, friends and neighbors offer constant encouragement to a writer—I am indebted to them all.

This book is dedicated to my son, David Malcolm Thompson.
Day by day, he makes it possible for me to continue to write and
illustrate my books, and I thank him for his constant encouragement.

THREE AT THE DOOR

1

"Honor!"

Brandon Lombard was yelling for her.

Honor Sloan was hiding—crouched behind a bar in a hotel suite. The University of Iowa Class of '55 had rented two rooms and a band. Tomorrow was Graduation Day, and the graduation party was on, wall to wall.

"Honor!"

Honor was tired, she was hot, she was furious, and she was wearing the garments of torture that college girls thought were absolutely necessary: spike heels, and (hidden from sight but hideously uncomfortable) a rubber "iron maiden" girdle with holes that left her body polka-dotted with dime-sized studs of pink flesh (how glad she was to hurry home after a date and *get it off!*), and a pointy bra that squeezed her breasts into two boned funnels strapped to her ribs.

The bar above Honor had empty beer bottles on it, and a plastic wedding cake. Brandon Lombard had left it there. Its plastic bride and groom watched her with flat black eyes.

The band stopped for a moment, and Honor heard Brandon laughing. She hadn't wanted to come to the hotel party; it would be wild—even wilder than others he'd made her go to—but this was her graduation.

She was too mad to cry. Ten minutes before, Brandon had grabbed her and jammed an engagement ring on her finger while the party crowd watched, clapped, shouted. He wouldn't let Honor go—he held her with one hand and waved the cake with the other. "Play the wedding march!" he yelled to the band, and he paraded Honor back and forth, yelling: *"Mr. and Mrs. Brandon Lombard, future bride and groom!"*

A month before she had told him she would never marry him.

Brandon was already drunk. He was shouting for her again.

Honor raised herself high enough above the bar to see him. Couples were trying to dance, but college boys had begun throwing furniture. She saw Brandon fall against an overturned table, then stagger away holding a chair overhead.

A half-dozen girls had joined the party now—they were wearing twice the makeup and half the clothes of the other girls. Honor crouched below the bar and crawled toward the door of the suite. Newcomers were coming in. Honor jumped up, pushed through the crowd, and was out of there…but what if Brandon had seen her go?

She looked down a hall that led in both directions—he'd see her running away.

Hide. Hide. A door across the hall was marked "Service." Honor yanked the door open, jammed her back against mops and brooms, pulled the door shut, and stood in the dark, listening to yells and the band's drum-beat from the suite's open door. She held her breath as someone ran past her hiding place. Brandon?

Was Brandon after her? She eased the closet door open. But the man running down the hall wasn't Brandon—he was bigger and taller—Brandon's brother, Joe Lombard. Had she seen him

2

across the room as she ran out? He'd come for his brother's graduation?

Honor shut herself in the closet again just as she heard someone dash past to the other end of the hall. When she opened the door enough to look, she saw Joe—again. Why was he running back and forth?

The closet reeked of soap and ammonia. Honor shifted her weight from one spike-heeled sandal to the other. She had worked all day filling suitcases and boxes with everything she owned. Her feet hurt. Her back ached. The footsteps died away.

Then she heard a steady creaking sound grow louder and louder under the party's noise. It came down the hall and stopped outside her closet. A woman's voice said: "You go on and look in there. Go on."

Another woman's voice said: "Yeah. That's some godawful mess. We'll be workin all night. Some of the stuff is busted."

"My kids are home alone," a soft, hopeless voice said. "No food, not since yesterday."

Honor could hear them breathing. She opened the closet door enough to see no one in the hall but three cleaning women and their cart, and came out to face them in her party clothes.

"Here," Honor said, "This is for you." She pulled some bills from her pocket, gave one to each woman, and ran.

Iowa City was soaked in a midnight downpour. Honor stopped under a shop's canopy to pull off her high heels and her best nylons. She'd paid too much for those shoes. Brandon had wanted her to buy them. She ran into the rain again—

And there, just as she reached the curb, was Joe, Brandon's big brother, driving up and opening his car door.

"Come out of the rain!" he called.

"Thanks," she said, and crawled in, trying to wipe her shoes with the tops of her nylons where snags might not run. Joe had come for his brother's graduation. Did he still believe she was going to marry Brandon?

They passed university buildings that were only blurs in the rain.

Joe pulled to the curb under her rooming house's dripping trees. He knew where she rented a room? What could she say except "Thanks"?

3

"Are you marrying Brandon?" he said.

She stared at him. "Brandon hasn't told you anything?"

"No.

" I told him weeks ago I wouldn't marry him."

"Never?"

"Never."

"He was playing a trick, then? Parading you around with the ring and the cake?"

"I'm sorry," Honor said. "You must have thought—"

"Yes."

"Never! No!" Honor snatched her shoes and nylons, said "Thanks for the ride!" and ran upstairs to her rooming house door. The blare of a loud radio met her, shouting about McCarthy and Un-American Activities. The widow who owned the place was nearly deaf.

Honor ran upstairs to her small room, and didn't turn on the lamp. Dim glow from a streetlight fell on suitcases in a corner and boxes stacked at the door. As Honor pulled off all of her wet clothes but her slip, something caught on the dress hem—it was the engagement ring Brandon had jammed on her finger, yelling "Bride and groom!"

Was Brandon too drunk to come after her?

Honor crawled across the bed to look from her window. A car turned the corner and stopped at the curb—Brandon! She leaped up to shut the door, but it didn't have a lock or key. Then she saw the car wasn't Brandon's—it was Joe again, alone at the wheel, looking up at her window.

She ducked out of sight on the bed. When she dared to look again, Joe was still there.

The rain had stopped. Joe had come back. Why? She lay down, listening for steps on the stairs under the radio's chatter.

"Stay away from my brother," Brandon had told her. "Joe always wants anything I've got, and he's taken boxing lessons. He's a botanist, for God's sake. Wild about *flowies*. Got nothing in his head but Latin names. Millions."

After a while she looked from the window again. Joe wasn't there. Gone back to his brother's graduation party. It wouldn't be over until dawn.

Honor was too tired to think. She hadn't slept the night before, packing everything she owned except her graduation clothes,

4

worried that Brandon would come. He trailed her everywhere—
he came to her room and wouldn't go home...drunk, of course.
He'd try to get her to make love, then pass out on her bed, and
sometimes he was still there when she went to class.

Brandon was pretty drunk now. She hoped so. But suddenly
she slid out of bed in her slip and ran downstairs to be sure the
front door was locked. It was. Her landlady had already put her
cat out and let him in again.

And where was she going to go now, when graduation was
over...when she had her poetry awards...when she had no money?
She wasn't going to her wedding. She wasn't going to Chicago
with Brandon to find an apartment while he began his new job.
No. Never. She crawled in bed, and fell asleep too soon to hear
the landlady put her cat out the front door.

Suddenly—horrible as a nightmare—someone was sprawling
on Honor, pulling down the blanket... she woke screaming
against a hot face and filthy words...shoving a heavy body away...

It wasn't a nightmare—it was Brandon—she saw his furious
eyes in light from the window. The radio downstairs was still
blatting as he yanked her off the bed to the floor.

"No!" Honor screamed. "No! Brandon! Don't—" but he
bruised her arms with hard hands. He was drunk and strong and
yelling dirty, awful, slurred words as she beat him with her fists—
he was so heavy—he forced himself between her legs until she lay
limp, afraid he would break them, or crack her spine. He hurt
her over and over, then crawled off, his whiskey breath hot on her
face, and ran.

Honor sprawled on the dusty rug. Her body hurt where it
had never hurt before. Her throat was raw from screaming and
begging and yelling. Footsteps pounded downstairs past the
widow's loud radio. The front door slammed.

After a while Honor pulled herself to her hands and knees and crawled on the bed. Dawn was breaking. The rain had stopped. The widow had turned off her radio.

When Honor stood up, her whole body ached. *Hurry*, she kept sobbing. *Hurry.* She wiped off blood, keeping watch out the window, and pulled on underpants and jeans, a shirt and sandals, then packed her party clothes in a suitcase, cramming them on top of white slippers, a wedding dress, a veil. Limping up and down stairs, she loaded her old car with all she owned. The sun came up as she pulled away from the curb, looking in both directions along the street.

First morning light struck campus buildings as Honor drove past—the dawn of graduation day. Streets were almost empty, but she kept watch in the rear-view mirror. At last Iowa City disappeared at the skyline. Honor was alone on a highway that was only a narrow crease through miles of spring corn.

She began to cry until she couldn't see the road. When she passed an overgrown farm lane, she turned around, drove down ruts out of sight of the highway, and parked. Her shirt was wet with tears, and stuck to her skin. A breeze blew through the half-open car window with the smell of plowed fields.

Her back hurt. Brandon's jaw had jammed into her neck, and his knees had ground against hers. She pulled up the legs of her jeans to see blue bruises. Her arms were bruised, too, and the rear-view mirror showed blood on her neck. The nasty names Brandon called her…what was he telling her, yelling, slamming her on the floor with the bleeding and bruises? Whatever he meant, he had meant to hurt her.

Go to her graduation? Look Brandon and his mother and his brother in the face as if she could fight back, even when she'd been raped? Limp up the steps of the dais to get her diploma and her awards? Listen to praise from Brandon and Joe and their mother—praise she would never hear from her own buried mother and father? Or would they already know she was going to walk away with her diploma and honors, and never see any of them again?

Salty tears ran down to her mouth. Should she go back, wear that robe, climb to that dais, let Brandon go on chasing her, begging her, raping her? Show Brandon she hated him while he forced her down over and over and filled her with absolute loathing—

He'd be after her.

When he was sober enough, he'd try to find her. Hurt her again.

What would a man like that do to his children?

Birds were twittering in bushes along the farm road. Morning air, blown through her car window, smelled of plowed earth. Too tired to think, too tired to cry any more, she folded her winter coat into a pillow, stretched out on the front seat, and fell asleep in sunlight flickering through leaves.

When Honor woke, she stared at a car roof, wondering where she was—something had happened...ah...her body told her when she tried to sit up. It told her she was somebody different, somebody who hurt all over and was parked in a farm lane, pushing a car door open, trying to stand, trying not to remember that she was on the other side of something she didn't want to remember. She pulled down her underpants and jeans and crouched in the ditch, painfully, found a tissue in her pocket, then pulled up her clothes and crawled behind the wheel.

A tractor growled somewhere in the farm fields. If a farmer found her there, he'd ask questions: *Who was she? Hiding from what?*

She looked at her watch. It was three o'clock. Her morning graduation had been over for hours. She hadn't worn a cap and gown. She hadn't climbed to a stage to get prizes and a diploma.

And Brandon would be hunting her.

Honor grabbed the wheel, started the car with aching hands and arms, turned around, and drove back to the highway. Her hand on the wheel wore a ring. An engagement ring.

She looked down the highway in both directions.

She would have to hide.

She hadn't told anyone where she was going.

She started for Cedar Falls.

A sign at the edge of Cedar Falls said: *Home of Iowa State Teachers College.*

Honor parked in front of the Black Hawk Hotel and went into the stale, smoky air of the lobby. "Do you have a town telephone book?" she asked the desk clerk. "I'm looking for a town address."

If there was no Vergilena Townsend... Honor's hand shook as she trailed her finger down a page.

There it was: "V. J. Townsend, 2309 Iowa Street."

Honor asked the clerk for directions, left the town's few blocks of false-fronted buildings, and drove under arching elms, street after street. In less than a mile, she turned a corner, turned another. She pulled up halfway along a one-block city park. A big, old-fashioned house across the street spread its porch and gables high on a bank.

Two flights of stairs to the porch...Honor ached with every step as she crossed the street, climbed step by step, and rang the doorbell. She waited, and thought she saw a curtain in a front window twitch.

A half-dozen children ran across the street. Park swings began their slow creaking back and forth in afternoon shade.

She rang again and waited. At last she turned the doorknob. The door wasn't locked. When she took a few steps through a front hall, there was a woman in a wheel chair staring at her.

"Forgive me for just coming in," Honor said. "I rang the doorbell. I was afraid you hadn't heard me."

The woman was swaddled in a shapeless robe that Honor's mother would have called a "wrapper," and her gray hair looked like a wig worn backward. She sat among piles of newspapers, magazines, stacked books and boxes and said nothing, staring at Honor with startled, angry eyes.

"Are you Vergilena Townsend?" Honor said. "I don't think we've ever met. I'm Honor. Your niece. Honor Sloan. My mother named me for your mother."

She took a few more steps into the room. The woman said nothing.

"I'm your sister Maryflora's daughter," Honor said after a few moments. "You're still living in Cedar Falls! I hoped you were. I've just come from Iowa City."

The woman looked Honor over, head to foot, that was all.

"Are you living alone?" Honor asked.

Suddenly Vergilena struggled to stand, then hopped a few hops, let herself down in an overstuffed chair, pulled a footstool nearer, put both feet on the footstool and looked at Honor over her old black slippers as if they were a picket fence.

"Did you have an accident?" Honor asked.

"Broke my leg," Vergilena said.

"What a shame," Honor said. "How did you do it?"

"Fell."

"Quite a while ago?"

"A month."

"Perhaps..." Honor began...

"I get along," Vergilena said.

9

For a minute or two the room was quiet except for the barking of dogs in the park.

"I'm so glad I found you," Honor said. "You're the only relative I have left, I think. You had another sister beside my mother."

"Dead."

"I'm alone, too, since my folks died last winter," Honor said. "I just graduated from the University of Iowa today. Class of '55." She waited for a while and then said, "Now I have to hunt for a job. I was going to marry a man named Brandon Lombard, graduating along with me." She held up her left hand to show the diamond ring. "For a while we thought we had our lives all planned, but it won't happen."

Vergelina said nothing. A living-room window was open. Children in the park banged on a slide with their heels, a drum roll.

"Vergilena..." Honor began...

"I'm Lena. Haven't been called Vergilena since I could leave home."

"Lena?" Honor said. "It's certainly a shorter name. I'm sorry I used the old one when I wrote you about the funeral for my folks. Last December. I hope my note reached you."

"I was in London. What happened?"

"To my parents? It was a heavy snowfall, and they skidded off the road, and were thrown from the car—"

"You aren't getting married?"

"We dated our senior year," Honor said. "It just hasn't worked out."

"You've jilted him?"

"Yes. Now I have."

"Why?"

"He drank."

Lena waited a while, and then said, "Good reason."

"I thought so," Honor said. Children shrieked in the park.

10

"Aunt Lena..." Honor leaned forward on the chair's shifting pile of magazines. "Now that I've graduated and won't be married, I have nowhere to go while I look for a job. Could I possibly stay with you for a few days until I find one? You've got a big city next door: Waterloo. And there's a state college here in town."

Lena didn't answer. Honor said, "I could help you around your house—I'd be glad to."

"I get along."

"I'd be so grateful," Honor said. "If you could possibly..."

"There's a bed upstairs."

"Oh, thank you! Thank you!" Honor said. "I'll try not to be any trouble." She limped out to her car and returned with a suitcase.

Lena looked at Honor over her large black slippers. "Front room," she said.

"You're so kind," Honor said. "I didn't have anywhere to go." Lena didn't answer.

Honor carried the suitcase upstairs, step by step, put it down at the top, and found a bathroom, an old-fashioned place with the toilet tank hung on a wall and lime-crusted sink faucets that dribbled. Then she peered into four almost empty bedrooms. They had views of back and side gardens, but the triple windows in the big front room showed Iowa Street and the park. There was an old double bed in a corner. Honor pulled the bedspread back to find two pillows without cases on a bare mattress.

It was dusty up there, but clean. Honor sat on the bed and looked at the shady park. A woman pushed a child on the park swings.

She limped downstairs after a while. Lena was reading a newspaper in her wheelchair. Honor waited until Lena finished a page and folded herself a new one; then she said, "Would you like me to make you some supper?"

"They already brought mine. 'Supper For Seniors.' " Lena rattled her paper.

"There's bedding and pillows in a closet upstairs. Is it all right if I make up a bed for myself?"

"Yes," Lena said. She tossed her newspaper on a newspaper pile, shut off her lamp, and rolled her wheelchair into what looked like a dining room. Its door slid from the wall; Lena pulled it shut behind her.

Honor went upstairs to a bare front room lit by a single light bulb at the ceiling. She spread a pad on the bed, shook pillows into cases, and tucked sheets, wincing with pain as she worked.

When she opened her suitcase on the bed, there was her wedding gown she'd bought months before, when Brandon had asked her to marry him. She'd often shut herself in her room those December days to smile and dream and stroke a second-hand, "gently used" dress from someone else's happy day.

The closet had a few hangers in it; Honor hung the wedding gown on one, shut her suitcase in the closet with it, undressed and climbed in bed.

Children called in the park. Swings creaked. A branch grated against a wall.

She was hungry. Food at the graduation party had been good, but Brandon hadn't given her time to eat it. She hadn't wanted to ask for dinner from a scowling aunt in a wheelchair. She had a bed. She had a place to hide. And Brandon would go to his new Chicago job, working for the rich father of one of his rich friends.

After a while she got up to bring the wedding dress from the closet. It lay beside her on the bed, pale even as the room grew dark: a white, empty shape of a woman with a wire hanger for a head.

Honor listened to small spring leaves tossing in the wind, and couldn't sleep. She was hungry. Then she suddenly remembered two candy bars in her suitcase, and ate them slowly, bite by bite, remembering how her mother and father had hated Lena for years.

For a long time, all her parents told her was that Lena was the middle girl of three Townsend sisters, Rosabella, Vergileana and her mother, Maryflora. All the Townsend girls had names from the heroines of romance books their mother read. The beautiful sister, Rosabella, had eloped at twenty—gone somewhere, or nowhere, who knew?

Honor nibbled at her last candy bar, looking through her windows to the park's glowing lights. Her mother had married young—too young to suit her parents. The Townsends wouldn't give the newly-wed Sloans a cent, or come to their wedding, because they were too young, and they weren't being married in a church. So Honor never saw her Townsend grandparents, though they lived only a mile away from the Sloans.

Then the old folks grew helpless, and the woman in the wheelchair downstairs had to take care of them for years—until they died, secretly rich, and Lena got all their money—went to Wellesley when she was forty, went on a trip to Europe, first class.

Down in the dining room, Lena lay wide awake. There was hardly room for a bed in that room —just a twin bed with a thin mattress. Her feet were almost jammed against an old buffet, and her head was in the corner.

After a while she crawled into her wheelchair, went to the kitchen and drank some milk. Going back to bed, she thought she heard sobbing upstairs.

That girl was one of those Sloans. She was limping. She looked like Rosabella. Another one of those Sloans—wanting something for nothing—never helping with the old folks, not for years... letting birthdays go by. Christmas. New Years. Easter. Never brought so much as a covered dish, or a diaper.

13

3

Early morning sunlight crept across the floor to Honor's bed. She sat up—where was she? Graduation...she must put on her black robe, walk to the platform—she almost leaped out of bed with the excitement—

No. Hard hands slamming her down. A woman in a wheelchair. A wrinkled wedding dress...sore...she was sore...

Birds were singing. The big, uncurtained windows showed her a green park.

Honor hung the wedding dress in the closet and limped to the bathroom, where the shower dribbled, but there was warm water and soap, and a towel on a hook. When she was dressed, she went downstairs a step at a time. The living room and kitchen were empty. She knocked on the dining-room door.

14

Lena, sitting in her wheelchair, slid the door open a crack.

"Would you like me to make you some breakfast?" Honor asked.

"Oatmeal," Lena said. "Orange juice. Coffee."

Honor found the kitchen. The counters were piled with canisters, boxes of crackers, prunes and oatmeal, knives, bowls, saucepans. Cabinet doors were worn white in places where they weren't scarred. Sagging curtains had a border of faded roosters pecking forever among gray sunflowers. She cooked oatmeal, poured orange juice, and found a placemat and silverware in the dining-room buffet. Flowers for the breakfast table? She went out the front door and around the house and found what was left of a big garden. Weeds had almost smothered flowerbeds and a patio, but a few violets were blooming. She picked some, and found a jelly glass for a vase.

Stacks of papers and checkbooks and ledgers covered the dining room table. Honor was piling them on one side when Lena rolled in from the hall, wearing a navy blue "wrapper" from neck to chin. "Well," she said, scowling at the half-bare table. "Just how am I going to find my account books and bills and letters in that pile you've made?" She parked herself in front of the placemat and stared at the violets.

"I'm sorry," Honor said. "I'll put your things back when you're through. Could you possibly let me see your newspaper when you've read it? I need to look for a job."

"Yes," Lena said.

When Honor had eaten at the kitchen table and washed the dishes, she said to Lena: "I'm going to shop for groceries tonight. Would you like me to shop for you too?"

Lena said No.

Spring sunlight shone on the park's greening bank as Honor went out to her car. She carried her second suitcase and her boxes up to her room, then drove around the corner to Seerley Boulevard. Only a few blocks along the boulevard, there was the Iowa State Teachers College campus! When she parked, she saw the library, close enough to limp to—there it was: her familiar home of bookshelves... worlds to explore... silence.

All day Honor wandered from library aisle to library aisle, stopping only to have lunch and supper at a nearby restaurant. A waitress told her there was a grocery store two blocks away, so at sunset Honor left the library to park in the grocery's lot, climb stiffly from her car—

Brandon was there! Brandon! He stood in front of Honor, blocking her way. "I can't stand it," he said.

"Go away," Honor said, trying to limp past him to the store.

He grabbed her arm. "I saw you coming from the library and followed you! We've got to talk." She could smell that he'd been drinking.

"Go away!"

"That deaf creature at your rooming house finally gave me your forwarding address—"

"Go home!" Honor yanked her arm away from him and found a cart.

Brandon followed her down an aisle. "You just ran away!"

Honor tried to turn a corner, but Brandon wouldn't let her pass. "I was drunk!" he yelled, holding on to her cart. "I know I was, and I shouldn't have done it, but why did you run away like that? You always said you loved me! I'm crazy about you, and I got the ring and the cake for the party, and planned the wedding march and all! Just for fun!"

"Fun," Honor said.

"But you ditched me at that party, and afterwards those guys gave me a hard time. You should have heard them! Brother Joe was there. They said I'd been left at the altar—and they bet I hadn't even laid you, and you probably couldn't get a man up anyway, and what dumb jock would buy a shirt without trying it on? They just got me so mad I socked them—couldn't help it— and Joe hit me and *called you names*—and I didn't know what I was doing when I came to your place, but what did it matter if we—" Honor turned to glare at him, and shoved the cart at him until he let her pass.

"We were planning to get *married*!" Brandon yelled after her. "Weren't we? I bought the ring and everything and my new boss in Chicago said we could use his church—and then you ran away! Even from our graduation! I thought you'd finally show up... everybody was asking..." his voice trailed away as he followed Honor. People were staring at them.

"I won't marry you. I don't want to see you, ever," Honor whispered, stopping to face him. "Ever. For your own good. I told you I wouldn't marry you. Weeks ago. And then you put a ring on my finger and paraded us around that party—and came

16

afterward—Oh! Get yourself straightened out before you ruin some woman's life along with yours. You're drinking your life away, but you won't drink mine." People were watching, so Honor whispered: "You called me terrible things. And then you..."

"I was really drunk."

"Milk," Honor said, and turned another corner to a dairy case.

"You were so beautiful...are so beautiful. I gave you the ring, didn't I? It's just that I couldn't—"

He stopped beside Honor, who was scowling at the price tag above the milk bottles. "I'm not going away!" he said.

"Here's your ring! Is that what you came for?" Honor yanked the diamond from her finger and threw it at him. It struck the milk case and rolled under it. Brandon groped for it on his knees while she grabbed two bottles of milk and limped off.

Brandon found the ring at last and followed her. Shoppers watched the limping girl and the shouting man. The louder Brandon yelled, the faster Honor limped. As they got to a rack of packaged bacon, Brandon was shouting that he loved her and she had to talk to him and how could she do this to him... and when he said that, Honor stopped and stared at him, and then grabbed a flat package of bacon and slapped his face with it.

Brandon's face got red, and he stopped yelling for a minute or two while Honor unloaded her cart and paid the cashier. But he started in again when she limped out the door with her loaded cart. Some of the shoppers stood at store windows to watch.

Brandon wouldn't let Honor load her groceries in her car. When she put one sack in, he took it out, and she put it back in. He stepped on a loaf of bread and squashed it flat, and cans fell out of Honor's sacks and rolled under cars.

Some shoppers in the lot stopped to help Honor. They couldn't do much about a broken milk bottle, or the bread. Brandon was shouting and slipping in spilled milk. Drivers and shoppers finally got Honor's groceries out from under cars and into the sacks, and shoved the sacks in her car, and crowded Brandon to one side while Honor climbed in, slammed her car door, and drove away.

Brandon got in his car and gunned it after Honor. He stayed right behind her until a truck cut in front of him and stopped him at a red light.

Honor drove down a block and swerved into Lena's narrow alley. Brandon caught sight of her as she turned, but she slammed to a stop in Lena's back drive, grabbed a sack of groceries, and started

17

for the garage built on to Lena's house. It had a side door, and she limped through, slammed the door and locked it. All Brandon could do was to pull in, park, and beat on the door, yelling.

"What's going on?" Lena asked when Honor came to the living room.

"The man I was going to marry." Honor was out of breath. "Brandon Lombard. He's banging on the door of your garage. I locked it. Don't let him in. I don't want to see him again. Ever."

Lena rolled her wheelchair to the front door and locked it. The doorbell rang. It rang while Honor put what was left of a sack of groceries on the kitchen table. It rang while she went to sit with Lena in a dark corner of her living room, because when Brandon stopped ringing the bell, he came to glare through the big living-room window, lit by the porch light.

"He's the one you jilted?" Lena said, while he banged on the glass. "Awfully good-looking. For a Peeping Tom."

"He chased me around the grocery store," Honor said. "Until he had to get down on his knees and find the engagement ring I threw at him." Honor stuck out her hand to show it was bare. "I slapped his face with a package of bacon and went out to my car with the grocery cart, but he wouldn't let me unload it. People helped me, and I got away."

"Wild man," Lena said. "What on earth—" Brandon began to ring the doorbell again, then knocked on the window while they stayed in their dark corner.

At last they heard more voices. Somebody called "Police!"

Lena rode her wheelchair to the front door and opened it.

"Ma'am?" the policeman said. "This fellow's worried about you. Thought something might have happened that you couldn't answer the doorbell. You all right?"

"I'm fine, but I don't want to talk to him," Lena said. "Tell him to go away." She shut the door.

Voices stopped. Car motors started.

In a few minutes Honor looked out the living-room window. "They're gone," she said. "Brandon still wants to marry me. That's what he's yelling about."

"I'm going to bed," Lena said.

"Aunt Lena!" Honor cried. "Brandon was so wonderful, I thought! We called ourselves the Perfect Companions last spring. Neither of us had any money, but we planned our wedding and our whole lives that summer! But when our senior year began last

18

fall, Brandon made friends with some of the football players, and started drinking. I tried not to notice that Brandon was turning into a drunk. I was so stupid....blind...but I got straight A's. Does that make any sense?"

"Not much," Lena said.

"And then—my folks died last December. I spent Christmas vacation and spring break doing all the things nobody else was there to do—bought the cemetery plots and the caskets, had the funeral, saw the lawyers, cleaned out their rented house..."

"Peeping Tom help you?"

"No. Never. One of his football friends invited him to Chicago for Christmas, and the spring break, too. I knew how much Brandon wanted to go—his friend's home was so fancy, so expensive. But Oh, Aunt Lena—couldn't I see...right then, after spring break? I've been so stupid! But finally, weeks ago, I gave back his engagement ring, and told him I wouldn't marry him. So I've 'left him at the altar.' The father of Brandon's football friend offered Brandon a job. Now Brandon has to tell him we aren't going to marry. And the football crowd made it hard for Brandon—you know how men treat a bridegroom who can't keep his bride! Brandon's furious."

"Well," Lena said. "I'm going to bed."

"I'm sorry to be so much trouble," Honor said. "I'll find a job as soon as I can, and rent a room somewhere to hide. Then Brandon won't keep you awake every night, banging on your windows and doors."

Lena watched Honor limp upstairs, then went to put on her nightgown and ease herself into bed. She settled her aching leg on a pillow. That girl looked like Rosabella, though she didn't have the red hair.

She heard what she thought was sobbing again. Rosabella would have thrown her engagement ring at a Peeping Tom, yes indeed, and slapped him with a package of bacon, too.

The next afternoon Honor looked from her bedroom window and saw Brandon getting out of his car.

She took the stairs down as fast as she could and found Lena. "Brandon's coming," she said. "Don't tell him I'm here."

Honor stayed out of sight, listening from the living room. Lena rolled herself out to her porch just as Brandon ran upstairs from the street.

19

"Hello," Honor heard Brandon say. "You're Miss Vergilena Townsend, I believe? Honor Sloan's Aunt Vergilena? I'm Brandon Lombard."

"I suppose you've come again to hammer on every window and door I've got," Lena said. "You're a nuisance that's not wanted."

"I'm awfully sorry about that," Brandon said. "I shouldn't have bothered you, but I'm desperate. I've come to see Honor. Her car's here."

"She's walked to a place to try for a job," Lena said. "And you're not coming in to wait for her, because I don't have a single bottle of whiskey or gin in the house. And you aren't welcome and never will be, not even with that smile."

"Aunt Vergilena—you've got to help me." He was trying to sound pitiful. "I love Honor. You know true love never does run smooth."

"You run smooth all right, but not smooth enough for me. Or my niece, either," Lena said. "I know a boy in the rough when

I see one, and you're just a kid. Going on thirteen, I'd say. You won't grow up—not until you've tried every other possibility. Out of the grubby age and into the grabby age—hell-bent after everything you don't know how to get yet. Think everything you want has your name on it, just because you're male. Your name's not on my niece, thank heaven. That girl's got sense. You go ahead and bang on every door and window in the world, and bust them, too. That's what teenage boys love to do. They're busters and breakers and wreckers and drinkers, and think it's such fun. Lord help a woman if one comes after her. Go home."

"You don't like me?"

"Are you in doubt? I can write you a note in words of one syllable and nail it on your chest to make an impression."

Brandon was quiet for a moment. Then he said, "Tell Honor I've come all the way from Chicago—"

"I'll do nothing of the kind," Lena said. "I don't know you. I don't want to know you. I haven't seen you. I hope I never see you again. Goodbye."

Brandon drove off.

Honor held the door open for Lena as she came from the porch. "Thanks so much," Honor said. "I was afraid he'd come here."

Lena rolled off to the kitchen. Honor stood for a moment, leaning against the closed front door, until the doorbell rang. Brandon!

"Supper For Seniors," a voice said. Honor opened the door, took the supper, thanked the woman, and carried the plate to the kitchen.

Lena was at the kitchen table. "He's back?" she said.

"It was just your dinner," Honor said. The two of them looked at the yellow-green, cooked-to-death vegetables, and a slab of gray meat.

Lena stirred the food on her plate with a fork.

"Do you really like these suppers?" Honor asked.

"No."

"And you don't like someone begging for a bed in your house and bothering you."

"No."

"But you like things clean and neat, don't you?" Honor said. "I can tell. The trouble is—you can't keep house much...not until your leg's healed. You could use someone to clean and cook ..."

"Everything's spread all over the place because I have to reach everything," Lena said. "And can't put away much. And can't clean much. And don't much care."

Brandon drove to Des Moines. He parked in the lot of The Hungry Chef restaurant, went around to the front, and saw his mother through the window.

"Mom?"

Emily Lombard swung around with a heavy tray of orders and cried "Brandon!" He followed her between tables and watched her serve dinners and salads to an old couple.

"Can we talk?" Brandon asked her as she carried away her empty tray.

"Take my key," Emily said, taking it from her uniform pocket. "In a half hour I'm free for the night. There's some soup and bread and cheese in my refrigerator...we'll have supper."

Brandon went around the corner, and unlocked the door to Emily's small room. It was nothing but a restaurant storeroom walled off, with its door facing the back parking lot.

Brandon sat on Emily's sleeper couch. Not much light came through the window. Her shower was in the corner near him, with a toilet and kitchen sink against the other wall.

After a while he took Honor's engagement ring off his little finger, turned it around, put it back on. What could he say to his mother? Didn't want to think about it. He went out to his car, got a bottle, had a shot, and lay on the sleeper couch. Tired out. Tired of running around banging on windows and doors.

"What a surprise," Emily said when she came in. "You didn't go to Chicago right away after your graduation?"

"I know where Honor is. At her aunt's in Cedar Falls. Near Waterloo. Old dump of a house on a park—talk about a friendly welcome—there wasn't one."

"What did you find out?" Emily sat down on her chair. "Is she sick?"

"Sick of me, I guess. Here's my ring." he held up his hand.

"Gave it back? Why?"

"Threw it at me. I almost couldn't find it under a milk case at the grocery store."

"At a grocery store..."

"Slapped my face with a package of bacon. Drove off to her aunt's house and wouldn't let me in."

"Wouldn't say a word?"

"Only a couple, while she kept running and yelling and slapping my face. But I went to her aunt's house this morning, and her aunt sure did some talking. I never saw Honor, but I got more than enough of the old witch in a wheelchair—she rolled out on her porch and called me every name she could think of."

"What kind of names?"

"I was waiting for Honor to come, so I hardly listened, until the witch said she was going to write an explanation in words of one syllable and nail it on my chest."

"Nail it...an explanation of what?"

"Don't know. I got out of there."

Emily put bread and cheese on her small kitchen table and poured soup in a pan. "Honor! I can't understand her at all. She took your ring and planned a marriage and then left half way through a party, missed her own graduation, disappeared without one word. What kind of girl would do that? I got a note from her."

"Let me see it." Brandon took it and read:

Dear Mrs. Lombard,

I am so sorry to have missed the graduation, and a visit with you and your sons. I was not well enough to come.

You have done so much for me: planning the wedding for Brandon and me, arranging for the invitations and the church—I deeply regret that it is impossible for me to marry Brandon. I informed him of my withdrawal from the marriage weeks ago, although he seems not to believe me. I am absolutely sure that we would have made each other very unhappy.

I must find a life for myself. I wish you and your sons good fortune, and hope all of you will forgive and forget me.

Sincerely,

Honor Sloan

"Who would write a note like that so late, after she'd ruined all our plans?" Emily said. "No explanation. Just says she was sick. Did she ever tell you weeks ago she wouldn't marry you?"

"She was just mad. That's what I thought. Didn't believe her. Still don't."

"Maybe you ought to believe it now." Emily cut a sandwich in half with a vicious slash of a knife. "Maybe you ought to be very glad you're not marrying somebody who acts like a lunatic. A graduation, a wedding, a good job in Chicago—what smart girl wouldn't want all that?"

"I don't know," Brandon said. "I'm going to Chicago."

After a week or two, Honor's bruises were fading and she didn't limp.

At suppertime one day she found Lena eating her Suppers For Seniors on her screened side porch.

Honor stood looking at the back yard. "Someone must have worked on your garden in the past," she said. "Before you came? When did you move in?"

"Two weeks before I broke my leg. Not much garden left. Just weeds."

23

"But you've got a strong six-foot picket fence all around," Honor said. "And a patio with brick edges. Quite a few perennials coming up."

"Perennials?"

"I saw them when I picked the violets. That big hackberry shades some of them."

"At least you know what perennials are, and what kind of tree that damn tree is," Lena said. "It's even older than me, or the house. Somebody planted a pear tree near it—crazy. Damned old tree scrapes the roof at night—it's alive. It'll outlive me, that tree. Look at it. It knows it. It's awake. Messy tree. Kills the grass." Lena grabbed her fork and empty aluminum plate and rolled into the house. "Can't bear to look at a garden of weeds," she said over her shoulder. "If I eat out here, I sit with my back to it. I'm going in."

The next evening while Honor ate her supper in the kitchen, Lena rolled herself out to the screen porch with her aluminum plate, and sat with her back to the garden. A sound like rushing water came from Seerley Park across the street: children were throwing park gravel on the slide, and then sliding down on it, screaming all the way.

Honor joined her on the porch. Lena scowled at the park. "Those kids'll skin their behinds on that gravel," she said, turning to Honor and glancing at the back yard.

Lena's glance turned to a stare.

She rolled herself to the screen door. "Looks like a lot of weeds in that garden have ripped up their own roots," she said. "And they walked all by themselves to that compost heap to die?"

"I did a little yard work early this morning," Honor told her.

"Perennials out there—thought they'd be dead and gone."

"Just smothered, almost," Honor said.

"Asters," Lena said. "Hosta. Peonies, looks like."

"And you've got a lawn mower in your garage," Honor said. "Would you like to have me mow the lawn? Pull the grass out of your patio?"

"Well," Lena said. "If you like hard work." When they went back to the kitchen, she said, "Thanks for weeding."

"I used an old knife and chopped the roots out, so they'll stay dead." Honor took a drink and splashed some cold water on her face. "I keep hunting for a job. You'll get better in a little while, but I'm here now. Could I possibly work for you? Just for my food and rent while I hunt? Clean up your garden? Cook? All you have to do is say you want something..."

"Bossy," Lena said.

"Oh, Lena!" Honor cried. "I don't want to be. Please don't say I'm bossy. Am I?"

"Sort of."

"Then tell me when I'm bossy and I'll stop. Will you? Honestly?"

"Makes me feel like a baby," Lena said. "Being waited on." She scowled. "You look like my sister Rosabella."

"I do?"

"She was bossy," Lena said.

"Your older sister?"

"Ten years older. Beautiful. Had red hair. And your mother was two years younger than me."

"My folks never talked about Rosabella," Honor said.

"I loved that girl. I think she died having a baby, and the baby died too."

"I never heard that! You lost them? How hard. To lose them both." Honor was still for a little while, sitting with Lena at the table.

Finally Honor said: "I do hate to bother you. I'm still looking for work. But the trouble is: I haven't much money. If you don't like your Suppers For Seniors, I could cook for you—I could, until I find a job. For my meals. I'm a pretty good cook."

"I get along," Lena said.

4

That afternoon Honor went back to weeding the garden. Hackberry shade quivered on the garden grass. Children called in the park. The earth was warm under Honor's hands as she knelt in dirt, knifing weed roots. Her back didn't hurt, and her bruises were gone. The air smelled like gardens she'd loved, year after year. Whether her family lived on the farm or in town, the Sloans always grew vegetables and flowers.

Then she turned her head and found a man at the open garden gate—a big young man with black hair and black eyes like Brandon's, and a shy, embarrassed look.

"Honor," he said. He took off his cap.

"Joe," Honor said in a cold voice.

Joe took a few steps toward her. "Beautiful garden."

She picked up a knife and trowel.

"I'm glad I've found you—it's been so long. That wild hotel pre-graduation party. You were sick and couldn't make it to your graduation, I guess. They called out your poetry prizes."

Honor said nothing.

"I just thought I'd see how you're doing," Joe said. "Drop in."

"Well, you've dropped," Honor said.

Joe took a few more steps toward her, slapped his cap against his jeans and said, "Would you have time for a dinner tonight, maybe? They're having some kind of fair in Cedar Falls. Downtown on the river. People packed in, block after block. Can't hardly get through. They've got all kinds of food and rides, and a dance floor, and a band, the signs say. You feel like a little country fare, maybe?"

"What for?"

"Old times sake?" Joe's black eyebrows rose over his dark eyes.

"Not really. Old times are just what they are. Old."

For a while there was no sound but Honor's trowel gouging a hole deeper. Finally he said, "You're all settled here?"

"Fine."

"Your aunt's house. Brandon remembered you mentioned her once. Got your forwarding address from your landlady and came to find you..." his voice trailed away as he turned to look at the house. "You've found a job?"

"Not yet."

"It's a tough time to find one," he said. "For you English majors. And for biology-zoology M.S.'s like me, too. I'm still living in Iowa City. Finishing my Berkeley Ph.D. dissertation there in the libraries. It's a lot cheaper here than in California, and I'm not halfway across the country from my mother."

Honor knifed a weed with a fierce jab.

Silence fell, except for cries from the park and robins squabbling on the patio.

She threw a dandelion on the grass, reached for another.

"Well," Joe said. "I guess you're pretty busy." He slapped his leg with his cap again.

Honor didn't look up.

"But I'll be back," Joe said.

She watched him go through the gate, climb in his car and drive away. *Those guys at that party gave me a hard time! Joe hit me and called you names.*

Honor went to the kitchen to wash her hands at the sink. Lena was there.

"Well!" Lena said, "That was another good-looking young fellow wanting to see you. Big and well-built, all right. The prettiest dark eyes. Polite. Came to the door—didn't bang on a single thing. Took off his cap. Man number two. You certainly attract handsome males."

"Joe Lombard. Older brother of Peeping Tom. He went to Berkeley after he had a B.A. and M.S. from Ames. Now he's in Iowa City, using the library there, finishing the dissertation for his Berkeley Ph.D.."

"Didn't stay long," Lena said.

"No. Brandon told me once that Joe was his brother from hell...always telling him what to do," Honor said. "Joe took boxing lessons, so Brandon had to watch out. When Joe was at Ames, he tried to date me, but I said No. Sometimes Joe came for one of my poetry readings—I'd look up, and there was Joe Lombard in a back row, watching me. I knew how Brandon felt about his brother. I'd pretend I didn't see him."

"Reading poetry?" Lena said.

"I write it sometimes," Honor said.

After another week Honor was still reading the want ads, and went once to an interview for a job as secretary, with no luck.

"Here I am, still being a nuisance," she said to Lena one afternoon. "Can I do something more around your house? Be some help to you? I grew up cleaning houses—I can certainly do it for you. I've found a vacuum cleaner that works, and pails and mops. You said you'd like to organize your kitchen a little? You said you couldn't sort things, but you knew where they ought to go."

"Well..." Lena said.

"Maybe, if we work together, you can decide what you want to keep," Honor said. "Or what to throw away, too, now that you've got someone to throw it?"

Lena grumbled, but in a few days she began to roll through the house in her wheelchair, saying she wanted to keep this and didn't want that. Honor took loads to the alley or St. Vincent de Paul.

"Disgusting," Lena said. "Most of this junk's not mine."

They rummaged and sorted. Honor began, day by day, to scrub and polish and mop. One morning Lena said, "I suppose you wonder why I didn't hire somebody to sort this place out after I broke my leg. Oh, I know why. I was so mad. I'd come home from a trip to London, all set to start fixing up this house. I had every detail planned, and then some cosmic joker tripped me on my basement stairs, broke my leg and dumped me in a wheelchair to show me I wasn't any luckier than anybody else. In a few weeks I was nasty enough to escape from one of those places they call a 'nursing home,' where people they call 'care-givers' shout as if you're deaf, and want your money at once, and your death as soon as possible."

They worked on, emptying and sorting. One morning Lena said to Honor, "You've been helping me. I left some money on the kitchen counter. Buy yourself some good food."

"Thanks!" Honor said. "Thanks so much. I'll shop, and then I'll walk to the library. Maybe they'll let me have a library card."

Lena said, "When I was shopping for a house, I found this one, and then discovered there was a library a few blocks away. Aha, I told myself—I'll buy this place and walk to the library every day, and read all of Trollope's horde of books. Every three or four pages of his, I have to stop and laugh."

Honor shopped, and got a library card for them both. She brought some Trollopes back for Lena, put away the groceries, and climbed upstairs with a load of books for herself.

There were no book shelves in her bedroom, or in the closet. She opened her closet door and looked at her wedding gown hung far back in the corner. White slippers touched toes forlornly under it. The veil trailed from its shoulder. It was almost hidden by shirts and her coat.

No shelf for books. But suddenly a small feeling of home came to Honor from her shirts and jeans and jackets there in the closet: the warm comfort she felt when she was in the company of her own belongings.

"Hold on to that," she said to herself. "Write it down." She'd always been a writer on the hunt, like somebody with a butterfly net, watching for natural, everyday things that suddenly meant more. Or like someone running around with a cage, trying to catch a bird. That last image wasn't hers, but it was fascinating. It was Kafka's.

She dug in her cardboard boxes for a pencil, then stopped and said out loud: "Oh—that desk. Yes!"

She'd remembered seeing a battered desk in one of the other bedrooms.

It was heavy, but she dragged it through the hall to her bedroom and her big front windows. Look at that—the oak desk was hard-used, but it fit just beneath her wide window sill, with drawers below, and such a view of the park!

After she dusted her new desk with an old sock, she dragged boxes from the closet. Unfinished poems and stories were in one: she put them on the desk top so she'd see them every morning waiting for attention, like cats sitting there, hungry for break-fast. Her pencils and pens, stuck in a bathroom glass beside them, waited, too.

Another box of hers (much smaller) was filled with her "hopefuls"—manuscripts she'd mailed to editors who hadn't answered her yet. They belonged in the first desk drawer, under her pressed and dried four-leaf clover. Blank paper filled the next drawer down. And, of course, the bottom one was the right place for all her rejection notes.

"Dear Miss Sloan, thank you for your submission. We're sorry to inform you..."

She unloaded the last of her belongings in a little dresser in the hall, except for her books. No shelves. She sighed, and stood her books on the floor like a regiment on parade: they marched along the wall, their spines out and their titles right side up. She added the new library books to the straight-backed line.

In another box were her diploma and her poetry awards. She'd sent for them from the university, but where could she put them? Finally she leaned them against the wall with the books, like bookends.

How still the old house was. She wandered from room to room. Everything she owned was unpacked and put away—hadn't she made her mark on this place—at least one room? Like a dog

30

marking a tree? The whole upper floor of a house just for her? That made her laugh, standing in the old bathroom. She hadn't laughed since the first hour of that hotel party.

Honor smiled at herself in the old bathroom mirror. *What are you so happy about?* she asked her face. The mirror had lost some of its silver, but it was still reflecting.

The last of June was hot, day after day. Sometimes Honor brought chairs to the wide front porch and sat with Lena watching the crowd across the street. Seerley Park was busy every morning now: summer-school students from the college had set up a children's art program there; they unloaded their supplies from a big green box. One day Lena and Honor saw children trailing scarlet and blue gimp over the grass: they were learning to cover coat hangers with braid, while their mothers perched on nearby park benches like a row of sparrows, chattering.

Honor was looking at the want ads, as usual. "I majored in *English*!" she wailed to Lena after a while, folding the paper with a rustle and dropping it by her chair. "That was my mistake. I should have been an education major—taken courses about *the attender and the attendee* so somebody would hire me. Here I am, almost through June and still on your hands. I'm sorry." She looked up at peeling paint on the porch roof. "I love this house. How old is it, do you think?"

"Don't know. Probably started out as just another one of those four-rooms-up-and-four-rooms-down Iowa houses," Lena said. "Until somebody tacked a big room on its rear, and then a garage. It's old—as old as I feel, I guess. It sure is younger than I look. After the folks died, I meant to buy a house, but decided to finish college first, and travel. Lucky thing I did, before I broke a leg. I came here because I wanted a college town. I saw this solid old Iowa house with a park right in front—no neighbors across the street—and the big back yard for a garden, and a college library just blocks away."

"So what did you plan to do to your house?" Honor asked.

Lena snorted. "The question is: Where to begin? But I had plans. Look at this front porch. Can't stand it! Somebody must have screened it, and then left the screen frames on those handsome pillars—slats nailed on the Parthenon!"

31

"And would you keep the big back room off the kitchen for a bedroom?" Honor asked. "Or a study? It's a delightful house! The basement has such solid limestone walls, and a cement floor, and the attic's huge, with those dormer windows that make it look like the house is raising its eyebrows. And maybe you'd enjoy a new fireplace that has fake logs and a real fire, so you'd never have to drag logs in and ashes out?"

At last Honor found a job.

A secretary for the dean of women at the college was leaving before Christmas. "I'm saved!" Honor told Lena. "I was so worried—and you were, too, though you'd never say so. A job for me right here in town! The only problem is...the position isn't open until the new year, and I have to keep going until then...on no money."

Her last words hung in the air between them...in the silence between them.

Lena waited. But the girl was happy at last. She sang around the house. She had a job.

Lena was mean enough, sneaky enough—she knew it—to wait and see what Honor was going to try, because she'd want to stay where she was until the new year. Where else could she go?

Lena didn't have long to wait.

The next evening Honor found Lena on the screened porch with her Supper For Seniors. The supper was particularly revolting; Lena stirred the mess around on the plate without taking a forkful. "I wish Supper For Seniors would at least bring these poor excuses for dinner at one o'clock, not six," Lena said. "The middle of the day's the right time for a dinner. A real dinner."

Honor watched Lena stirring and stirring. Finally she said in a faint voice: "I *could* make your meals for you. If you'd want me to try. Whatever time you want them. While your leg is healing."

"Well," was all Lena said, but she looked at the plate with the face that says "Ugh!"—crinkled-up nose and tight little mouth.

"I could certainly do better than these suppers," Honor said. "You'll have to admit it wouldn't be hard. I'm a decent cook."

Lena just sat there, trying not to smile.

"We can make a list of the foods you enjoy," Honor said. "I can shop if I go to the store right now, and cook dinner for you tomorrow at one o'clock. I'll be careful what I spend. My family never had much money. I learned how to cut corners."

Lena looked at the plate and said, "Well..."

"I'll get paper and a pencil," Honor cried, and ran to the kitchen. In a minute or two she was asking Lena what she liked and making menus and grocery lists. Lena gave her the money for the first dinner. "I hope you'll survive my cooking," Honor said. "You've been eating dry meat loaf and watery potatoes and wobbly gelatin for months. It hasn't killed you yet." She was smiling.

Honor shopped, and the next morning she made breakfast and then shut herself in the kitchen. Lena read Trollope's *Barchester Towers* on the front porch, chuckling from page to page: Eleanor Bold had been proposed to by three men in a single day, and she'd slapped one of them, the hideous Mr. Slope. Good for her.

At exactly one o'clock Honor came to say that dinner was ready. Lena rolled her wheelchair up to the old dining-room table that Honor had polished until it looked pretty decent. Honor had found Lena's sterling silverware, and a nice place mat with a matching napkin.

Honor came from the kitchen with a plate and put it down before Lena—roast beef in nice thick gravy. The green peas were still alive and green—not pale, boiled marbles—and the whipped potatoes were real ones, with a crown of real butter and no lumps.

Honor went back to bring Lena a dish of fresh fruit salad, and sat down across the table. "Would you like to read while you eat?" she asked. "I can bring you the Trollope book you haven't finished."

"Where's *your* dinner?" Lena said.

"I didn't think I should—"

"I'm not going to eat here all alone!" Lena cried. "Dish up some for yourself."

33

Honor came back with slices of beef and some beans on a plate. "You're having nothing but that?" Lena said.

"I just cooked enough—"

"I'm not going to dine by myself like some Queen Elizabeth First or Second," Lena said. Set a place for yourself and eat."

"Thank you," Honor said, going to find more silverware and a placemat and napkin. "Thank you so much."

When Honor sat down, Lena took a bite of each thing on her plate and then said, "It's good."

"I do so love to cook!" Honor said.

Sunshine shot a golden bar across the dining- room table. As Honor carried the empty plates away, she said: "There's a dessert," and came back with two big pieces of apple pie.

Lena took a bite. "It's still warm." She took another bite. "And this pie's not from any bakery."

"No," Honor said.

Lena took another bite and rolled it around on her tongue. "It's not sickly sweet. And it's got a lard-butter-flour crust that maybe just a few old women still remember how to make."

L ena ate the good meals and smiled to herself. Honor had managed to make herself useful. The girl was smart.

But then, one morning at breakfast, Honor changed the game. "Aunt Lena," she said, and stopped. "I don't know how...I don't know what..." Both her hands were fists on the table. "I have to tell you: I'm pregnant."

Lena didn't know what to say.

"Maybe you've heard me being sick in the morning?" Honor asked.

"No," Lena said. "Peeping Tom?"

Honor nodded.

"He got drunk, you said."

"He—Oh, Aunt Lena! Oh!" Honor laid her arms on the table and hid her face.

"Drunk. Took advantage of you."

Honor sat up and looked at Lena. "*Yes*," she said. "That's why I ran away from him—ran here to you. I'd told him so many times how I felt! I told him how much our waiting until after the wedding meant to me! I said he'd be my first, and wasn't I worth waiting for. Wasn't I?"

"Yes," Lena said.

"*Perfect companions*"—that's what we called the two of us: the Perfect Companions." Honor said. "There was nothing Brandon and I couldn't discuss, I thought—we talked for hours about Brandon's business major, and I read him my stories, and my poems. But he started drinking. His football-player friends thought drinking was the 'Man Thing' to do, I guess—and so was sleeping with any woman they could catch. They must have made Brandon feel he had to do it with me...he kept talking about it... tried to make me feel so selfish...so prudish..."

She rubbed her eyes. "Some of the football players wanted to date me, and Brandon's brother Joe, too...the one who found me in your garden. But I wouldn't go out with any of them—I loved Brandon. So his brother Joe was mad. (That's what Brandon told me when he caught me shopping for groceries.) Joe taunted Brandon at a party the night before graduation, when I ran away home—hit him! Brandon's football friends—and his brother Joe, too—told Brandon they bet he'd never slept with me, or I wasn't any good, and a man was pretty stupid if he bought a shirt without trying it on...they were all so drunk. Joe called me names. Brandon fought them, I guess, and then came after me."

Lena said nothing, and Honor rushed on: "Joe and the others made Brandon so mad—I wonder if they goaded Brandon into doing that to me. I'll never know, I guess. But months before that, Brandon had started arguing that we were going to be married, so what did it matter if we... I saw how he'd changed. He started taking me to the football team's parties—Oh, Aunt Lena!"

There were tears in Honor's eyes.

"I knew boys do silly stuff," Honor said. "Childish, messy, dumb things they think are so funny—spoiling and dirtying and never cleaning up. They enjoy it. Why? But I found out there were college men like that! To them it was such 'fun' to fill dormitory halls with water and soap and slide in it, or throw a box full of light bulbs out the window and watch them smash on the traffic passing underneath. College men! And Brandon took me to parties. I don't drink, so there I was, watching people I thought I knew getting so drunk they turned into somebody else. I do hate that.

"And Brandon changed. The party before graduation was the worst—when he wouldn't believe I didn't want to marry him, even though I'd told him so, weeks before. I said, No— No—I wouldn't marry him—ever. He knew it. He heard me. And then he came to my room afterward...hurt me...it was..."

She stopped again to rub her eyes. "Oh! Attacked by someone I trusted. And now a baby's coming. You're the only one I can talk to...I'm sorry I have to tell you all this. I thought I knew what my life was going to be, and was looking for a job, but now I can't work. Where can I go? Maybe there are homes for unwed mothers in Iowa somewhere? I won't ever marry, I don't think— I'd never marry Brandon. If he hurt me like that, he might hurt our child. If I could find a good job...but how can I?" She gave a soft sob. "I'd never get rid of the baby. I couldn't."

"No," Lena said.

"So my baby's the only thing I have now," Honor said. "And my baby doesn't have anybody but me." She left the table and ran upstairs.

A few days went by. At meals, Lena and Honor kept up the only conversations possible: a bland question here, a short answer there. Was Honor hunting for a place to stay? Lena saw no sign that Honor was leaving. Where would she go?

One morning at breakfast Honor said, "I hope you don't mind. I used your typewriter in the back room for this." She put a sheet of paper in front of Lena.

Lena pulled her glasses out of a pocket. "Looks like a poem." She picked it up. "It *is* a poem."

HACKBERRY

Bark sags in folds from the crotches down
to where the roots begin secretly, deliberately
to suck water out from under the lawn.
Children know how the knotholes seem to shift
sometimes. (Do gnarled sockets darken
when we walk between it and the young pear?)
Our living room is dark. We wish the tree weren't there.

It's alive with ants. Brisk birds creep
upside down on its hide all day, grooming.
Twenty feet up, squirrels, grubs, beetles
hang with thick shade over us, a ceiling
(tiny breaths, droppings). One dead limb creaks
just over our bench. Wasps dive
sizzling from it. Green leaves fall near us. It's alive.

It never seems to sleep. We hear how it tests
its tether out there, restlessly. All night long
it rubs against the roof. We think it remembers
old years before we were born.
It's killing the grass.
We talk in bed about chain saws, ropes, danger. We take
care not to be heard. It's alive. It's awake.

Lena read it over three times while Honor watched her, and
their coffee got cold. Finally Honor said, "I write poems all the
time. None of them are what I'm trying to say. Not one. But I've
had quite a few published after I gave up on them...just in university journals."

Lena read it again, and said, "I wrote poems when I was young.
I used to write poems for my older sister, Rosabella. Your aunt."

"I never heard about her, except for her name," Honor said. "To
think that I don't have one memory of her. And she liked poetry?"

"She liked mine," Lena said. "And I loved her. She was so
beautiful."

"Where is she now?"

"I don't know. I never have," Lena said. She read the poem
again. "I wrote poems, but I didn't have what you've got."

"Me?"

"Look at this." Lena tapped the paper. "You got my hackberry.
Right there."

"*You* said it was alive and awake," Honor said. "Only a poet
would say that."

"But I'd know that tree anywhere," Lena said. "The lines jut
out, rhyming just at the right place where you don't expect it, like
a tree spiking into a view. And it's a person. You got it. But it's
still a real tree." She ran a finger from line to line. "It's saggy.
It's sneaky. It's sucking water and killing my lawn. It's like an old
lecher, looking over that young pear tree. It's a dirty old man,
messing up my grass, and it's too old to sleep well any more. It
feels tied down. It rubs against the roof—it does—and thinks
about the past, and knows I'd like to cut it down. It knows."

"*You* know," Honor said.

"*A tree that will in summer wear,*" Lena warbled.

"*A nest of robins in her hair,*" Honor sang. They were giggling
now.

37

"Upon whose bosom snow has lain."

"Who intimately lives with rain." They laughed, howling over Kilmer's bad poem and their cold coffee.

"You've got to send this poem out," Lena said. "Someone will print it."

"But I gave it to you." Honor stirred her soggy cereal around in the bowl. "It's a kind of going-away gift, I guess—I'm so thankful that you've given me a home for a while."

5

The next morning Lena said to Honor: "Shouldn't you go to a doctor? To see if everything is normal?"

"Go to a doctor?" Honor cried. "I can't go to a doctor. I couldn't. I'm healthy…I feel fine, now that the morning sickness has stopped…"

"But you'll have to go, sooner or later," Lena said. "What if—"

"I'm not *married*," Honor cried. "I'm—what am I? An 'unwed mother'? That's the polite name for it, I guess…there are lots of nastier names—but they all mean that you're *out of society*. You know how it is." Honor walked around and around the kitchen. "If you don't have a husband, you're lucky if you can sneak off somewhere and have the baby and find someone to take it. A couple of girls in my high school simply disappeared as if they'd never been born, but everybody knew why—they were 'used goods,' packed off to some relative. Nobody wanted to have anything to do with them...nobody wanted to even *look* like they were their friend, even when they were, because people might think that they were that kind of girl." She stopped and looked at Lena. "Won't you be glad to be rid of me? A relative of yours who let herself get..." She couldn't go on.

Lena didn't know what to say. Did Honor expect her to talk about unwed mothers and fatherless children, and even say she might marry a man who was responsible for all this, but still wanted to marry her?

Lena couldn't. She'd called Brandon Lombard "Peeping Tom," and a nuisance that wasn't wanted, and a buster and breaker and wrecker and drinker, which he certainly was.

For a day or two they just tiptoed around it, but the problem was not going away—it was scheduled for delivery in less than seven months. Lena kept still, waiting and watching. Honor had already managed to stay under her roof a long time more than her "little while," and now she had free food. Honor didn't say much, but Lena thought she knew what Honor was planning.

The next day when they had eaten Honor's delicious chicken dinner, Honor gave Lena a worried look. "While I'm cooking our meals... doing whatever else I can to help before I leave, I wonder what you'd think of a crazy idea of mine."

"What?"

"It's just a crazy idea. You've got every right to say it's not my business," Honor said. "So tell me if it isn't. But...you do have some money to spend, don't you? And you do like living in this house?"

"Love it."

"You want to live here always."

"It's my home."

"Then, while I'm here to help... do you think you might like to fix up your house a little?" she said. "You've told me so much about your plans for this place—would you like to start? While I'm here? You've said you miss taking a shower. What about putting one in your downstairs bathroom—they've got new kinds that you can step right into. You've said you hate sponge baths."

Lena just sat there.

"And you might want to make your big first-floor room off the garden into your bedroom?" Honor said. "You can't quite go upstairs yet, but in the downstairs back room you could wake up every morning to see your garden, and your shower would be right next door. We could go to Waterloo and look at showers."

Lena licked the last bit of pie from her fork. "I don't look decent enough to go shopping for showers or anything else."

Honor cooked good dinners, and kept quiet. Lena was trying to use a crutch now, and walked around the house. Now and then Honor caught Lena looking at her reflection in a window as she hobbled past. One day when Lena glanced in a mirror, she caught Honor smiling. "My hair's a mess," Lena said. "But what does it matter what an old lady looks like?"

"Who's old?" Honor said. "You're not old. You're in the prime of life!"

"At fifty? Certainly not!" Lena said. "Never have been."

But Lena was disgusted with her hair. Finally she said she ought to have it cut, at least.

"There's a nice little beauty shop on Main Street right here in town," Honor said.

It took Lena a day or two to think about it. Then she said, "I guess I ought to have my hair cut." So Honor loaded Lena and the crutch in Lena's car, drove them downtown, and unloaded them at the beauty shop.

Lena complained all the way to the door that she was as ancient as a mummy and looked like one. But the beauty operator—who couldn't have been more than seventeen—started to work as if she had some hope, and Lena had to admit that it wasn't so bad. When her graying hair was cut short, it turned to waves. And then the girl used some cream to cover dark circles under Lena's eyes and some more to make her "blush," and powder to top it off, and even lipstick of a "mature pink," whatever that was.

On the way home Lena admitted the trip was worth the money, maybe. She said, "Nobody will know me. But nobody's seen me much around here anyway."

"You can keep up that pretty hair style yourself," Honor said. "I can show you. And now—clothes?"

"Clothes!"

"Wouldn't you like some light jackets for summer, maybe, and heavier ones for fall—jackets with beautiful patterns? And some full skirts?"

41

"Maybe slacks. Not skirts," Lena said. "Skirts hike up in back when you hobble around with a crutch, and show your petticoat under. But no jeans! Jeans make you look like you're on your way to plow a field or break stone on a road gang! Teenagers have got to have them, I suppose, but I've even seen T-shirts and jeans on people my age! Do they ever look at their behinds in the mirror? A little bitty T-shirt hiking up in back—they *always* hike up in back—over a pair of wobbly blue watermelons."

They went shopping a few days later. Sometimes Lena was so disgusted that she leaned on her crutch and lectured salesladies. "Don't you know that there are mature women with money who can't find clothes in your stores?" she told them. "I need low-heeled, high-fastening shoes, so they'll stay on and I won't break another leg. Clothes with no low necks. No princess seams. No three-quarter sleeves with lower arms flapping underneath! Sleeveless? Don't even think about it."

Lena said she felt like her house—she was a work in progress. "I've got decent clothes now, but stairs are such a problem," she told Honor. "I can't navigate the front steps to the street. If I want to get into one of our cars, I have to use the back stairs, hanging on to you. It's scary."

"A ramp?" Honor said. "Right at your kitchen stoop in the garage? Bannisters on both sides? Then you can use your crutch to go down the ramp from your kitchen door right into your car."

So Lena ordered a ramp. A cement truck the size of a dinosaur came down the alley with its belly revolving and groaning. Men paved her back drive, built the ramp and bannisters, and even put in a new garage floor for the two cars while they were at it. More men came to install her new downstairs shower.

Honor wanted to know how Lena liked her first shower bath. "The pleasure of not having to clean yourself at a sink, limb by limb," Lena said. "And handles, so you can get in and out. Stayed under water too long—I'm an old, wrinkled prune."

The next week Lena said she was losing her mind at fifty. She said: "That new shower looked so crazy in a bathroom with cracked walls and worn-off linoleum—and the upstairs bath's ancient, too. So they're going to put up new walls in both bathrooms, and new floors. And I ordered a shower and bathtub for the upstairs bathroom, and sinks and toilets for both, too. Streamlined toilets, like a new car. And the sinks are almost too fancy to wash in."

42

Now plumbers swarmed all over the place, but Lena couldn't stop. The carpenters said her leaky windows weren't much use against heat or cold. But if she installed new ones, she wouldn't have to hire somebody to lug storm windows in and out every Iowa winter. "So," she told Honor, "can you believe it? I'm going to have all new windows. Big ones. Twice the view in every direction. And now the contractors tell me the house is pretty old, as if I didn't know. It doesn't heat right, and it's hot and damp in summer. So what did I do? Decided on a new furnace. No drafts creeping across my floor and freezing my ankles in winter. And then—I couldn't believe it—I ordered air-conditioning, so I won't have fans all over the place in hot weather."

"Air-conditioning," Honor said. "Isn't that awfully expensive? I've never been in a house that had it."

"Some of the big houses in Waterloo do," Lena said. "Why not us?"

It was like a disease, Lena told Honor. Making an old house over. It crept up on you and wouldn't quit, and it certainly made a mess—like a disease. Day by day, workmen filled the rooms with noise, hideous smells, and tracked-in dirt. But Honor got up early to open the door for the work crews, and cleaned up all she could after they left at the end of the day.

One day Honor drove Lena to choose a floor covering for the kitchen.

The salesman spread linoleum samples on the floor. Honor crawled over them, lining up a mosaic of the ones Lena liked best.

"We had such worn-out floors in our house on the farm," Honor said. "My mother and I tried to keep them clean, but you'd get splinters in your knees."

"I remember that farmhouse you lived in—I drove by it sometimes," Lena said. "I saw you once when you were a child, did you know that? You stood at the gate of your farm road with a cat in your arms as I drove past."

"And you didn't stop?"

"I didn't think I'd be welcome," Lena said.

The next day Honor and Lena wandered down the aisles of a carpet store. And then another, and another. "My father sold rugs for a year or two." Honor ran her fingers over soft, thick carpet pile. "Mother always said he could sell anything. He had a way with people. He taught me games, and we camped, hiked..."

"I hardly ever spoke to my father," Lena said. "I sometimes thought he didn't remember I was there."

Another afternoon they shopped for dishwashers, following a salesman down a long, gleaming row as he recited the virtues of each, until they wondered how they could choose among them. They went back to the car, and Lena said, "Dishwashers. When I was in London, I had dinner at a London friend's home, and afterwards I helped wash the dishes. She gave me a dish towel, rinsed the dishes under the faucet and handed them to me."

"No soap?" Honor said.

"I didn't know what to do. I didn't dare say a word. We 'washed' them all and put them away."

"England!" Honor said. "How I've always dreamed of going there." She started the car. "Always. Where did you stay?"

"Crosby Hall. The oldest domestic architecture in London. They moved that huge treasure—I don't know how—to Sir Thomas Moore's garden on the Thames in Chelsea, and added dormitories to it so that college women from all over the world could stay there. We ate our meals by a stained glass oriel window in this great hammerbeam-roofed hall. The stone doorsill was worn to half its height from centuries of passing feet. Royalty had dined there."

"Splendid!" Honor cried.

"Horrible food," Lena said. "Ancient bathrooms. Furniture out of some second or third-hand store, and one clean towel a week. Right on the bus and subway lines to anywhere you wanted to go. And cheap."

"Those big red double-decker buses."

"If you can get the front seat on the top floor of those buses, it's like flying through the city," Lena said. "They go fast—on the wrong side of the road. On one of my first English days, I took a bus tour to the Lake District."

"Wordsworth! Coleridge. You saw where they lived?"

"Southey. De Quincey. Beatrix Potter...and her Peter Rabbit," Lena said. "And I thought I was going to die—quite a few times."

"What?"

"Those buses. Sit way up on top in front of their front window, and pretty soon you'll see another double-decker on the country road, coming from the opposite direction! They pass with a few inches leeway. You shut your eyes and wait for death."

Lena's kitchen was down to the bare walls for weeks. Lena ordered a hot plate for the back room, and Honor cooked as well as she could there. She used the downstairs bathroom to do dishes and get water and "make do," as Lena said. They laughed about it, squeezing past each other, hanging wet towels on the screened porch, doing laundry in the bathroom sink.

Lena walked with her cane from room to room, watching her old house change. The weather was hot, but the air conditioning would soon change that. New windows, so wide, so high, brought the colors of her garden in, and the deep green of the park. Lena watched Honor wandering the house, too, looking out the new windows, thinking who knows what. She had a baby coming, but she wasn't "showing" yet. She wouldn't go to a doctor—she'd have to use her maiden name at the hospital—what else could she do? Make up a husband's name? That wouldn't be right, or legal, probably. Peeping Tom might never know he was a father. He'd banged on doors and windows and never come back.

Lena had known girls who "made a mistake." Two of her high school friends were in school one day and gone the next. Finally they came back after "visiting relatives," but who leaves school in the middle of the year to go "visiting," when there's been no catastrophe in the family—except their own? They never went back to school. They couldn't. They were farm girls, and they stayed home, and never married, that she ever heard.

Honor went up each night to her almost empty room. Her clothes were in the closet. When she went to bed, she had the company of her books and prizes, and her diploma standing along a wall.

August came and broke heat records. One hot morning Honor went to get the mail while Lena sat in her living room that was filled with rolls of carpet.

"That mailbox was almost too hot to open," Honor said, settling beside Lena on the new couch. She put the mail in Lena's lap, except for one envelope. "A letter for me," Honor said, opening it.

"We should think about some mother-to-be clothes for you. Most of your outfits will be riding up or falling down before long," Lena said. "Let's buy you some nice ones. It'll be my treat."

"Thank you! Thank you so much!" Honor looked up from her letter, her eyes wide and dark blue. "I may need something new to wear, all right. I've got an invitation here." She took a deep breath. "I'm invited to a wedding on the twentieth. In Chicago."

"A college friend of yours?"

"I didn't really have close friends in college, except Brandon," Honor said. "I had to get top grades because of my scholarships, and I had two jobs, too. Most of the time I was too tired to make friends." She put the invitation back in the envelope. "The bride must be from Chicago. I don't know her. But the groom..."

Lena thought Honor had tears in her eyes.

"I know him quite well," Honor said. "He wanted to be *my* groom..."

Lena stared at her. "Peeping Tom?" she said, but Honor was already on her way upstairs. Lena heard Honor's bedroom door close.

L ena sat in her living room, wondering what on earth she could say.

At last Honor came down. Lena could see she'd been crying.

"Tell me what you think," Honor said.

"I can't believe it—Brandon sent you an *invitation*?"

"But why?" Honor's eyes were wide and blue. "Would I do that to him, if I'd found somebody else to marry after...how long? How long does it take to fall in love again? From May to August? Is there anything friendly about this? I have to decide...I've got to give him any kind of credit..."

"Give him credit for revenge? Getting even?"

"Is that how it seems to you? Isn't there any excuse for him at all? I did 'jilt' him," Honor said. "It was so hard—Why? Did he believe I wouldn't let such a handsome man get away—just never believed I really could?"

"If you were going to marry somebody else this month, would

46

you send Brandon your wedding announcement?"

"No." Honor stared at Lena. "I couldn't. I never would, if I'd done something that hurt him so much that he wouldn't marry me, and it was my fault. No. I'd have to write him a letter and say I was going to be married. I'd try to explain that I knew I'd hurt him, and was sorry, and hoped he'd be happy when he found someone else to love, too."

She got up, walked around the room a couple of times, and came back to Lena with red cheeks and narrowed eyes. "Revenge," she said.

"Brandon?"

"That's what Brandon's after," Honor said. "This Katie Bushnell that Brandon's marrying…"

"She's got herself a real prize," Lena said.

"I hate Brandon," Honor said. "I never dreamed I would—but I do."

"Just think if you'd married him," Lena said. "Before the honeymoon was over, he'd be revenging himself for something *else* that was really his fault, and you'd have to creep around with a wedding ring on your finger and a baby coming."

"Trapped," Honor said.

"Good and trapped. Married. The worst kind."

"But I'm not, am I?"

"No."

Honor went into the kitchen. Lena heard her opening the new refrigerator. In a few minutes she supposed Honor was starting supper, but what on earth was she *chopping* like that: carrots, cabbage, celery? Raw meat? Whatever it was, it was certainly going to be minced.

But the chopping must have done Honor good: she was calm when she came back to say, "The invitation talks about 'formal attire for the dinner and the evening.'"

"Fancy affair," Lena said.

"A long red dress, don't you think?" Honor said, sitting down. "Scarlet woman? Scarlet letter?" She glared at Lena. "No. Don't give him a chance to call me nasty names again. Pink? Isn't pink an innocent color?"

"Well," Lena said. "Pink. Yes! With diamond earrings. Diamond necklace—Yes! I've got diamonds. I've got just the thing."

It seemed to do Honor so much good to be mad, Lena thought. Being mad was a whole world better than moping and weeping.

"I'll go to Chicago," Honor said the next day.

"Brandon won't expect you to come, will he?" Lena said.

"Too bad," Honor said.

Lena was mad—as mad as Honor was. She said she'd pay for everything for Honor's trip to Chicago—air fare, hotel, maternity clothes. "Nothing but the best for Peeping Tom and that name-calling Joe!"

"How wonderful of you," Honor said. "At least I'm not bulging with the baby yet."

So they went to Waterloo stores, and then drove to Des Moines.

New clothes thrilled Honor. She tried not to show it, but Lena knew Honor well enough now: she watched Honor's glances as they lingered on silk...her hand smoothing a coat's wool sleeve. What had Honor done for her high-school clothes? College clothes? Dresses for dates? Lena didn't want to ask herself that. She watched salesladies zipping and buttoning, admiring Honor's hair, praising her pretty face, and remembered a child by a farm gate, a cat in her arms, watching an aunt she'd never seen drive by.

"Do you like this one?" Honor asked Lena, turning to show all sides of the long rose-pink evening dress.

"Just the thing!" Lena said. A saleslady praised Honor until she blushed. But having a baby *was* making Honor twice as beautiful, Lena thought—she'd lost that skinny, hungry, people-are-no-damn-good look she'd had the day she came. She wasn't "showing" yet, but she was filling the top of her dresses very nicely indeed.

6

In a few weeks, unbelievably, Honor was flying for the first time—flying above a green patchwork Iowa she could never have imagined, flying over a rounding globe of a world she had only seen in pictures. She stared from the plane window, wondering how people around her could talk of ordinary things while the earth dropped out of sight like a stone. She found a notebook in her purse and scribbled:

> We filed in, sat down to read by small
> dusty windows. The seats reclined
> with the passengers. Nobody seemed to mind
> when the plane revved up, screamed at the sight
> (I thought) of so much sky, and then all
> at once earth tipped, was gone.

As usual, words would have to be worked and reworked. They had to be jerky with shock and amazement to catch what she felt, and keep that faint chime of rhymes at the line-ends that you hardly heard, but were charmed by just the same. And that little "all" that rhymed with "small"—see how the line-end hung there? And then—between "all" and "at once" (while your eye went from line to line)— the earth was gone!

The plane slid from clouds and returned the world to her, and she hardly recognized it. She took a taxi to a very expensive hotel, feeling dazed—she was a speck of a person in a city that was a speck on a world that was a speck in the universe.

It was Brandon's wedding day. She checked into the hotel, slid her room's door chain shut, and sat on the bed's quilted satin. The room was splendid, the kind that college boys would love to wreck.

A rose lay on the pillow, cradled in spreading leaves, courtesy of the management. Their note said that she should telephone the desk if anything at all was not perfect.

So far, her plan was perfect. In a few hours Brandon would be standing at an altar. She wouldn't be there to watch the bride that was not Honor Sloan come down the aisle to be his. Or had he slept with Katie Bushnell already? But then the reception line would form in the ballroom downstairs: guests for the wedding dinner-and-dance for Mr. and Mrs. Brandon Lombard—and she would be there. *She had an invitation.*

Honor put the rose in a glass of water, unpacked, and found she had a headache. A bathtub with bubble bath in it…yes. She undressed and sank into that comforting pleasure to think. She didn't want to think. The bathtub was fluffy with soapsuds as white as clouds from a plane window.

But she had to think. What on earth was she doing here?

In an hour or so Brandon would come from his wedding to the hotel, a bridegroom in white, no doubt, to match his white bride. Honor stripped soapsuds off her arms as if they were thoughts that didn't matter. What mattered was the question: What should she do?

Why ask that? Hadn't she decided? Her soapy washcloth circled around the island of her stomach in the bathwater. That island was still flat, but it held an invisible human being ringed by rainbow bubbles. A baby was under there on that island… half Brandon…a small person hidden in her—a castaway. A Crusoe… secret, determined to stay alive.

50

A hot jet of anger made her finish her bath and climb from the tub. Anger told her she must look as beautiful as possible—beautiful and icy. That was what she had come for, and that was what Brandon would see.

Her makeup must be perfect; she took great care. By the time she pulled the long silk dress down her body, there was nothing but revenge in her head.

She brushed her hair until it shone, and braided it around her head like a crown. Brandon would see her face framed in the glitter of Lena's diamond earrings above a low, low neckline and the matching glitter of a diamond necklace, all cold as ice: the look of a remote Madonna.

Outrage crept through her. As she left her room, she was aimed like a gun at one thing: the stunned look she meant to see in one man's eyes. Brandon had invited her to his wedding. She was here.

The wedding reception line was long in the big ballroom. Ushers in tuxedos were first greeters. Next came four small girls in ruffled pink, hitting each other with their nosegays, while some of the bridesmaids next in line whispered to them: "Stop that! Your poor flowers."

"Oh-oh," said Mary, the first bridesmaid.

Ann, the next bridesmaid, said "What?"

"Look who's in the doorway!"

"The gorgeous one in pink?"

"She belongs up there with the groom," Mary said.

"What?"

"She's the one that didn't want him. Honor Sloan. You should have been at the Iowa U. graduation party—I was there with one of the football players. We were dancing, and all at once Brandon told the band to play the wedding march because he was going to marry this Honor Sloan. And he put the ring on her finger in front of everybody, and waved a fake wedding cake around..."

"What did she do?" Joan said. Honor had reached the line of ushers.

"Left the party. Just like that. Left town. Didn't even go to her own graduation."

Ann stared at Honor. "A handsome guy like Brandon?"

"The guys at the party gave him a hard time," Mary said. "She'd left him at the altar..."

51

"He didn't go after her, find her?"

"I guess he did, but I heard she threw his ring at him and slapped his face."

"Then what's she doing here?"

"Rubbing his face in it, I guess. The bride certainly comes in second to *her*."

Anne giggled. *"See me and weep. Look what you could have had."*

Honor reached the row of bridesmaids just as a large woman began shooing someone through a far door. It was the bridal couple—Brandon and small, blond Katie Bushnell—taking their places at the end of the reception line.

The line was moving now. Joe Lombard was giving the guests' names to Mr. Bushnell. Men ran their eyes over Honor, but she was ice-cold as she took step after step, pink silk rustling around her as she left the last bridesmaid behind and came to Joe.

Joe's tuxedo made him almost as handsome as Brandon, Honor thought, if she was thinking at all. He gave the name of the last guest to Katie's father and turned...

"Honor Sloan," she said.

Joe's black eyes were wide open. "Honor!"

Honor waited.

"Honor?" Joe said. Still staring, he turned to Mr. Bushnell. "Honor Sloan," he said.

Katie's father had never seen Honor. He shook her hand and said they were glad she had come. Mrs. Bushnell said the same thing, shaking her hand, and so did the bride. But Brandon, turning toward Honor, heard Katie as she passed the next guest along: "Honor Sloan."

Brandon's mouth opened. That was all. He froze, his hand held halfway out. Honor heard Brandon's mother gasp.

Cold as ice, Honor passed Brandon's outstretched hand, shook Mrs. Lombard's hand, and walked away across the small dance floor to the tables.

She saw what she wanted: a chair with its back to the reception line. She sat in it, quivering all over, and folded her hands on the table to steady herself.

A waiter came with a glass of wine. Honor asked for water. The huge room was only a flood of chatter in her ears.

She drank the water slowly, sip by sip, wondering if she'd ever grow warm. After a while she glanced back to see that the reception line was ending, and soon would be gone. The band began to play. Guests were settling at tables.

Someone said her name. She turned around and said, "Joe." Her voice was cold, and there was a tinge of "Oh, no!" in it.

"Would you..." He looked embarrassed as he came around the table to face her. "Would you mind if I sit down?"

"You must be with friends...your mother—"

"No," he said, and pulled up a chair to sit down without looking at her.

They said nothing more, for the band started a number.

A waiter brought a glass of wine to Joe, and took their order. Honor said, "The filet mignon, please," over the band's wailing and tooting. She was glad of loud music: conversation was impossible. She glanced behind her once, and saw the wedding party seated hardly fifteen feet away.

Brandon's eyes were on her. She said to herself: *If Joe asks me to dance, Brandon can watch us. Let him.*

The band stopped with a last clash and bang as the waiter set their dinners before them. Joe said, "I never expected to have supper with the most beautiful woman in the room."

"I was invited," Honor said. "Brandon sent me an invitation." She raised her chin and stared at him. "So here I am."

Joe stared back. "He...invited—"

"Yes," Honor said. "He did."

They ate their dinners in silence, for the band drowned out talk. But when their music changed to a softer, sentimental number, Joe said, "I'm hoping you'll be in town tomorrow." He hurried on: "How long can you stay in Chicago? Could I show you some city sights?"

For a second Honor felt nothing but a blazing desire to yell: "Go anywhere at all with you! You called me names—" She stopped without a word at the look in his eyes.

Joe's mouth was on his wine glass, but his black eyes over the rim said he saw nothing but Honor Sloan. They said, in that second or two, that he was so sorry, that he was so angry, that all he wanted to do was to block everything in the world that might try to harm her.

"I...I'm sorry," Honor said to that look—those eyes above the wine. "I fly back to Iowa after breakfast tomorrow."

"Breakfast then? Better than nothing," Joe said.

The band began to play loud jazz again, drowning any conversation. How glad Honor was to hear them wail and thump. She could hardly speak sensibly to Joe—Brandon and his mother were so close...She sat rigid in her chair, hardly breathing, trying to take a few bites...

She heard Brandon's loud laugh. Soon Brandon's voice was louder still. He wasn't laughing; he was arguing. She knew that sound. But the band was louder than he was.

Brandon glared at his mother. "I didn't invite Honor! Why would I?" He scowled at the wedding dessert the waiter set before him, and wondered who'd want to eat sugar-frosted doves on top of some kind of yellow stuff.

"You're married to Katie now. You'll have a fine honeymoon and a new house and a job...don't let Honor upset you," Emily said. "And don't drink any more, you've had enough. Honor just came to embarrass you—she's so obviously mean and nasty. Pretend you don't know her. Don't spoil your lovely wedding."

Honor gave a quick glance behind her. Brandon and his mother were looking at her.

Let them. Honor leaned across the table and smiled at Joe, and suddenly she felt such triumph that she was almost dizzy. *I imagined what I'd do, and I've done it.*

The band played on, to her comfort. She ate a bite now and then, but hardly noticed when her plate was taken away. They ate the lemon tarts topped with white frosting doves and drank their coffee, and then Joe half-shouted over the howl of the band: "Dance?"

Joe took her hand. In a moment they were among the dancers, only a few feet away from the bride and groom. Brandon's eyes were on Honor as she tipped her head, the diamond earrings shooting fiery sparks, and smiled at Joe. Then she whirled away in his arms, pressed tightly against him in the crowd.

When the band gave a last flourish, Honor went back to their table with Joe. He said, "I'm going back to California next week. I'll stay in Berkeley for a while to check on my thesis."

"Why didn't you go to Iowa City for your master's and doctorate?" Honor asked.

"Berkeley has a reputation in botany and zoology, and I had a wonderful scholarship, and a girlfriend there," Joe said. "She got over me before I got over her, but I soldiered on, and I'm almost done."

The loud music began once more, hooting and banging and howling, and Honor and Joe could see why: the band was trying to drown Brandon's yells.

People stopped talking to watch as Brandon pulled his bride to the dance floor. She was struggling to unpin her immense veil. Her mother hurried around the end of the table to help, but Brandon tripped on Katie's cloud of tulle before the women reached him, and fell on his back among startled dancers.

Brandon tried to get up. He couldn't. Two men grabbed him under his arms, but he fought them off with his fists. The band banged and clanged and shouted lyrics while the dance floor turned into a punching match surrounded by fleeing guests.

"Brandon's been drinking," Joe said, standing up beside Honor. People at other tables were on their feet. "I'll have to do my duty as best man," Joe said, "but would you like to go somewhere to dance afterward?"

"Oh, no. No. Thanks," Honor said. "I flew in this morning, and I'm so terribly tired—I wouldn't be good company. But thank you."

"Tomorrow for breakfast, then?" Joe said. "I'm staying here. Call me when you're hungry? What floor is your room?"

"Three."

"My floor, too," he said.

"I'm very tired," Honor said. "Goodnight."

"Tomorrow for breakfast," Joe said. "I'm in room 321. When you're ready in the morning, call me."

"Thanks so much," Honor said, and went upstairs to lie on her bed in the dark, too exhausted to turn on a light or take off her dress.

Then satisfaction swept over her, head to foot, like a sizzling ripple of fire. She'd done it! She'd gone down that line! Brandon had watched Honor Sloan dancing with his handsome brother... dancing cold and safe and out of reach!

Joe Lombard. She couldn't have dreamed that he'd be so helpful. She'd imagined herself all alone at Brandon's wedding.

"Can I do it?" she'd asked Lena. "All by myself?"

Joe's look over his wine glass.

She could have breakfast with him. He'd said horrid things about her, but he seemed so shy...

But it was over! She'd done it! It was over! She took off her clothes, put on a nightgown and robe, and fell asleep in the dark, murmuring, "Over..."

It was still dark when Honor startled awake, sat up. Someone was pounding on her door.

Open it? In the middle of the night in a strange room in a strange hotel?

Now she heard a man yelling—someone drunk: he was slurring his words.

It was Brandon.

He sounded wild. Honor turned on a light. The door was chained; she opened it a crack and saw Brandon's red cheek and one eye through the narrow space.

"Honor! Lemme in!" he shouted.

"No," she whispered. "Go away."

"Lemme in!"

"Go to bed."

"Honor! Oh, Honor!" Brandon slid a few fingers along the chain, and Honor saw the glint of his wedding ring.

"I should have had a chain on my door last May," Honor whispered.

"I w'drunk!" Brandon yelled. "I wouldn'done that to you, but I w'drunk!"

Anger swept through Honor, but her voice was cold and bitter and clear through the chain: "Go away."

She heard another man's voice down the hall: Joe. Joe came close to say, "Let's go, Brandon."

"Go t'hell!" Brandon yelled.

Now Honor heard a young woman's voice; it came close to the gap in the door and whispered, "Come on, Brandon."

"Go 'way, Katie!" Brandon yelled, pounding on the door. "Honor! And you left! You never gamee a chance—"

"Let's go, Brandon," Joe said.

"Go t'ell!" Brandon yelled.

"Come on," Katie said.

"I said I wassorry!" Brandon shouted through the door crack. "Didn't I? Over'nd over. And we were going to gemmarried, weren'we?"

Honor heard a heavy thud, and then a scuffle. Katie's voice. Joe's voice saying, "Come on now. Come on."

"Joe Shtop me? Joe? Old pansy-waist? Old Flowwie-kisser?" Brandon giggled. He pressed against the door chain, and snarled, "Stay'way from Honor!"

Then Brandon's voice seemed farther away, still yelling "Honor! Honor!" Other voices joined it down the hall—fainter, as if they had turned a corner. At last they died away.

Honor shut her door and sat on her bed for a while, trembling. Someone tapped on her door. A low voice said, "Honor?"

It was Joe. She slid the chain back and opened her door. He whispered, "Are you all right?"

"Yes," she whispered back.

"Then I'll see you in the morning. Call me," he said.

What could she say? *I don't want to see you? I don't want to see anybody—I'm going home?*

"No," she whispered. "I'm sorry. No breakfast...I just want to go home. But thank you. Goodnight."

"Goodnight," Joe whispered. "I'm sorry."

Honor locked and chained her door, turned off her light and crawled into bed, but how could she sleep? She lay in the dark for hours, it seemed, listening to the constant sounds of a city, until the roar and honk of Chicago traffic grew louder under her window: it was dawn. She got up and hurried to pack and put on her travel clothes while daylight crept into the room.

When Honor went downstairs, a sleepy hotel clerk yawned and shoved her receipt across the desk. Brandon's shouts seemed to follow her through an almost empty hotel lobby. How many people had heard Brandon outside her door? Joe! Katie! She couldn't face any of them. Swinging doors opened to the street, and she left the hotel behind her...left Brandon's wild voice: *I wouldn'done that to you, but...*

A restaurant full of strangers—that was what Honor wanted. She found a small place open a few blocks away. At first, setting her suitcase down at an empty table, she couldn't think of eating. Then the luscious pictures on the menu told her that she was very, very hungry.

Honor ordered an omelet that spilled out cheese and bacon....
puffy rolls glistening with brown sugar and butter...hot coffee
topped with a swirl of cream.

L ena met Honor at the Waterloo airport. "Well," Lena said
as they drove home, "How did it go?"
"It went...exactly as planned," Honor said. "The planes, the
lovely hotel room...my beautiful dress and your diamonds..."
Lena had tea ready, and they sat at the kitchen table. Honor
described the faces of Joe, Brandon and his mother in the receiv-
ing line...dinner and dancing with Joe...Brandon flat on his back
on the dance floor, tangled in Katie's veil. "Oh, my," Lena kept
saying as their tea cooled. "Joe? After he called you names at that
party?"
"He acted as if he were trying to help."
"He's sorry for what he said about you?" Lena said.
"Last night wasn't over yet," Honor said. "Brandon came after
midnight: hammering at my hotel door, but I'd chained it. And
then Joe and the bride came, while Brandon yelled how sorry
he was for what he'd done to me. They heard it all—until they
dragged him away for his wedding night, I suppose."
"Oh, my," Lena said.
They sipped their tea in silence for a while. Then Honor said,
"I did just what I meant to do."
"Good for you," Lena said.
"But it wasn't what I thought it would be."
"Not at all?"
"No."
"You never expected to have Brandon hammering on your door
on his wedding night."
"I didn't. No. But all the way home on the plane I thought
about what I really went to Chicago for." Honor put her teacup
in its saucer with a clatter. "I hated Brandon, didn't I? And Joe?
Revenge! That's what I was after. I felt as if they'd ruined my life,
killed all my hopes and my chance to be free—didn't I?"
"Well, of course, you must have—"
"Wanted revenge! Yes! And I got it. Brandon and I managed
to ruin both our lives! Can you imagine just how much harm I did
to him...coming to Chicago on his wedding day...letting his bride
and family know—"

"Honor—"

"I read a warning in some book: *Before you embark on a journey of revenge, dig two graves.*" Honor laid her head on her arms beside her empty cup.

7

October came: beautiful leaves against blue skies. Lena's house was becoming a different place: the wide oak baseboards, door frames and doors had been stripped and sanded and varnished until they gleamed, and cracks in walls and ceilings had disappeared under plaster, paint and wallpaper. Old furniture had come with the house...soon it was gone. Carpets went down. Dark walnut kitchen cabinets went up. Honor told Lena that the new kitchen made her a better cook, but Lena said Honor was good enough already.

They ate in a splendid dining room now: men had carried Lena's Jacobean oak dining-room set down from the attic. She said her father had always hated the lumps in the chair backs, so she had them sawed off and the whole set refinished, and she'd bought more fine furniture when she was in London, and a cut-glass dining-room chandelier.

The deep green living-room carpet went down. The fireplace had a new fire in it: fake wood blazing with real flames. Carpenters built bookshelves in the living room, and Honor brought boxes and boxes of books down from the attic.

"My passion—leather bound books!" Lena said as they unpacked authors they knew and loved: Austen, Dickens, Colette, Conrad, Hardy, Hemingway, Montaigne—shelved alphabetically, shelf after shelf. "Acid-free paper! Sewed pages, not glued in!" Lena said, chanting the alphabet to put her beautiful library in order. "Gilded leather covers and gold edges all around! Ribbon page markers! Marbled end papers! Illustrations!"

Now her gilded books, row after row, lined the walls where they sat by the fire. "You have so many authors I love," Honor said one night. "Would you mind if I borrow a book to read every now and then? I'd take good care of it."

"Help yourself," Lena said. "Choose one. Maybe we should read it to each other to begin? A book by my new fire! The perfect evening! Choose."

Honor walked along the shelves. Her figure was definitely expanding now. "Do you like Jane Austen?" she asked, coming back to the A's.

"*Emma*?" Lena said.

"*Emma*!" Honor cried. "Don't you love her? Making all her mistakes so blindly, with such good intentions? Looking right past the one man who's perfect for her? Rushing about trying to arrange marriages, poking her nose in everyone's business, while a secret love affair goes on right under that nose?"

"I wish Austen hadn't called Emma's lover 'Knightley,'" Lena said. "Because, obviously, he is. A loving knight of a gentleman who will always care for her, and knows right from wrong. I've always thought he was too good for Emma."

"You don't like her?" Honor asked. "Didn't Austen say she was afraid her readers wouldn't like Emma? I know Emma's young, and seems too rich and high-handed and quick to judge. She hurts a good old friend. She almost keeps another friend from a true love. But Emma can learn. She does."

"At least she cares for that old father of hers, who's fixated on his health and his chicken house," Lena said. "Emma has to live with him—care for a creaky, cranky old man. But she won't leave him."

"And when Knightley says to Emma: 'How could you be so unfeeling?' I think it's the only time in the book that Emma cries." Honor took the red and gold book down from the shelf to turn pages. "And listen to some of the hidden warnings Austen puts on the first page: *"Emma Woodhouse, handsome, clever and rich...seemed to unite some of the best blessings of existence; and had lived nearly twenty-one years in the world with very little to distress or vex her."*

"*Seemed*," Lena said. "What a warning! And do we really care for Emma and her blessings and her lack of trouble? Turns the reader right off, wouldn't you think?"

"But that first page isn't over—it says that Emma has ceased to have *'any restraint'* on her, *'the shadow of authority'* over her having *'long passed away.'*" Honor said.

"Handsome, clever, rich, and nobody has any power over her. Sit down and read," Lena said. "Emma is in danger."

So Honor sat down and read. When her voice grew husky, Lena took over. Evening after evening, they stopped to argue, leafed back through the book to check, and laughed at the deliciously funny, happy ending when Emma persuaded her father to let her marry. Her father was afraid for his chickens—but if Emma married, he'd have a young husband in the house to save his chickens from the fox.

Lena said, "You love books as much as I do. I wish I'd known how you read and read as you grew up. I'd have sent you books, guessing what you'd like...so many fine children's books. But maybe your folks wouldn't have let you keep them. They certainly wouldn't have let me see you, probably, and I wouldn't have wanted to see them. They never helped me—they took my best years, and my chances."

"How could they?" Honor said.

"They could and they did. They had reasons."

"Reasons?"

"Your grandparents didn't want your mother to marry your father," Lena said. "Maybe you've heard that. Your folks weren't going to marry in a church, and your mother was so young. Your father didn't have a shoe without a hole in it, but he rented a farm the neighbors called 'The Swamp,' because it was such low land, and cheap."

Lena sighed, closed *Emma*, and stroked the leather cover. "Your grandparents had all that money, but they told your mother and father they were poor, and said the newlyweds had made their bed and they could lie in it. 'That farm won't make you potatoes,' the grandparents told Maryflora and John. They never gave your parents a single thing or a single cent. I remember your mother crying. Your folks rented a terrible farm. After you were born, they had to move to town at last, and get work."

"Dad had a lot of different jobs," Honor said. "I went to a little Lutheran college in Nebraska for two years, until the folks said they couldn't pay for any more college, but I got a scholarship at Iowa."

Lena sighed. "I worked, in a library, so I couldn't pay for college, and then your grandparents became too sick to live alone. Somebody had to nurse them. But do you think that your folks ever...all those years...helped me take care of the old folks?"

"I guess my parents hated yours for never giving them any help, so they weren't going to do a thing for those grandparents, ever," Honor said.

"Not ever. Your folks never came to the shabby old farmhouse the three of us lived in, or brought us a single plate of food. They were just a mile or two away. They stayed away, and let me do everything. For years."

"They never told me anything about it," Honor said. "I remember my mother and father running around yelling at each other, or crying, that's all."

Lena said: "They certainly weren't crying about your grandparents being dead. I didn't cry either, but I had reasons not to, and one reason was that I didn't have to feel selfish and mean. *I* hadn't taken years of anybody's youth away, or ruined anybody's chance to get married, or left my parents for my sister to take care of!"

"I suppose you did feel it wasn't fair," Honor said. "Who wouldn't? You were going to get married?"

"I worked in the library for years, and met Jack Trowbridge. He was forty-five, and I loved him. I wanted to spend my life helping him. It wasn't that he was handsome—although he was—but we were so alike, loving books, planning to travel and have a family. He went on to be a professor somewhere in Ohio, and has a wife and children."

"How miserable you must have been," Honor said.

Lena ran her hand along a shelf of books; their gilded backs shone in the firelight. "We had our wedding planned. We'd already rented a house, and set the date. But there my folks were, all alone and sick and poor."

"You couldn't get married?"

"Jack was so decent, and tried his best to keep us together. But he had to get his doctorate, and there was so little money to keep four people at my grandparents' farm. We cried together, and tried and tried to find an answer—but why would a man want to spend the first years of his married life in a ramshackle farmhouse with crutches and bedpans and two old folks who yelled from their beds that their daughter didn't come fast enough with the food or pills or clean sheets?"

"I'm so sorry," Honor said. "I never knew any of this—except that you got all my grandparents' money."

"That wasn't my fault," Lena said. "Nobody knew the old folks had any money at all…until they died. Then a lawyer told me that your grandparents hadn't needed me to live with them—for years! They could have paid for luxuries and caregivers, and I could have married, and even gone to a really good college, they were so rich. I never knew they had money." Lena sat looking at the fire, not at Honor. "But your father and mother must have thought I did."

"What a sad story," Honor said.

"But there's justice in this world," Lena said. "Justice may drag its feet, but it finally gets where it's going, I guess. I'd saved my parents from spending money, day by day and year by year, and at last that money was all mine. Maybe I'd lost my love, but I sold their farms, and graduated from Wellesley, and traveled abroad. I lived!"

Late autumn brought rain, week after week, but the last day of October the rain was gone. Honor and Lena were getting supper, and Lena said, "The rain's stopped! The little kids will be so thankful."

"Thankful?" Honor said.

"It's Halloween!" Lena said. "I've got a basket of candy and pennies and gum ready. We've got lots of kids in this neighborhood." She brought a basket full of treats from a closet, and after supper she turned on the porch light and went out with Honor to wait in the dark, fresh, rain-washed air.

"Here they come," Lena said in a few minutes. They watched a slow procession walk uphill past the park corner: a group of adults and children. Plastic pumpkins bobbed among them, glowing like orange fireflies. Soon they halted in front of Lena's house, and adult voices called "Trick or Treat!" but only three small people came up Lena's stairs one by one—small, strange shapes.

"Happy Halloween!" Lena called. "Come and choose your treat!"

The three climbed slowly out of the dark into the porch light. The first small figure was a witch. It was all in black, and the mask under the pointed hat was menacing—fangs, great nose, empty eyes. Behind the witch, a ghost yanked a sheet away from its sneakers and almost fell flat, its black eyes and gaping mouth half covered by its shroud. Last came the skull: a bony, white and grinning Death.

They stood in a row and said nothing.

Lena held out the basket, and small hands reached for treats.

Then the three turned away down the creaking stairs without a word. Darkness gathered them in.

When Honor came down to breakfast the next morning, Lena said: "You look tired. Did I hear you walking in the hall around two o'clock this morning? All those trick-or-treaters last night?"

"I finally came downstairs and used your typewriter," Honor said. "I couldn't forget those first three Halloween beggars last night—you remember?"

"A skeleton?" Lena said. "And wasn't there a ghost? A witch? Three little haunts. Couldn't have been more than four or five years old. What a crowd we had…candy and gum and pennies, all gone."

"You call them 'little haunts,' and they were." Honor handed Lena a paper.

"A poem!" Lena said.

TRICK OR TREAT

The ghost is a torn sheet,
the skeleton's suit came from a rack in a store,
the witch is flameproof, but who knows
what dark streets they have taken here?
Brother Death, here is a candy bar.
For the lady wearing the hat from Salem: gum.
And a penny for each eye, Lost Soul.
They fade away with their heavy sacks.
Thanks! I yell just in time.
Thanks for another year!

"Ah," Lena said after she'd read it twice. "The Fates. The Furies."

"Yes," Honor said. "Threatening."

"People used to put coins on the eyes of the dead to keep them closed."

"Yes."

Lena read the poem again, and said, "Lost soul. Death. Witchcraft. The Dark Powers on All Hallows' Eve."

"That's what I felt when I saw them standing there on the porch," Honor said. "They were so still. And you see it! The Dark Powers. Almost as if they had come to tell me, without saying a word: 'See what a trick we've pulled on you this year, just when you never, ever expected it? But it might have been much, much worse. *You could be married! Be thankful.*"

"Maybe they're always at our door," Lena said.

"Just little children."

"*But,*" Lena said, "*who knows what dark streets they have taken here?*"

The days cooled. Nights came earlier.

"This great big baby of mine must be twins—and it's not due until the middle of February!" Honor said. "I can figure that date out with no trouble. My graduation day. But look how I'm expanding. I'm so glad winter's coming."

Lena stood on her side porch steps, watching Honor rake leaves. It was growing dark, but the weather was warm for the last of November. Honor was wearing old sneakers and too-small jeans and a shirt that the baby was straining at every seam.

"Glad? For winter?" Lena said. "You're an Iowa girl! Aren't you acquainted with ice and snowdrifts and below-zero wind—"

"But I can *hide* in a coat," Honor said.

"A big coat," Lena said. "My treat. Let's shop on Saturday."

"Thanks," Honor said. "Thanks so very much."

Just then a wind from the park hit Honor's big leaf pile, spun it like a dervish, and sent half of it back to the cleared grass.

"Darn!" Honor said, and that was all, because Joe Lombard was standing at the garden gate.

66

For a moment no one said anything, until Honor said, "Joe."

He looked stunned. A leaf from the hackberry fell on his curly black hair. He didn't notice it; he was staring at Honor. "I... told you I'd be back," he said.

For a moment there was no sound but the wind in leaves. Then Lena said, "Joe! Come right in—I remember you! You're the other Lombard fellow. The polite one. Come sit by my new fire and have some cider."

Joe was the polite Lombard: he took off his cap and asked how she was, and then held the porch door open for her—and Honor. Honor had to pass close by him, bulging shirt and all.

Honor could think of no word to say, not one, but Lena saved her—Lena was so warm, so friendly to Joe all the way from the yard to her living room. She didn't fool Honor. By the time they settled in chairs by the fire, Honor knew quite well what Lena had in mind, and would have said, "No! No!" if she'd had the chance.

But Lena chattered at Joe and smiled at Joe. Joe pretended to admire the colors Lena had chosen for the living room, and the books in their bookcases—Honor admired his presence of mind. But his eyes were on her every time she dared to look, and she thought he didn't see much except her, because his eyes were full of fury. Pity. Shock.

"Green and blue," Lena said, gazing at handsome Joe, while Honor's bulging front seemed to turn everything Lena could say into desperate babble. "That's what I wanted all over this house," she said. "Nature colors. Not all those dreary, tired, 'fashionable' shades: grayish green, brownish blue, faded pink! And I won't have any tan or brown or beige! Nature hardly uses them, except for fur, mud, rot, tree bark...I've seen whole houses decorated in those 'trendy' colors—floor to ceiling. Drab, drab, drab."

"You have a fine view from these big windows," Joe said, but he was looking at the rug, not the view.

"The first time I saw this house, there was a Christmas tree in that window," Lena said. "There won't be a Christmas tree there this year. We won't be climbing ladders..." she changed the subject: "I'll bring some cider—it's warm on the stove." She hurried off to the kitchen.

Joe and Honor sat looking at the fire. Children were playing in a pile of leaves in the front yard. Their cries were the only sound in the room until Joe said, "Honor..."

She wouldn't look at him.

"Brandon?" he said.

"Yes," Honor said.

The children yelled. The fire snapped. "Does Brandon know?"

"No."

"That was why you ran away from the party, and graduation?" Joe asked.

"I'd told him, weeks before, that I couldn't marry him. But at the party he stuck the ring on my finger and paraded around with that wedding cake and me. You brought me home in the rain, but later he came my room," Honor said. "He was still drunk. He called me awful names." She was almost whispering, her eyes on the fire. "I couldn't stop him. He was too strong. I couldn't marry him. Not ever."

She wasn't looking at Joe. He wasn't looking at her.

Lena came in with a tray. "You've finished your dissertation?" she asked Joe.

"It's been approved. I'm doing the last work on it," Joe said in a low, flat voice.

They drank the cider and ate the cookies while Lena said he was certainly welcome any time he was in Cedar Falls, and asked if his mother was well. Joe said she was, thanks, and he'd just dropped in. It was his mother's birthday, so he was on his way to her apartment in Des Moines.

He got up. "Thanks for the cookies and cider." Lena and Honor went to the door with him, and watched him take the stairs to the street two at a time. He ran to his old car and drove away fast, as if he felt glad to be gone.

Joe drove fast around the corner of Seerley Park, but he slowed down, turned another corner and parked. When he left his car and sat on a park bench, he could see the big white house, high on its bank. Lena's porch light was still on.

He sat a long time with his head in his hands. Dead leaves blew around him on the dying grass.

Windows in surrounding houses began to glow as the last daylight faded. Mothers called their children in. Smoke rose from chimneys: families were eating supper.

November wind rose with the dark. Joe shivered and stood up. Lena's porch light was off. His mother's birthday was almost over. He took the highway to Des Moines.

68

Emily Lombard had spent most of her birthday waiting tables at The Hungry Chef. Now it was closing time. She walked around the corner to the parking lot and her room in the restaurant's back wall, crawled on her sofa bed, and lay back with a deep sigh.

Miles to walk all day: kitchen to table, table to kitchen. Heavy trays. Chattering people. How quiet it was in her small room. Lanterns in the parking lot glowed through her one window. She closed her eyes and heard nothing but a car leaving the lot.

Joe would come. He'd drive in before long. He never missed her birthday.

She wouldn't see Brandon. He was settled now with a wife and a well-paying job and no time to drink, she hoped, and he wouldn't come from Chicago today just for her birthday. She hadn't seen him since that awful wedding breakfast, and might not see him for a long time—perhaps not even for Christmas.

She stared at the ceiling. Brandon at his wedding party—on his back and tangled in a veil—his new in-laws and Katie crammed in an elevator because he said he had to talk to Honor—pounding on Honor's door...

And that wedding night. Brandon was still yelling while they got him to the wedding suite and put him on a huge, satin-sheeted bed festooned with bouquets and wedding bells. And then that breakfast the next morning, where everybody pretended that dinner dance hadn't turned into a brawl...

Honor Sloan. Joe had said he was going to an appointment in Cedar Falls...was he going to see Honor? She was there...so cruel, so mean. But Joe was smart...

Emily fell asleep, until Joe knocked at her door.

"Hi, Mom," he called. "Happy birthday. Sorry I'm so late."

"Joe!" she cried, opening her door and hugging him. There wasn't much space in her little room for a man as big as he was, and when he shut her door on the November night, there seemed to be no room at all.

"Thank you for the beautiful flowers," Emily said. "I put them on the desk at work where everybody enjoyed them." She kissed him and hung up his coat. He was smiling, but she thought he was sad. "Are you staying the night?"

"I'm afraid I can't. But I didn't want you to spend your birthday evening alone."

"The cook at The Hungry Chef baked a cake for me," Emily said. "He always does. Have you had supper?"

"I ate before I left," he said, sitting on her sofa bed while Emily sat on her one chair. "I've been struggling with my bibliography all day."

"What you need is some coffee and a piece of my birthday cake," Emily said. She spooned coffee into the coffee pot and put two big cake slices on plates. "You've been in Cedar Falls?"

Joe said, "Yes," and Emily asked: "You didn't run into Honor, did you? Have you seen her since the wedding?"

"Mom..." Joe said. He turned his empty cup around in his hands.

Emily sighed. "She broke Brandon's heart. I've often been so glad he didn't marry her. Now he's got a wife who loves him, and a new house, and a good job..."

Joe put his cup down and said, "Mom, I came with some news for you. I didn't know I'd be bringing it on your birthday, but it's...important. I guess it's a present, all right, but it won't be coming for a while."

"Never mind. Presents like that are special, aren't they?" Emily said. "Something to look forward to?"

"I guess," Joe said.

"You don't seem very cheerful. I noticed it the minute you came," Emily said. Something's happened? Is Brandon all right?"

"*He's* all right."

"Is Katie all right? She isn't sick?"

"Not that I know of." He took her hands. "Mom..." he stopped, and she saw how sad he was. "I just have to say it right out: You're going to be a grandmother."

"Grandmother!" Emily cried. "Then Katie is expecting? Oh—"

"It's not Katie," Joe said. He squeezed her hands hard. "It's Honor."

Emily stared at him. "Honor? Honor Sloan?"

"That's why Honor ran away," Joe said. "I didn't know. You didn't know. She never came to her own graduation with Brandon, or went up to the platform that day to get the prizes she won for her poetry. We couldn't understand it. When we asked him then, Brandon told us he didn't know anything about it."

70

The two of them sat there, gripping each other's hands.
"Brandon's baby?" Emily said. "Brandon's..."
"Yes. She told me so this afternoon."
"We were so surprised she wasn't at her graduation!" Emily cried. "She was going to marry Brandon in a few weeks, and then she..."
"Brandon told us she jilted him," Joe said. "Honor did jilt him, and no wonder. She'd found out too much about him, and he'd come to her room...and he married Katie in a few months!"
"And now..."
"Having his child," Joe said.
"Oh, Joe!" She couldn't say anything more.
They sat together for a while without speaking. Finally Emily asked: "Does Brandon know?"
"She's never told him. He's never seen her since she ran away from him, except when he found her in a grocery store soon after she hid with her aunt. But I stepped right into the middle of it this afternoon," Joe said. "I was in Cedar Falls for a meeting at the college, and went to see Honor and her aunt, even though I knew I wasn't welcome—I told you how she'd hardly talk to me when I visited her in July."
"And she told you?"
"She didn't have to. I found her in her aunt's yard, raking leaves, and she looked...far along." Joe was squeezing Emily's hands hard again. "Her aunt invited me in, but I was an absolute marble statue—could hardly talk sensibly. Or make any sense of it. Honor didn't say a word. Lena kept a conversation going— told how Honor helped her redecorate her house, and the colors she'd chosen. But all I could think of was Honor sitting there, so...pregnant...saying nothing, not even looking at me. We sat by Lena's new fireplace, and Lena went to get cider and cookies for us."
"And Honor told you?"
"I don't think we said a dozen words. I didn't know how to begin—I just blurted out 'Brandon?'—I can't believe that I was so..."
Joe dropped her hands and walked the two steps to her window, looked out, walked back, stood looking down at Emily as if he didn't see her. "And all she said was *Yes*. And I said, 'That's why you ran away?' And she said *Yes*."

71

"That was all?"

"Then she said, *Brandon was drunk, and he said awful things. He came to my room after that party. I couldn't stop him. He was too strong. I couldn't marry him. Not ever.*"

He sat down and took Emily's hands again. "She's there in Cedar Falls...no job..."

"She came to Brandon's wedding!" Emily said. "July, August, September...she must have known by then, but she wasn't showing it yet, and she just walked down that wedding line—"

"So regal!" Joe cried. "So full of hate! I saw it when she looked at Brandon."

"And today she was the same?"

"Lena did all the talking, until we were alone for those few minutes."

"What did you say?"

"Her aunt came back. She said they were glad to see me. I told her it was your birthday and I was going to see you."

"That was all?"

"That was all."

They sat for a while looking at empty plates and coffee cups.

"I don't suppose she ever leaves her aunt's house," Joe said.

"No," Emily said.

"She can't go out in public looking like that," Joe said. "She had several jobs in Iowa City when she was a student, but she can't work now. Not with a baby coming. All she can do is stay with her aunt if she can...like you lived with your folks when Dad left you and Brandon and me. She doesn't have anyone else to help her, and I can't imagine she has any money. Her parents barely made ends meet, and they died last year."

"Brandon's baby," Emily said, staring at Joe. "And he doesn't even know?"

"First of a new generation of our family. But she'll be an 'unwedded mother,'" Joe said. "You know how people feel about that kind of girl. Maybe she can give the baby away..."

"Oh, no!" Emily cried.

"At least she hasn't gotten rid of it," Joe said. "I know her. She'd never do that. But, of course, she's so ashamed. She wouldn't even look at me. Ashamed of what Brandon did! Ashamed of what people will think she did. And what can girls like her do? She'll have no married name at the doctor's, or at the hospital. No father's name on the birth certificate. No last name for the baby

72

but hers." He stood up. "I have to be going, I'm afraid, but will you try to think of some way to help her?"

"I'll...try," Emily said, helping him on with his coat.

Car lights swept by Emily's window. Then they heard a car door close. Someone pounded on the door and shouted, "Mom!"

"Brandon," Joe said. Emily opened her door.

"Happy birthday, Mom!" Brandon cried. "Joe's here?"

"Yes," Emily said, and the very way she said it stopped Brandon halfway through the hug he was giving her.

"Sorry, Mom—Sorry I'm so late," Brandon said. "You must be mad at me, but I had to come from Chicago! It's easy for Joe. He's practically next door."

"Yes," Emily said.

"I don't have a present for you now, except me, but I'll send it later."

Brandon just stood there. They looked at him.

"Never mind," Emily said. "You've already given me one."

"A present? I have?" Brandon said. "When?"

"When you graduated," Emily said.

"I did?"

"When you made me a grandmother."

Brandon stared at her.

Joe said, "You bastard."

Emily had never heard Joe say that word. He shoved Brandon against her kitchen sink and yelled: "*You did that to Honor!*"

Three canisters above the sink dumped raisins in Brandon's hair and flour on his shocked face as he fell backward. He managed to get to his feet. The room was so small with three people in it — the furious faces of the two men were only inches apart.

"Get out!" Joe yelled.

"We'd planned our wedding!" Brandon rubbed the flour on his face. "I was drunk, that's all! And she left the party—just ran off—and you guys got on me, saying I was left at the altar, and you bet I hadn't even—"

"You did that to her!" Joe yelled. "And then *invited her to your wedding!*"

"I was mad, that's all! I found her in Cedar Falls, and she threw my ring at me and wouldn't talk—"

"And what can Honor do now? Where can she go? Her folks are dead! She's going to be an unmarried mother! She doesn't want you, whether you're married or not—what woman would?

73

But you know what people will call her! And how can she work when she has a baby?"

Brandon, powdered with flour, yanked Emily's door open, ran for his car, and was gone.

Joe put his arms around Emily. After a while he said, "What a birthday you've had! I'm sorry. I shouldn't have yelled..."

"He let us think Honor was to blame for jilting him," Emily said. "Never told us why she didn't go to her graduation. Why she's hiding with her aunt. Too ashamed."

They sat down and looked at each other.

"But we'll have a new generation in our family," Joe said in a little while. He knelt to pick raisins off the floor. "So we've got to think how to help Honor... save her from having to hide...being left out... being called names..."

"She's so alone!" Emily said. "Such a beautiful girl. Coming down that line to look Brandon in the eye. And think of it—she couldn't even go to her graduation—was so hurt. Where could she go, after such a night? Her aunt's taken her in, but the baby won't have a father, or a father's name...people will have a name for *her*. And how can she get a job, alone with a baby. I know how that feels."

"But you were married," Joe said. "You could always say that you had a husband. You had Dad's name."

"But people always wondered about me," Emily said. "Divorced women weren't as bad as unmarried mothers, of course. But it seemed like there were very few, because divorced women weren't seen much—certainly not at church. Or much of any place, except if they could find a job. Everyone asked, 'Are you married?' when they met you. If you said you were a teacher or secretary or nurse, you probably weren't married...hardly any married women worked...and unmarried women had to be watched."

"You've never talked about it," Joe said.

"Women without husbands were dangerous, you know, like foxes circling a henhouse. A woman who hadn't caught a man lost the only game in town." Her voice was bitter. "Never mind that your husband drinks, or spends all the money, or knocks you around. And times haven't changed that much."

"Mom," Joe said, and put his arms around her.

"*Your little boys don't have a father*, people sometimes said to me." Emily sighed. "It was painful. I hated to lie. Finally I found a perfect and truthful reason for not living with a man who loved his bottle."

"Kids asked where my father was, when I was growing up," Joe said. "But I never knew what people said to you."

"It usually happened when I was at work," Emily said. "But if people asked questions, I told them my sons and I were lonely, of course, but my husband had perfected a new way to empty liquids quickly, and was perfecting his invention abroad because—they would certainly agree—a man had to support his family, even if he were half a world away."

Joe hugged her. "And they always agreed that he did," Emily said.

"Happy birthday, Mom," Joe said. He put on his coat and opened her door. "I have to be getting back."

"Thanks for the roses," she said. "And for that news. I guess."

She watched him get in his car, raise his hand a little in goodbye, and drive away.

8

O ne morning Joe woke before dawn, and found he'd
been dreaming of pregnant Honor...and Lena, saying:
*The first time I saw this house, there was a Christmas tree
in the window. There won't be a Christmas tree there this year."*

Yes! A Christmas tree! Yes. He'd buy Honor and Lena a tree—
show them he hadn't just run off—run away when he saw Honor.

That afternoon he went to a tree lot and bought a big Fraser
fir (Lena's ceilings were high) and a small one, and a wreath for
Lena's front door. Before he'd loaded them in his car, a blizzard
began.

The first heavy snow of the winter. He drove into a blast of
driven white. Two Christmas trees filled the car with their rich
scent, and poked bristles down the neck of his jacket.

Traffic was creeping along Iowa roads, but at last he reached Lena's house. He dragged the big tree up on the porch and rang the bell, and Lena opened the door and said, "Joe! Come in! Come right in!"

"Thank you, ma'am," he said, "but I've got some company with me. Do you think you've got some space in a corner for him? I figured the two of you might not have your tree yet, and I brought one along."

"A Christmas tree!" Lena said. "Come in! Bring your big green friend. Take off your coat and warm up." Honor peered from the kitchen doorway. "Honor, Joe's brought a Christmas tree!" Joe stood the tree in Lena's front hall, and she hung up his snowy coat while he took off his boots. "Sit down by the fire, Joe, and you'll certainly stay for supper, with such weather out there. Honor's an amazing cook, and I can peel potatoes. We're having coffee. Would you like some?"

"Yes, thanks, and I'll put up your tree," he said. When Honor brought his coffee, she hardly gave him a look. Lena said, "Honor, can you find my tree-stand upstairs in the smaller back-room closet?"

Honor found the stand and brought it down. They drank coffee and watched snow dim the windows. Forest scent and winter cold breathed from Joe's tree.

"I'll get your fir on his feet," Joe said to Lena when the coffee was gone. "Where do you want him?"

Lena looked around the room. "Between the front window and the stairs? Folks can see him from the street then."

"I brought a wreath, too," Joe said. "Left it on your porch. Thought you'd like one for your door."

The fir was heavy, tall and broad; Joe lifted it high enough to get its trunk in the water pail, and crawled out of sight to fasten chains while Honor held the tree straight and Lena said, "Lean it a little more toward the windows...that's it...a little more..."

"Perfect," Lena said at last, looking at branches that rose from the new carpet to a firelit ceiling.

"And do you have ornaments? Lights?" Joe crawled out from a roof of green to brush needles from his hair. "I can buy some."

"In the attic under a window," Lena said, so Joe followed Honor upstairs, and brought down box after box. "Those belonged to my folks—lights and ornaments and stand." Lena said. "Didn't think I'd ever use those again—imagine an old lady with a broken leg wrestling with a tree. Joe, you simply can't go out in that weather—we can give you a bed—I've bought two new ones! That storm's going to last all night."

"It *is* pretty bad out there," Joe said. "I was afraid you might not have a tree this year, and I thought I'd just get your tree put up and then go—"

"Nonsense," Lena said. "Haven't you ever heard of Yule, as in 'Yule stay for supper, of course.'"

"If Yule have me," Joe said, grinning.

"And Yule stay the night too!" Lena said. "It's Yule!"

The boxes were full of ornaments, and a mass of tree lights. Lena went off to peel potatoes, and Honor and Joe untangled strings of bulbs and spread them on the new carpet. Joe found a stepladder, hung a silver star on the tree's top bough, and began hooking lights to branches as Honor handed the strings to him. They rummaged through tissue paper to find ornaments and hooks; before long the tree shone with lights and bright-colored balls from ceiling to floor.

The scent of the fir tree filled the room. They shut boxes and stacked them, and Joe carried them to the attic.

He came down to Honor at the foot of the stairs.

"I wanted to kill Brandon, that's all," he said in a low voice. "Still do."

The sad and angry look in Honor's eyes— Joe saw it, and said more than he meant to. "Brandon's crazy!" he said, leaning down to whisper, his mouth almost touching her dark hair. "You're so smart and talented and beautiful—don't you know how many men would marry you in a minute?"

He heard her take a deep breath. "If that's so, I wish it weren't," she whispered back. "I'd like to be stupid and ugly, if only I could be without any men at all—ever. Free."

"Hey, you two!" Lena called from the kitchen. "When you're finished, we'll eat!" She came in and clapped her hands. "What a beautiful tree!" she said, and went to her front window. "It's glowing over my porch and down the bank and halfway to the park!"

After supper they sat in the living room, lit by the fire and tree. The good food had tasted like dust and ashes to Joe— all he could hear was Honor saying: *If only I could be without any men at all—ever.* He tried to act cheerful. He said to Lena: "I've just enjoyed an early and delicious Christmas dinner. Never thought, driving in that storm, that I was coming to such a welcome."

"Any time," Lena said. "Even without a tree."

Honor was staring thoughtfully at the fire, her hands folded over the top of her round lap. She said, "Can the two of you imagine how thankful I am tonight? Last December I'd just buried my parents and cleaned out their house, and was sitting by their empty fireplace on Christmas Eve."

Joe's spirits lifted a little: she was talking to both of them. "Alone?" he asked.

"Brandon was invited to Chicago for Christmas with three of his college friends," Honor said. "He loved going there—they have every luxury you can imagine."

"They didn't invite you?" Lena asked.

"I don't think they knew about me, or our plans to marry. To them, I was only one of Brandon's girlfriends. And my parents had just died. And I couldn't have left my job in a florist shop— they had almost too many orders to fill. But the boss gave me Christmas off, and I finally finished clearing out Mother and Dad's house."

"I wish I'd known!" Joe said. "I'd have come to help."

"But you've brought us this beautiful tree," Honor said, "and Lena's given me food and clothes and a home—think of that! When I knocked on her door, I thought there was no place in the world for me."

"It's hard to imagine being as lost and hopeless as that," Joe said. The three of them watched the fire for a while without a word.

"Well," Lena said finally. "Joe—you've put up our tree and eaten with us, but I really don't know much about you. Start at the beginning. Tell us about yourself."

"The very beginning? Can't remember it," Joe said. "There must have been a hospital, and piles of diapers, don't you think? Let's see…Christmas. I believe one of the first things I remember is my fourth Christmas. I yearned for just one thing."

"A puppy?" Honor said.

"A bicycle?" Lena said. "Too young? A train set?"

"You might guess all that. I suppose I wanted those things, too. But what I wanted most was a big green plant that I'd seen at a florist's shop. A philodendron taller than I was. My mother bought it and hid it under an old bedspread in the basement until Christmas morning."

"What did your mother think?" Lena asked.

"She was used to me by that time. She lived with her folks and Brandon and me in a little town near Traer after my dad left us. My mother's father had a big garden, and spring, summer and fall I was there more hours than I was home. My other grandfather was a gardener, too, and I grew up believing it was what men did: garden." He watched the fire quiver and spark. "I should have been born in England."

"England?" Honor said.

"In America, gardening just isn't the thing. Not for most boys. Heaven help you, no—not for boys. Not even for men, really. Have you ever heard a group of American men at a party talk about gardens? Hardly ever, and not for long, even in Iowa. They'll talk about crops and yields, maybe, or politics, or the stats of athletes, maybe. But how about garden fertilizers...choosing flowers that deer and rabbits won't eat...grafting plants..."

"England's different?" Lena asked.

"I found that it was. I went there for a summer after a year at Berkeley. My mother thought I was crazy, but I'd saved up enough money to take a cheap trip."

"Oh...I would love to go to England!" Honor said.

Joe smiled at her. "I went to all the beautiful gardens. England gave that art to the world: landscape gardening. I went to Sissinghurst Castle."

"Virginia Woolf's lover. Her very own castle," Honor said.

"Yes. Vita Sackville-West. I saw her White Garden, all white or green...no other colors in sight. And I pinched one of her ivies."

"Stole it?" Lena said.

"Pinched it. Literally. A lush ivy, like clusters of holly. Huge. In the center of the White Garden. I backed up to it. No one was looking. I pinched off a bit, and carried it home through customs in a secret pocket under my arm. Pinched it. You should see that plant now."

"And how did you learn what English men feel about gardening?" Honor asked. "They didn't pinch you for pinching their greenery?"

There was coolness in Honor's voice. Joe thought he understood it—he was Brandon's brother. "I'm glad to say they didn't. An English lord led our tour. Can't remember his illustrious title.

80

He knew that garden—every leaf and bloom. The tour group had a lot of English men in it, and they were gardeners too, I soon realized. And they were there for the gardens—they didn't want to hear about Virginia Woolf, or even Bloody Baker, a past owner. I couldn't believe what I heard. More than a dozen Englishmen were asking this lord about the smallest details of Sissinghurst plantings...arguing among themselves and with him! I talked with most of those men before the tour was over, and almost all were serious gardeners."

"But that's why they were there?" Honor said. "A select group of hobbyists?"

"I thought so," Joe said. "But I was curious. I started listening to Englishmen in clubs and pubs and theater lobbies and subway cars. I went to agricultural fairs and flower shows—the Chelsea Flower show—I think I was following some very deep feeling in myself...I know I was, because I felt at home. Gardening is what English men love to do, and they admit it."

"But American men love gardens," Honor said. "Some of them, at least."

"If you think they do, try asking them about it in mixed company," Joe said. "They may be devoted gardeners, but I'll guess that they won't talk about it very long, especially if other men are listening. Try it. And heaven help any first-grade boy when his teacher asks her class to describe their hobbies, and he says: 'Flowers.' I said that just once, and I paid for it."

"They bullied you?" Lena asked me.

"Couldn't live it down."

"Maybe you couldn't live it down, but you took it up. Your life's work," Lena said. "Why did you go clear out to California for your doctorate?"

"U.C. Berkeley is known for their emphasis on the biological sciences, and California has the largest number of native plants of any state in the Union. I wanted to get my doctorate there, but California was expensive, so I lived in my car."

"Your car!" Lena said. "All the time?"

"California's pretty warm. I ate on campus, and showered in the dorms or took sponge baths in a lab...did my laundry there, too. And once I began my Ph.D. dissertation, I was alone in my car in the desert for months. Had a few close calls. You don't want to hear about those."

81

"Yes, we do!" Lena said.

"I stepped on a rattlesnake once; he was hidden under leaves. The only thing that saved me was the winter weather—he was too cold to strike. And one day I was driving slowly, thank heaven, sitting in the driver's seat with the car door open, looking for plants. But for some blessed reason I stopped looking sidewise to glance at the road ahead, and it wasn't there—that road ended at a steep cliff that was about twelve feet away and a hundred feet down."

"Oh!" Honor and Lena said.

"But the strangest escape I had still seems like an even greater miracle to me," Joe said. "One of my desert days I left my car and couldn't find it when I turned back...the desert looked the same in all directions. I walked and walked and walked in blistering heat. The water I had was gone. And then I came to a road. It wasn't much of a road; it looked like no one used it. I crouched under a bush for hours, looking at the one mark of civilization I could see...that empty road...as if it could save me. And it did. Just before sunset I saw a black speck on it. I ran into the road, waving like a fool at nothing larger than a gnat. But it grew into a truck, and it stopped, and the driver said, 'Get in.' He had to help me climb in—I was so dried out and weak. He was a local man. He gave me water, and said he knew where my car was, and he did."

"A miracle," Lena said.

"Yes. But it was even more of a miracle when he told me that he only drove that road once a month."

The three of them sat looking at the fire. Then Honor said, "You were alone, and almost out of hope. I guess we've all had that feeling."

"Yes," Joe said. The three of them were silent for a while, watching the fire. Then Joe said in a happier tone: "But I soon found out that botany wasn't the solitary kind of study I thought it was. When I began requesting loans of specimens from institutions, I found that thousands of Americans have been, and still are, amateur botanists. They go on walks and identify plants—that's their hobby—and they're good at it. They preserve specimens and deposit them at these institutions."

"A hobby," Lena said. "More than that. Who knows what wonderful new medicine is hiding in some plant?"

"One amateur botanist that I found was amazing," Joe said. "I can hardly believe it yet. A plant species I was studying hadn't been seen for over twenty-five years. I called the botanist who had collected that species, and he told me he knew exactly where it had grown years before. When I visited that old, white-bearded farmer, he took me to a corner of his land and pointed, and I shoveled up several sacks of soil. I took it back to Berkeley and spread the soil on wooden flats in a greenhouse, removed all the weed seeds I could find, and watered it...waited...hoped. I knew what the seedlings would look like; I'd studied the plant's closest relatives. And one morning, there the green leaves were—that rare, long-lost plant!"

The blizzard finally blew away the next afternoon after lunch. Joe shoveled Lena's steps, sidewalks and driveway, and Honor followed him with a broom. Lena insisted that he stay for supper.

"We'll give him that hearty soup we made yesterday," Lena told Honor. "I can put a meal together. But you look tired. Why don't you lie down for a while?"

"I wouldn't mind a rest," Honor said, and went upstairs.

When they heard Honor shut her bedroom door, Lena beckoned to Joe. "I've hoped we could talk," she said. "Come here." He followed her to a corner of the kitchen.

"You're a good friend to us," Lena said in a low voice, "and I don't know anyone else I can ask for advice."

"About Honor? I'm so sorry for her," Joe said. "Mother, too. And worried."

"She won't go to a doctor," Lena said. "She says there's nothing wrong with her, but now the time's so short—the baby's due in February. She needs a check-up—she must realize that."

"She won't go?"

"It's sad. Such a shame. But Honor's not married. She's hiding here...never goes anywhere now...won't see a doctor. I can hardly talk to her about it, of course, but I can see how worried she is."

Joe didn't look at Lena; he looked at her kitchen floor. "I'm so ashamed," he said. "I've told my mother, and I think she has an idea we might try."

"Honor can't go on hiding."

"I don't think Honor likes me very well," Joe said. "I'm Brandon's brother. She told me last night that she'd be happy if she could be without any men at all, ever. Free. She's got every right to tell me to shut up and get out."

"Talk to her," Lena said.

Lena's hot vegetable soup tasted good on that winter evening. When it was gone, along with Honor's cinnamon rolls and dishes of fruit, the three of them sat by the fire.

Joe took a deep breath and said, "Honor...I brought that tree because I wanted to talk to Lena and you. Lena can help us, give us her own ideas."

"Ideas?" Honor said.

"I've had some," Joe said. "Wanting to help. Brandon's my brother. I can imagine how many worries you have... misgivings...."

Honor was silent, gazing into the fire.

"You might feel like you want to hide," Joe said. "You might not want to see a doctor."

Honor gave Lena a glance. Lena looked guilty.

"You must feel..." Joe stopped and stared at the fire, then said: "I hope I can understand this, a little. You must feel that because of what Brandon did, you have to bear everything by yourself. Alone. With people not knowing..."

"Yes," Honor said in a low voice, her eyes on the fire.

"Then perhaps I can help, if the three of us can look at a possibility. Do you mind if I tell you about it?"

Honor shook her head.

"I've thought so much about you, and so has Mother. I had to tell her—I hope you understand—I couldn't think of what to do."

High winds sent drafts down the chimney. No one spoke for a while; they watched the flames twist and flare.

"Your mother...how is she?" Honor asked. "How does she..."

"She loves the thought of her grandchild," Joe said. "And she loves you for having it. The Lombards go into the next generation with your baby, so now you're part of our family. She wants you to know that, and so do I. You and Lena aren't alone. Never will be."

"Oh!" Honor cried.

"Mother and I have talked and talked, trying to think how to help you," Joe said. "And we've discovered some things you might want to consider."

He twisted his hands together and stared at the fire. "We've discovered that there are two kinds of marriages in Iowa. One of them is the usual one: ceremony and license and all. But there's another kind. If there's a reason why a man and woman want to share a last name, they can."

Both women stared at him.

"I know you aren't fond of me. I know that," Joe said to Honor in a low voice. "And I'm intruding so much in your affairs, when I haven't a right in the world. But I'm daring to ask you, Honor— will you take my name?"

"Your name!" Honor looked dazed.

"Once upon a time you'd have been 'Mrs. Lombard,'" Joe said. "It's my brother's fault that you're not."

"Give her your last name?" Lena said.

"The baby's half a Lombard, after all," Joe said. "Lombard may not be a famous name, but it's an honorable one." Joe kept his eyes on the fire. "Or was."

"A 'common law marriage.' That's what you mean?" Lena's voice had doubt in it.

"Iowa is one of the states that allows it," Joe said. "If a man and woman want to use a single last name, both their names must be on some document—a birth certificate…a bank account. They must live together for a time, and show the community that they consider themselves married, and tell people they are. That's all. It's legal."

Lena and Honor sat silent, looking at the fire.

"If Honor will use my last name—if she's 'Mrs. Joseph Lombard'— it will be easier for her to go to the doctor, and the hospital," Joe said to Lena. "I'd need to be seen at your house whenever I can be here, so that people will think I'm living with you and my 'wife' Honor, but working on my dissertation at Iowa City." Joe looked at Honor. "You're welcome to my name as long as you need it—if you want it. It's a disgraced name now, but it's all I have."

"*You're* not disgraced," Lena said.

"But I want to add a last thing," Joe said. "My true word to Honor. If she's willing to take my name, I promise she'll be my wife in name only. I'm not asking for a single right as a husband. I'm only asking to help her." Joe shrugged. "It's the least I can do."

"The least!" Honor cried. "The least? You'll be a man with an illegitimate child! Your name will be on my baby's birth certificate! How can you want that? What if you want to marry someday? Have a real marriage?"

"I've thought of all that," Joe said. "I wouldn't have said a word otherwise."

For a while no one spoke. The fire leaped and flared. They could hear a snow plow scraping its way down Seerley Boulevard.

"I won't blame the two of you if you don't want anything to do with anybody in my family," Joe said.

"There's a name for women like me," Honor said. "And that's what people will call me. Brandon's family and friends would."

Joe said, "Not me!"

Honor's eyes followed a flow of sparks spilling from a log. "But your mother! How does she feel?"

"You're having her grandchild."

"I'm sure she'll care about that," Honor said. "But not quite enough."

"Enough?"

"I've *got* to be honest with you. I must!" Honor said. "I don't believe your mother will tell you: 'Please marry Honor—a real marriage. I want her for my own daughter.'"

"Don't think that!" Joe cried. "Don't ever—"

"What mother would want her son to marry a …woman like me? Maybe it would only be a fake marriage, but how is she going to explain that to her friends and family? At the very best, they'll think you and I…."

"It happens all the time, doesn't it? Babies 'born early'?" Lena said.

Joe got up to walk around the room, and stopped as far from Honor as he could get. "I've told my mother why we can't have a real marriage. My mother understands. Honor herself told me why last night—she said she'd be happy to live her life without any men at all. Ever."

Joe sat down again and stared at the fire.

Nobody said much for a while. Lena gave a little "humph," that was all.

"I can't do this to Joe!" Honor said to Lena. "How can I make myself his common-law wife, just like that? Have a baby that everyone will think he fathered? People will be sure he did." She looked at him. "Brandon's wife...and his new relatives...they might think *Joe* made me pregnant and that's the reason why I wouldn't marry Brandon...or why he wouldn't marry me! They'll blame Joe!"

"Well," Lena said. "People will always talk."

"And what can I tell the baby?" Honor said. "What can I say, if I've taken Joe's name? That it has two fathers? And they're brothers?"

"Maybe two fathers are better than one?" Lena said.

Honor sighed. "Two men claiming the baby?"

"Two fathers are better than *none*, don't you think?" Lena asked.

Honor didn't answer. She kept her eyes on the fire as if she were talking to it, not anyone else. "I can't do anything else, can I? I have to wreck Joe's life to make the world think my baby and I are respectable..."

Lena said, "Joe, I have to say that I'm very grateful to you for this offer. I think Honor will be, too, when she has time to think about it."

"He's my brother," Joe said.

He's my brother. That was the worst excuse for a marriage proposal that Joe had ever heard. He went to put on his boots and coat and hat. "Thanks for the warm bed and good food," he said. "I'll try to come again next week for Christmas Eve, but I promised my mother to stay that special night with her. I don't want her alone on Christmas morning."

Joe opened Lena's front door to the wind and a white world. The door wreath he'd hung was dusted with blown snow. "Goodnight to you, Lena, and Honor."

The snowplows were out. Joe crept behind one as he took the highway to Des Moines. His car heater didn't work. Bitter-cold wind hurled snow across the road.

Night was black and white on the highways, but when Joe reached Des Moines, suburban houses blazed with Christmas red, blue and green. He took a road the snowplows wouldn't clear for days, and was glad he didn't have much farther to go, bucking and sliding.

The parking lot of The Hungry Chef restaurant had only been shoveled near the street. He pulled in. Emily's door was half-hidden in a snowdrift and her apartment window was dark. Emily wasn't home from work yet.

He parked, left his car's headlights on, and unloaded a snow shovel. His boots weren't high enough; they filled with snow as he cleared his mother's door, and a path for her to the sidewalk. Then he dragged the tree with its little lights out of the car, along with the good, strong stand he'd bought for it. Emily didn't have room for a tree anywhere in her apartment, but she'd find some Christmas cheer waiting for her when she came around the corner after work.

A rust-streaked "Free Parking" sign stood by Emily's door. Joe wired the tree to the pole. He had the key to her room; he ran the tree lights' cord through her window.

All the small bulbs flickered and lit, showering Emily's door and the parking lot with twinkling stars.

Joe was shivering. He got back in the car, kicked off his boots, stripped off his wet socks and put on shoes. As he drove along ruts to the main road out of town, he looked back. Very small and far away, a Christmas tree in a parking lot shone gold, red, green, blue.

Snow fell on Iowa, day after day. Iowa City streets sparkled with lights strung on house after house. Everywhere Joe saw pictures of madonnas with infants, of course. Holy babies everywhere. "Away in a manger, no crib for his bed" kept playing on the radio. After all, Joseph had married an 'unwed mother.'

At last it was Christmas Eve. Joe drove to Cedar Falls at dark, and saw the lights from Lena's tree spreading a brilliant shimmer of colors over her porch and lawn and stairs, all the way to the street. Lena opened her door when he rang and said, "Welcome!"

Even before Joe had shed his coat and cap and boots and the three were settled by the fire, Joe sensed the change. Every face showed it. They passed ordinary words back and forth gingerly, as if "How-are-you" and "Fine, thank you" were hot potatoes. Glasses of eggnog were a relief: they could sip eggnog with only a few polite words said.

Finally Honor reached for a wrapped present on the hearth and handed it to Joe. "My present to you," she said.

"Me?" Joe said as he ripped off ribbon and paper to find a handsome leather jacket.

"If you don't like it, she can take it back," Lena said.

"Read the card," Honor said. "Out loud."

"To Joe Lombard from Honor Lombard."

Honor smiled at him. "As Lena says about that jacket, if you don't like me, you can always take me back."

"Thanks!" Joe said. The look on his face brought Lena to her feet. "I think I'll turn in," she said. "But Joe, tell your mother how thankful we'll be to have her experience with babies in our family! Babies are an unknown country for me. Being an aunt was hard enough to learn!" She smiled at them. "May I offer a downstairs room and bath for Joe, my new nephew? You're welcome to a bed tonight, or any time!"

"I promised Mom I'd be with her tonight," Joe said. "But thanks for the standing...or should I say sleeping?...invitation."

Lena went upstairs. Joe put the coat on, and it fit. "A fine present," he told Honor. "Thank you. The leather's handsome, but it seems like 'cloth of gold' to me, considering what its message is."

Honor and Joe were quiet for a while, watching the fire. Finally Honor gave a little laugh. "I don't really know how to talk to a husband. I've only had him a few minutes."

"I wish I could give you the white dress and the bride's bouquet and the walk down the aisle," Joe said.

"A balloon bride, I'm afraid."

"No one would notice. You'd be as beautiful as you were in Chicago, walking down that bridal line. I'd never seen such courage."

"You can do anything when you're mad enough. I can't tell you how much I regret it. It was a sad, mad, bad, mean thing to do," Honor said. "Your poor mother! I wasn't thinking of anyone but myself."

"She admires you!" Joe took Honor's hands to pull her to her feet, and they stood close together in the firelight. "Mother wants you to know that. She sent you a Christmas present." He unbuttoned his shirt pocket, and firelight sent sparks from his hand. In a moment Honor wore a wedding ring on her finger, a platinum ring studded with diamonds.

"Oh!" Honor cried. "So beautiful!" Staring at the ring, she had come close to Joe; the baby almost pressed against his red shirt.

"It was her mother's ring," Joe said, looking into Honor's eyes so close to his. "You're a married woman now."

He reached in his pocket again. "And this was my grandmother's, too. It's the love ring, the engagement ring that says that someone loves you and wants you to be his."

Joe slipped the engagement ring on Honor's finger to join the wedding ring: a platinum setting surrounding a single fine diamond.

He knew Honor could see what he felt. Her beautiful blue eyes were shining in firelight. Would she put her arms around him? She was so close…

The moment trembled between them. Honor stepped back.

Joe turned away. "It's so late," he said. "I'd better be on the road."

He put on the jacket, went to the hall and pulled on his boots. He shrugged into his coat.

"How can I say anything at all?" Honor said in a low voice. "Nothing but Thank You? I can't even begin to say…" her voice trailed off.

Joe opened the door. Snow was falling again. "I have to thank *you*," he said, stepping into the cold and dark. "It's the merriest Christmas I've ever had, Mrs. Lombard."

9

Brandon and Katie had Christmas decorations in every room of their house. There were parties every night, even Christmas Eve, and Brandon had had enough. He told Katie he was feeling sick and was going to stay home. So away they all went to another party, and he could sit with a bottle by his huge fireplace flanked by his two huge Christmas trees, and think.

He hadn't minded being married, for a while. He honeymooned with Katie at Florida nightclubs, and tanned on Florida beaches. They never talked about their wedding. Katie said she just wanted to forget it.

That was all right with him, because he could only recall snatches of it anyway. He remembered the church all right, and that reception line with Honor so suddenly *there*—there in the line of hand-shakers! And then she was dancing with Joe! But after that he only remembered lying on a dance floor with faces looking down at him, but Joe wasn't there—he remembered that. So he bet Joe had left his own brother's wedding party when it got wild, and was off having a good time with Honor somewhere—Joe had always wanted Honor—that "flowee lover" brother of his, the first Lombard to get a M.S.—in botany! Botany!

And then he could remember crouching at a door that was chained to keep him out, and Honor whispering through the crack, and him yelling at her. And then they dragged him off to a "wedding night,"—passed-out on a fancy bed in a room full of flowers, and everybody as cold as the North Pole when he woke up the next morning.

But after a day or so, lying on a beach with Katie, he figured he'd come out of the whole mess without too much damage. He'd been drunk, pounding on Honor's hotel door. Katie and Joe had heard what he was yelling, he supposed. He'd been so soused. But he remembered telling Honor he was sorry.

When their honeymoon was over and he went back to Chicago with Katie, her sisters wanted to talk about Honor Sloan. He didn't know why, but they did. He tried not to say a word. One of his sisters-in-law said Honor was good-looking, all right, but was obviously showing off, and where did she get those diamonds— they looked real. It did make you wonder. Another sister-in-law asked him how Honor got invited to his wedding. He said he didn't know—some mix-up by the wedding planners. The youngest sister-in-law said she'd heard that Honor couldn't take a joke—did Honor run away from Brandon when he was parading her around a graduation party with a fake wedding cake? He told her he'd just been having fun.

Those Bushnell girls...mean, always yapping and stabbing each other. They said Honor was so gorgeous in pink with diamonds. Wasn't Katie jealous, they kept asking, and wouldn't quit. Wasn't she? They screeched like cats on a fence.

K atie cheered up when she got to choose their new car, and the new house her dad paid for. She filled every room of that fancy place with new things, right and left, and threw parties every weekend. Sometimes the parties were no fun at all. Businessmen and their wives came to his house and sat around a huge table loaded with all the silver and glassware and china that Katie and her mother bought. The food was good, but who could enjoy it in a starched collar, trying to look like you're listening for hours to short, bald, middle-aged men talking about Big Ideas? Sometimes he could almost see Big Ideas full of hot air, floating up to the ceiling.

At first he wore his new tailor-made suits and was a kind of receptionist for Carl Bushnell, showing people into Bushnell's office: it was as big as a barn and filled with expensive paintings and custom-built furniture. After a month or two Bushnell told his secretary to give his new son-in-law an all-around introduction to Bushnell Kitchenmaster. Bushnell had a lot of pet expressions— when he told this secretary to give Brandon a "good feel for the business," the secretary and Brandon tried not to laugh.

Brandon tried to get a good feel of Bushnell's business. Before long he got a pretty good one from the pretty secretary, and she liked it. He told her he'd get on top of Bushnell Kitchenmaster after a while, but right now he was interested in her, and also a new Harley. Bushnell was giving him a nice salary, so one day he bought that Harley—top of the line—and rode it home.

It was great. Katie and her friends heard Brandon when he roared into his driveway, and they came to chatter and coo over his "big machine." They followed him into Katie's expensive new house, and perched on her expensive new couches to giggle and shriek about nightclub shows and movie stars and expensive beaches and new books packed with sex…new, expensive, expensive, new. Their expensively made-up faces looked Brandon over: Katie's new and expensive Brandon Lombard.

And then he finally went to Iowa to see Emily, because it was her birthday.

What a night that was. Joe shoved him into a sink. Honor was pregnant. He was going to be a father in February.

He got out of there, went back to Chicago. What else could he do? His own baby—would he ever get to see him? Chicago was the windy city, all right, with Katie breathing down his neck, telling him to stop moping around and being late to the office all the time, always yelling at her, and drinking too much.

Day after day, he tried to call Honor. Finally he got the old biddy aunt. She said, "Lena here. How was your honeymoon?"

in a voice as sweet as vinegar. Before she could hang up, he said: "Lena! Can you do me a favor? Even if you're probably mad at me? Honor won't take any of my calls, but could you let me know, you know, when the baby..." She hung up.

Brandon kept calling. When February came, he called hospitals in Cedar Falls and Waterloo every week. At last the Cedar Falls hospital told him that someone named Honor was in the maternity ward there. "Honor Sloan?" he asked. They said they were not allowed to furnish last names. But who else could it be?

He didn't tell anybody he was going. Katie would have a good sulk with her mother and sisters if he told her, and her father would tell him to stay home. Bushnell's favorite solution for trouble was: *Let sleeping dogs lie.* Maybe it was good advice, but not this time. Was Brandon Lombard supposed to let his son or daughter go out of his life like a play ticket he'd lost in the trash, maybe, or his watch left behind on a sink somewhere? And what about Honor, stuck in a hick town with a witch? He loved Honor. He couldn't let her go through this alone.

A blizzard started before Brandon left Chicago; there was a foot of snow by the time he parked at the hospital in Cedar Falls. He slogged up hospital steps no one had shoveled yet. The halls were pretty empty and nobody stopped him; finally he came to a sign that said "Maternity Ward."

There was a big glass window. Inside was a row of bassinets holding white bundles. Each bundle had a pink face like a little dried-up apple. Which apple was his?

The parents' names were lettered on cards and stuck at the feet of the bassinets, like price tags on store bins. Honor's name would be alone there on a sign: "Honor Sloan."

He flattened his nose against the glass to read the price tags.

The last label in the row read: *Dr. and Mrs. Joseph Lombard.*

That card seemed to grow larger and larger to him: DR. AND MRS. JOSEPH LOMBARD. As Brandon stared at it, the baby in the crib opened its eyes.

His baby! *His baby!*

Its small eyes shut tight again, and the baby screamed. The scream hardly reached Brandon through the glass, but he could see a small body jerking under the blanket.

His baby screamed and screamed. Why didn't someone come? His baby—with Joe's name on the label!

94

Nobody came to the row of bassinets. His baby's hands were cased in tiny white mittens, and they struggled like mice in a sack. His baby did not like this world, he could see that. Nobody cared. Nobody came when you called.

His baby twitched and jerked and yelled. Where were the nurses? He looked down the hall in both directions and, for a second, saw a man where hallways crossed: a man with an armful of flowers. Joe.

Before Joe could turn his head and see him, Brandon got out of there—took the stairs, ran through halls to the door. Snow hit him, thick and heavy; he was plastered with it when he crawled in his car and turned on the heater.

He waited half an hour, keeping a car window clear, watching the hospital door. Finally Lena and Joe came down the steps. They huddled together against the wind, and climbed in Joe's old car. When they drove off, Brandon took stairs and halls to Honor's door.

A fragrance drifted from her room. Honor was asleep there, surrounded by flowers.

He hadn't brought any flowers. He came closer to the bed. Honor was holding a baby! Brandon tiptoed over to look—a girl? A boy?

Then he saw Honor's hand. She was wearing his grandmother's wedding and engagement rings! As long as Brandon could remember, Emily had worn those rings, because the father of her boys hadn't given her any.

Honor must have felt cold winter wind breathing from his clothes—she opened her eyes, then clutched the baby close to her.

"I came," was all Brandon could think of to say.

Honor said nothing.

"I had to come," he said. "You know I had to come. He leaned over her. "Our baby," he said. "A girl?"

Honor moved her head side to side: No.

"A boy?"

She didn't answer. Brandon grinned. "Has he got a name yet? I thought—"

"He's named for my grandfather," Honor said. "Donald. Donald Joseph Lombard."

For a moment Brandon said nothing, while snow struck the windows. Then he asked, "Can I hold him? Just hold him a minute?"

Honor tightened her arms around the baby. "Go away."

"He's mine, too!"

"No."

"He's got a father! He's even got my name!"

"Not yours."

"He's got 'Don'! He's got 'Lombard'!"

"The 'Joseph Lombard' is from Joe, not you. Someday I'll have to tell my baby why it's not your name."

"I'm his father! You know that I—"

"No. Go away."

"You can't just run around choosing a father for him!"

"I wasn't very good at it the first time." Honor reached for a button on the bedside table. "And now I have to protect my baby. His father raped his mother. How would his father treat a baby?"

"I was just crazy!" Brandon yelled. "So mad and crazy that you left that party! And the guys saying I'd been jilted! Then Katie got me on the rebound. I don't know why. I don't know why I did anything! I'm so *sorry*!" He pulled both of them into his arms against his snowy coat; they lay there together, though Brandon was halfway out of the bed. "Marry me!" he cried. "I can get a divorce!" He kissed them. "I don't want Katie—I want the two of you! Can't we be a *family*? Father...mother...baby boy! I love you! You know that! I'm so *sorry*!"

"I'm sorry, too," Honor said. She closed her eyes. "You invited me, but I shouldn't have come to your wedding. Katie and her family would never have known...only your mother, and she'd never tell. That was the way I planned it. But you yelled the whole story in the hall." She hid her face against the sleeping baby and whispered, "I never should have come to Chicago. I'm sorry. Can you forgive me? I'm so very sorry."

A nurse must have noticed a light above Honor's door, or heard Brandon shout. Now she stood in the doorway, scowling at a wild man who had pulled a new mother and her baby halfway out of bed. "Please leave at once," she said, hurrying in. Brandon put Honor and the baby down and got off the bed.

"Yes. Please leave." Honor said.

"You married *Joe*?" Brandon cried. "You married—"

"This man was just leaving," Honor said to the nurse. "I'm very tired. Will you see that he goes?"

"You shouldn't be here," the nurse said to Brandon, grabbing his arm. "Visiting hours are over."

"I love you!" he cried to Honor.

"Come this way!" the nurse said, shoving Brandon out the door. "Follow the exit sign at the end of the hall."

"Honor!" he yelled, but the nurse held on. Finally Brandon shook her off, but she stood watching until he went down a flight of stairs and out of sight.

Snow. More snow. Brandon drove to Lena's house. He didn't know what he thought he was doing—they wouldn't let him in. But just as he parked around the corner, Joe came down Lena's porch stairs, pulled his jacket collar above his ears, and sprinted around the corner to Seerley Boulevard in the pelting snow. He was taking his daily run, late. Probably heading for the campus where the walks would be shoveled.

All right. Joe was the one he was after.

Brandon drove slowly, following his big brother along Seerley. Joe wouldn't see him even if he looked back: it was snowing so hard. When Joe crossed College Street to the campus, Brandon parked and followed him. Joe had boots on, but Brandon didn't, and his shoes slipped and slid, but he kept Joe in sight.

Joe stopped and looked up at the brick campanile. Then he must have heard Brandon coming—he turned and said, "What in hell do you want?"

"What do you think?" Brandon said, getting close enough to Joe's scornful look to give him one of his own. "Some explanations from you."

"Nothing to explain," Joe said. "You've explained to the Bushnells, haven't you? Told them all about Honor, one of those loose women who runs around having babies by every man she meets. Now leave her alone!"

"I've been to the hospital to see *my son*!" Brandon yelled. "He's not yours—never will be! You can plaster our last name all over him, but he's mine! Go ahead and give Mother's rings to Honor, but he belongs to me!"

Joe glared through the snow. "How about our father? We belonged to *Dad*, didn't we?" he said. "*Two sons*. And what did our father do? He gave us this name you seem so proud of—but he didn't stay with Mom, did he? Help her? Raise us? Support us? Have you given Honor a single cent?"

"I tried!" Brandon cried. "*Honor* ran away, not me! I couldn't find her, hunted and hunted, and then she'd hardly talk to me, threw her engagement ring at me, wouldn't explain why she—"

"Explain?" Joe shouted. "Explain?"

"—Why she ran off, why she hid, why she didn't even go to our graduation! We'd planned our wedding...I already had a job! Explain! And then she came to my wedding and loused it up, really gave me and Katie a hell of a honeymoon. Now she won't even let me hold my own boy. Good luck with that bitch! You wanted her, and you've got her. You've got her *now*." Brandon's breath steamed between them on the cold air.

Joe moved closer. "I can certainly 'explain' why she'll never marry *you*—you got drunk and slammed her on the floor and tore off her clothes while she screamed and begged—"

"I was drunk."

"Just tell me," Joe said. "How would you feel if some big guy slammed you to the floor and called you every filthy name he could think of? What if he pulled down your pants and did what you did to Honor? Would he be your best friend? Would you live with him the rest of your life? What in the hell do you think women *are*? Not like you? Just pretty dolls you can throw across a room and they lie there and smile?"

"I was drunk!" Brandon yelled. "She didn't understand—"

"She 'didn't understand'? Didn't understand rape? It's one of the oldest crimes in the world! If that man raped you and he was drunk, would you forgive him? Or would you beat him to a bloody pulp, if you could? What in the hell do you think 'rape' *means*?"

Brandon scraped at snow with his shoe. "Well, she ought to—"

"Forgive and forget? Is that it? Or is rape more like *Hate and remember forever, even when you try to forget*? When Honor—all through her life—looks at the boy you want so much to call your son, *what will she remember?*"

Suddenly the campanile began to drop heavy bell strokes through the snow.

Joe turned and ran off down a walk, his boots leaving deep scars on white.

Brandon went back to his car and sat there. He had a son, named for him— half his name, at least. They wouldn't want two Joe's—they'd call that baby "Don," wouldn't they? Half of his daddy's name!

Honor had chosen "Donald." Brandon liked to think about that. She'd used part of his name. And she'd come to his wedding. She had courage, all right, but what else was she going to try?

Well, she'd grabbed Big Brother. Joe was wild about her—the fool couldn't hide it, even though Little Brother told him to get lost. Even their mother knew what Joe wanted.

Emily must have helped Joe bring off the whole thing! She'd always liked Joe best, and she'd been fond of Honor when Brandon brought her to visit her once. Emily had given Honor her rings! Now Honor could be a married woman, and his mother would have her first grandchild, and Joe would have a son who wasn't his, and just where did that leave the baby's father?

Brandon drove back to Chicago. Katie grabbed him and asked where in the hell he'd gone, and he yelled back at her that he'd been to see an old classmate who was in the hospital, which was true enough. Bushnell didn't ask.

Brandon drank too much. He knew it. He wanted Honor. And his son.

He bought himself a red Corvette, and one weekend in March he left town. He didn't tell Katie where he was going—it was none of her business. He made good time from Chicago to Cedar Falls, parked near Lena's, and waited until dark to sneak along the alley to her house.

Brandon knew the outside of Lena's place pretty well: the year before he'd raced around it, banging on windows and doors. The brick walk along the side of it was muddy; he slipped and slid, ducking under Lena's kitchen windows, glad that the house next door was empty—nobody would see him from there. He tiptoed up the side porch steps and crouched under her front window where the porch railing hid him from the street.

The wind was cold. He gripped the window sill and raised himself to take a quick look inside. Honor was sitting by the fire! *Honor.* Dark brown hair, blue eyes...so beautiful...

When he raised himself to his knees on the icy porch, he saw Lena holding Don. There he was! Don still looked a bit like an old, bald geezer, but he seemed much bigger already, and happy, blowing bubbles and pumping his arms and legs.

Honor was reading to Lena, just as she'd read to him their senior year. A lot of times he'd hardly listened...he just drifted along on the sound of Honor's voice, wondering what she'd be like in bed.

He shivered in cold wind. Think of it! He couldn't knock on the window. He couldn't ring the doorbell. They wouldn't let him in. He couldn't tell Honor he wanted her. She knew he did. He wanted to hold their boy!

But at least he'd seen that Honor and his baby were all right.

He crawled off the porch, ran down the alley, and drove to Iowa City in the dark. It was late when he went into the rooming house where Joe stayed: an old house with baby carriages and bicycles on the porch.

He climbed stairs and opened Joe's door. Joe was working at a table piled with books. He got up and looked at Brandon without a word. "Doing an all-nighter, Brother?" Brandon said.

Joe rubbed his eyes. "Writing an article on Virginia Woolf."

"Some bitch who breeds ' flowees'?"

"No. An upper-class English suicide and great writer. Honor's fond of her, so I told her about my day in England at Sissinghurst castle. Woolf's lover helped design the world-famous gardens. A prof in the English department at the college here heard about my trip. He wants me to write an article about Sissinghurst for the university journal. Honor's going to help."

"Seeing a lot of Honor?"

"Some," Joe said.

Brandon laughed. "You followed her around our whole senior year like—"

"Did you see her poems in the university quarterly that year?" Joe scowled. "Go to her readings for the English Club?"

"Yeah, I guess. Don't remember."

"She's a writer. I bet you never noticed the middle finger of her right hand."

100

"What for?"

"She's got ink ground into the knuckle," Joe said. "Stay away from her."

"Yeah? I saw her hand, all right! She's got Mom's rings on. She's got your name on. And it's all lies! She's had *my son*!"

"You got too close to her once," Joe said, and stepped close to Brandon. "Don't get anywhere near that close—"

"Donald's *mine*! She won't let me see him."

"Your fault. Live with it. Go home. I'm busy."

"I can't even see her, or my own kid."

"No."

"My own kid!"

"That's right." Joe scowled. "So you're here, sneaking around. Don't you have a job?"

"Yeah," Brandon said. "I'm my father-in-law's front man: I usher people into his presence, like he's the president or something."

"Well, he is," Joe said. "Of his company."

"Right. And when I'm not glad-handing, I spend hours with worksheets and sales charts. Bor-*ing*. I'm being 'groomed,' my father-in-law says. I feel like a horse. But you can't beat the salary he pays me." Brandon scowled. "Stay away from Honor. You've loaned her our name, but you haven't a hope in hell of getting her down the aisle. You're the guy that called her some pretty names at that graduation party, and she knows it."

Joe stared at him.

"At that jock party the night before graduation. After she ran off and went home, the guys said my bride had left me at the altar. You, too. Oh, yeah, dear brother—everybody at that party heard you laugh at me, and bet me that I'd never ...well, don't think she doesn't know it, because I told her."

"Know what?"

"You were mad, weren't you, because you couldn't get her? Everybody knew it!" Brandon yelled. "Everybody heard it! I was so mad—I hit you, and you used some of those boxing lessons you took to floor me—you ought to remember *that*!" He laughed. "So I left that party and went off, so drunk and so mad at you— I went to her place and just lost—"

Joe shouted: "You're lying!"

"You can't remember?" Brandon grinned. "You were drunk!"

101

"I don't drink."

"Well, you were."

"*You* were the drunk," Joe said. "You're making this up."

"I was just drunk enough to take you on at the party! You sure weren't going to say those things about Honor!"

Joe stared at him. "You told her this?"

"Somebody did. Isn't she as cold as six feet of snow when you're around?"

"Get out," Joe said. "Go home!"

"Who says?"

"Get out! Leave her alone! You had your chance, and you lost it," Joe said.

Brandon grinned. "Yeah. I had my chance, all right. Maybe I lost her, but I had her! How do you like going to bed with a second-hand—"

"Get out!"

Joe shoved Brandon out the door and locked it.

Brandon went back to Chicago and had a big fight with Katie.

"You run off!" she yelled. "All the time! You've got a job, you know! You've got a wife! So where did you go this time?"

"To a hospital in...Joliet. Had to see one of my good friends from Iowa."

That wasn't really a lie, or not much.

They had a lot of battles that spring. Katie yelled that Alcoholics Anonymous hadn't worked because Brandon didn't go to the meetings, and her sisters didn't want their friends to see him drunk and puking around all the time, and she was sick of it—sick of it—sick of it! "You may be the handsomest man at parties, but you're hardly there, or else making a scene!" she shouted. "You fell down-dead-drunk at your own wedding, and you've been doing it ever since!"

Sometimes she cried. Sometimes she was mad, and wanted a divorce.

"Not even a year married and you want to break it up?" Brandon said.

Katie glared at him. "Just exactly what is there to break?"

So they didn't talk at all...walked around pretending they were invisible.

Finally Bushnell came into Brandon's office and said, out of the blue: "How would you like to take over our new office in Rockford?"

"Well, sure," Brandon said. "Sounds good."

"Katie doesn't want to have all her friends ninety miles away, she says, so she wants to stay here, at least until you're settled," Bushnell said. "Johnson had the Rockford office, but he left last month. It's so new that you won't have much business at first—nobody knows we're there yet. But you'll have a chance to show what you can do."

Brandon couldn't believe it.

He couldn't believe it in a week, when he was out of Chicago and in the Rockford apartment that Bushnell Kitchenmaster Incorporated found for him.

The apartment was great. It didn't have Katie in it, for one thing, and he hoped it never would. She told him it never would when she said goodbye, but he couldn't trust her.

The view from his big apartment windows was like a double-page spread of a city in a travel magazine, except that it moved: traffic went by below, day and night. His office was fine. Just an office—desks...chairs...files...and another pretty good view—but it had one big asset: his secretary. When Johnson quit, his secretary stayed: Trisha Boyle. She told Brandon she had an afternoon job typing in a room full of secretaries, but she could work for him in the morning. He said her schedule suited him just fine.

Trisha Boyle was young, and she was pretty, but the thing was: Trisha knew how to run the office—not that there was much to run. Bushnell had told him: "Lombard, your new office will keep you busy, and you can prove yourself." Prove yourself? After a week or two, Brandon wondered how he was going to prove much of anything there. The phone hardly ever rang, no one came, and letters were mostly from Bushnell's office about Bushnell meetings and Bushnell "Big Ideas."

Not that Brandon minded the peace and quiet: it didn't have Katie in it. Every weekday morning he came to work after a gym workout and a late breakfast, and read the paper while Trisha ran the office without a hitch—typed letters for him to sign the same day he got them—especially the ones from Bushnell about the business. Pretty soon Brandon started picking her up at five when she got off work at her second job, and they had a really good thing going.

The thing was: he felt like Trisha appreciated him like nobody ever had. She was young and pretty and good in bed, but the main thing was that she appreciated him. He was on his way up, she told him. "Look at your office!" she said. "Look at your apartment! Look at you!"

But he thought about Don. His own son—fat little belly, blowing bubbles, pumping his arms and legs. And he couldn't even hold him, couldn't give Honor any money for him...somebody would find out. She could stay with that yapping aunt of hers.

Wait until Don was older, and his real father could tell him everything. And his real father would have money enough for his son to have a first-class education.

Money enough, all right. He gave Trisha some, and she bought new clothes. They did the Rockford scene most nights (or drove the ninety miles to Chicago and back on weekends), and ended up at his place. She promised she'd make him so comfy that he wouldn't want too much whiskey, and she sure knew how.

10

A baby. Honor had never thought much about babies, or known a woman who had given birth, except her mother, who would only talk about God's will. Pregnant women stayed out of sight. She'd imagined that giving birth would be like going to sleep and waking to find herself thin at last, with a baby.

So that was the way it was—except that she didn't sleep. She hurt. She yelled. Finally, yes, her stomach was flat, but they put something small and screaming in her arms. It was as ugly as an alien from space, and they said it was hers.

It was so loud. So terrified. It had gangling legs and flailing arms and a streaked red body. You could see that it had been dragged from its known world through a hole that was way too small. It gave horrified gasps and stared into a blazing light that it could never have imagined. And she knew she had writhed and screamed like that once, and had forgotten.

They wrapped it in a blanket. It was quiet at last, lying beside her in bed. Its hands, crawling about like aimless crabs, couldn't grasp anything.

And then it opened its eyes. They stared at her long and hard. "So there you are," they seemed to say. And there she was, a mother with a son, thinking the same thing.

Lena said she'd never been near a baby, except for her younger sister, and she couldn't remember that. But Lena couldn't stay away from Don. Messy diapers, fountains in your eye, yells in the night didn't bother her. It wasn't at all like taking care of old folks.

Honor and Lena read baby-care books, asked the doctor questions, and in a few weeks they couldn't imagine the house without Don.

That baby despised being wet. He loathed being messy. He hated being hungry, or alone. He might as well have been stuck in a wheelchair, he was so helpless, and he sang long, angry songs about it, sometimes in the middle of the night.

Lena often heard him yelling in the dark before Honor did, and one spring morning Lena sat up before dawn, listening.

What had she heard? A call? Someone was calling, she thought. A voice she knew, but far away, like smoke blown through the air...

Rosabella?

She held her breath, listening. All she heard now was Don, complaining in his crib next door.

Lena crawled from bed, but before she opened Don's door, his angry fussing stopped. She stood in the hall, listening. There in the dark, silent house that baby began to coo and chirp...happy sounds he made whenever he saw that someone had heard him and was there.

So Honor was with him...she'd must have heard him crying. Lena opened Don's door, taking a breath to speak to Honor, but Don was alone. Faint light from the hall showed Lena the baby in his crib, his arms and legs in happy motion, looking up at no one... cooing and chirping to no one.

Lena changed Don's diaper while the spring wind howled, and he fell asleep before she was through. She went back to bed and slept until breakfast time. The night had been a dream, it was nothing—

Then Honor came down to find Lena in the kitchen. Honor said, "I thought I heard you get out of bed last night."

"Yes," Lena said.

"Don was crying," Honor said. "I almost got up."

"Yes," Lena said.

Honor sat down and poured her coffee. "I heard Don fussing in his crib and I sat up in bed. But then he stopped. It sounded as if someone were with him, I thought. He cooed and jabbered—the way he does when he's been crying and someone comes."

"Yes," Lena said. "Both of us thought somebody was there with him."

"But you went in? Changed him?"

"Yes." Lena was quiet for a while, looking out a kitchen window at budded trees in the first sunlight.

"I want to show you something," she said at last. "After breakfast. You've finished the Virginia Woolf article?"

"I didn't help Joe much with it," Honor said. "Looked up some data in the library for him. I've done the proof-reading."

"Well then, let's go for a ride," Lena said. "We can take Don, and go to Beverley, the little town where I grew up. It's a beautiful morning."

A world of fresh green surrounded them as they left with Don. "You drive," Lena said. "We'll take my car."

Farmland striped with young corn was all they could see as they took the highway out of Cedar Falls. Don sat on Lena's lap and chortled to himself, blinking his beautiful dark eyes in the sun.

"Did you ever visit your grandparents?" Lena asked.

"We never did," Honor said. "Mom and Dad were pretty angry—they'd hardly ever talk about you, or their parents."

"Just like my mother and father...your Grandma and Grandpa. They couldn't forgive your folks, or my sister Rosabella," Lena said. "Maybe being unforgiving runs in the family."

"Rosabella? What were they mad about?" Honor asked.

"My mother and dad were religious...the hating kind of religious—sure of heaven and prophesying hell for the slippers-and-sliders-away from the true word."

"That's where my mother and father got their ideas about religion, I guess," Honor said. "Not much about love. Lots about damnation."

"It was worse than that with my folks. I've always wondered if those ideas killed Rosabella," Lena said. "We three girls had fancy names from novels, but it always seemed to me that 'Rosabella' was right for my big sister. She was a beautiful redhead with skin as pale as my mother's 'company dishes'—white china painted with roses that we weren't allowed to touch. Your beautiful aunt. Rosabella."

"She ran away from home, you said."

"I dreamed of her last night," Lena said. "Don was crying, but he stopped. I thought you'd be with him. You weren't. But it seemed as if someone had been..."

Birds in flight unfurled from a field as they passed, like a shimmering veil of wings.

"I suppose I should tell you about my parents and sisters," Lena said. "I don't know whether your mother ever talked much about what kind of family we were. It really wasn't what she might want to tell you, I'm afraid. She probably just said we lived on a farm, and then moved to Beverly where our father worked at a grocery store."

"Yes," Honor said. They passed a long fringe of crows on a telephone line.

"Religion," Lena said. "That's where it started, I think. On Sunday our family went three times in the day to a country church with a few dozen 'believers.' We heard brimstone and hell-fire sermons—our howling, jumping minister fired 'thou-shalts' and 'thou-shalt-nots' at us like bullets for most of one day every week."

She smiled over Don's head at Honor. "How that preacher scared your mother and me when we were little! We had to sit on a hard bench for hours, absolutely sure we'd be lost forever in hell if we wiggled, or even scratched an itch. But that minister never once frightened our big sister. When we had nightmares about hell and devils, Rosabella climbed in our bed to whisper the most outlandish sermons to us, and we'd laugh until our stomachs hurt and our nightmares went away."

"Mother never said much about Rosabella," Honor said. "Only that there was another sister in her family, and she'd disappeared. That's all I remember."

Lena hugged Don for a moment, and closed her eyes. "When I was ten, I was sure my big sister was the most beautiful woman alive, and I loved her more than anybody in the world. I was ten years younger than Rosabella, and your mother was two years younger than me. Maryflora and I followed Rosabella around, listening to books she read to us, learning poems by heart, chanting away in chorus. The three of us loved each other—the only kind of love we had."

A school bus on the road ahead pulled up at a farm lane, and Honor stopped behind it. Two small boys ran from their uphill house and climbed on.

"The girls at school were jealous of Rosabella," Lena said. "It wasn't just that she was so beautiful—it was the way the boys followed her around. The girls called her names, and wrote notes about her, and did all the nasty things girls do when they're burning with envy. Rosabella always had the most valentines, and the boys kept asking to walk her home or buy her ice cream. Even when she graduated from high school, our parents wouldn't let her go to dances, or date boys. Your mother and I heard our father shouting, and Rosabella crying."

The school bus was slow; Honor passed it after a half mile. "Welcome to Beverly, Iowa" said a sign by the road.

"The owner of the town's feed store had a handsome son," Lena said. "Rosabella climbed out our window at night to be with him, and your mother and I helped her do it. He couldn't take her on a date because he didn't go to our church—my parents wouldn't let him put a foot in our door. When Rosabella was twenty, she ran away with him."

"Where did they go?" Honor asked.

"We never knew."

"Didn't Rosabella write you?"

"She wrote, but our parents wouldn't give us her letters. Her soul could never be saved, they said. She was lost forever, and she'd lead us into sin. Mariflora and I had to tell everyone that Rosabella had found a job in California. We weren't allowed to say her name at home. She'd gone to hell, Mother and Dad told us. We'd all be turned out of our church and go to hell too, if anybody knew that we were such a God-forsaken family."

"My mother never told me a word about this," Honor said.

"Then, after a year, Rosabella came home late one night in summer. Maryflora and I heard her voice, but we weren't allowed to see her. My parents locked her in her room. All your mother and I could do was push notes under her door late that night. She sent notes back, and one of her notes said, 'I'm not married, but

109

I'm going to have a baby. I'll try to run away when I can. I love you both.'"

They came to Beverly's main street. "Go right on First Street," Lena said. "And take the alley to the right, halfway down the block. Just stop there in the alley, along a white picket fence."

Honor turned, turned again. She drove down the graveled alley and parked. "That house there," Lena said, pointing. "The one with the swing set in the backyard. That's where our family lived for years."

The house had a fresh coat of paint, and the back lawn lay smooth and green. Two swings dangled back and forth on their chains in the spring breeze.

"Did Rosabella have her baby?" Honor asked.

"Your mother and I thought she did. The folks gave us some food and told us to stay out all day and play. When we came home at dark, we could hear Rosabella screaming. Mom and Dad couldn't hide that, and we heard them talking about the baby when she stopped yelling and crying. They gave us supper in our room and then locked us in."

"You never saw the baby?"

"No," Lena said. "We were sure we heard it crying, but we never saw it. We never saw Rosabella. Never again. Your mother and I lay in bed, listening to the screaming, and then a baby crying. Finally we went to sleep."

"So Rosabella had her baby?"

"We thought she had. I don't know. The next morning my parents told us that our sister had gone away, and we must never, ever say one word about her to them or each other or anyone. The door to her room was open, and it looked as if she'd never been there. We went to school, and did our homework that evening. They sent us to bed, and we whispered together before we went to sleep, wondering where Rosabella had gone, and whether her baby was a girl or a boy..."

Lena sighed and turned to look at the house.

"I'm so sorry," Honor said. "You've never tried to find her, or her baby?"

"Where would I start?" Lena asked. "But it's only right that you should know about Rosabella. She was your aunt. Her baby would have been your cousin."

"The man she ran away with," Honor asked. "Didn't he come back to Beverly and ask about her?"

"Never heard of him again. I'd only been ten years old when we lost her, and it seemed like a dream. I buried the memory deep in my mind, or tried to."

"How heart-breaking," Honor said after a while. "Rosabella had no place to go. I certainly know how she must have felt. How sad."

"When I heard Don crying this morning, I thought of my sister," Lena said. "Rosabella with her little baby. How could my parents do such a thing? And then I thought about what I was doing. No wonder I couldn't sleep thinking of Rosabella."

Honor said nothing. She stared at the road ahead.

"So I wanted to bring you here and tell you what my parents did to my sister," Lena said. "Because I didn't make you welcome either, did I? I was selfish and nasty and unloving, wasn't I?"

Honor said nothing.

"You'll never have to beg to stay with me again. You and your baby," Lena said. "Never." She smiled at Honor over Don's head. Honor smiled back.

Summer rains brought flowers to Cedar Falls gardens, and turned the park lawns a thick, intense green. Lena could walk now, so she went to the park with Honor and Don every fine afternoon, and lounged afterward on her front porch. Workmen had painted the porch pillars and ceiling, walls and railings, and sanded and sealed the floor. The pillars were white columns stripped of their ugly frames. Lena bought pots of scarlet geraniums for white wicker stands, and matching lounge chairs with green and white cushions.

Hot weather came. University students began to teach crafts to children in Seerley Park every weekday afternoon. Boys and girls crowded around a big case of art supplies under the trees, or sat at picnic tables, pummeling balls of clay, weaving baskets of paper strips, or painting drippy masterpieces in washable paints.

One day, walking in the park, Honor and Lena stopped to introduce themselves to women sitting on benches. Two were college
students, and the other three were mothers who had children busy
at the craft tables. "We've seen so many trucks at your place," one
young woman said to Lena one afternoon. "Carpenters. Plumbers."

"You've made that whole house over?" asked another.

At first Honor didn't want to stop, or talk, but Lena did, and she
said to Honor: "When we walk in the park, why don't you tell those
young women that I'm your aunt, and you and Don are staying
with me while your husband finishes his Ph.D. in Iowa City."

One afternoon the air was hot and heavy.

"Let's wait to walk until it's cooler," Lena said. Honor turned
on the big porch fan, and they sat on the lounge chairs, watching
the park. Some of the young women on benches waved when they
saw Honor and Lena.

"It's so hot in the park," Honor said to Lena as she waved back.
"Why should those women sit on those uncomfortable benches?
If they come to your porch, they can still watch their children
from here. Should I go over and ask them?"

"We've got some lemonade and ice," Lena said. "And your
sugar cookies." She watched Honor cross the street to the women
sitting in the shade. She knew their names now: Barb, Sandra,
Amy, Rafaela and Charlotte. In a few minutes she saw some of
the women talk to their children, pointing to the porch across the
street, and then they spoke to the students who were in charge. At
last the five of them crossed the street with Honor.

"My," Charlotte said, climbing the porch stairs and looking
around. "How pretty it is here."

"And cool," said Amy; she settled in a lounge chair with a sigh.

"We asked the students in charge to watch our children," young
black Rafaela said. "If the kids want us, we told them to stand at
the curb and call, but never cross the street."

Barb sat down and sighed. "Three kids under six! If you don't
think I'm glad to get away from them for a while..." she laughed.
"Monsters."

Sandra perched on the edge of a chair, twisting her long blonde
ponytail.

"Would you like some lemonade and cookies?" Honor asked.

The women smiled and said Yes! and Uh-huh! Barb said, "Just
don't let the kids see us having a party."

Hesitant at first, the young women came to the park the next day, and waited for Lena or Honor to wave them over to Lena's porch. But in a week or two, they began to leave their children in the park and climb Lena's steps by habit, settling into soft cushions to eat and talk. Sometimes they brought cupcakes or fruit or a jug of iced coffee, and washed glasses and cups and plates in Lena's kitchen. On blistering-hot days, they sat in Lena's air-conditioned living room, and watched their children from her front window.

One day Amy handed some iced coffee to Honor and said, "I can see this house from my kitchen window, and I've noticed your awfully big, handsome husband at your place. Tall and dark. He was dragging a Christmas tree out of your front door in January, and then he was helping you with ladders and paint cans a while ago." She hesitated, then said, "I wonder if the two of you would like to have me babysit for you sometimes?"

"That's a nice offer," Honor said, "Sometimes my aunt and I like to go somewhere together, or the three of us when Joe is here."

"I can use the money," Amy said. "I'm living at my grandmother's with my little girl while I go to college and my husband works in Milwaukee. I'm so close to you—less than a block away—down there on the corner. I could babysit for you any time I don't have classes. Grandma can watch my Stella."

The young women talked of their children and their husbands... how expensive food and gas were...their classes nearby at I.S.T.C., or their husband's classes, or both, lazing there together, laughing and teasing and interrupting each other. They ran up Lena's porch stairs with smiles, and left for home reluctantly when dark began to fall.

Joe rang Lena's doorbell one warm, rainy night.
      Lena answered and said, "Joe! Come in!"
"Sorry I couldn't drop in for so long. I tried to phone you often," Joe said. "My only excuse is that it's official now: I've got my doctorate."

"Congratulations!" Lena said. She called upstairs: "Honor! We have somebody named Dr. Lombard down here!" She smiled at Joe and said, "You'll stay for supper?"

Joe smiled said he would, thanks, and Honor called, "*Doctor* Lombard! Joe! You've got your Ph.D.!"

"At last!" he called. "Can I come up?" Honor said yes, so he climbed the stairs to find Honor beside Don's crib in one of the bedrooms.

"How proud you must be!" Honor said to him. "Congratulations!"

"It was a long haul," Joe said. He looked at the little boy in the crib, asleep on his back with his fingers curled at his ears. His toes curled, too, at the hem of his white gown. "What a beautiful child," Joe said.

Don's eyes opened. Honor picked him up and held his small face against hers. "I love this little boy. I never imagined how much I could love a child of my own. He's all I have in the world, except for Lena."

"And me," Joe said. "Count on me, and Mother, too." He touched the baby's cheek. "Can I hold him?"

She gave Don to him. "Donald Joseph," Joe said. "Welcome to the family." Two pairs of the Lombard dark eyes looked at Honor. "Your aunt's fascinated by him, don't you think?" Joe asked. "So Don's got two mothers to love him—he's Ruler of the World already." Joe walked around the room with Don in his arms, looking at walls that had once been papered, a scarred linoleum floor, and two pieces of furniture: a table and a crib.

"Don hasn't got a very fancy nursery," Honor said. "I cleaned out this storeroom, and Lena bought the crib and table."

"I thought you and Lena had redone the whole house," Joe said.

"Not on the second floor, though the bathroom next door is all new."

"Nothing else upstairs?"

"No. We haven't done Lena's bedroom yet, although she can climb the stairs now. And we've never done my bedroom, or this room. I didn't think I should…" Honor's voice trailed off. After a moment she said, "It's not my home, you know."

"But Lena's given you a home. She's your aunt…"

"I had nobody else when I ran away from Iowa City. No family but Lena. No job. No money." Honor moved to the uncurtained window to look at back gardens in the rain. "I didn't have a choice. I shoved my way in here—that was what I did. Lena didn't want me."

"I can't believe that."

"She was in a wheelchair, of course, but she didn't offer me anything. I had to ask for food, and find a bed for myself—I didn't know I was pregnant. She spoke in words of one syllable for weeks, if she spoke at all, and she glared."

"But she was all alone," Joe said. "In a wheelchair. Wasn't she glad to have company? Somebody to help her?"

"No. She was curled up in herself—a regular porcupine, all her spines on end, determined to take care of herself, thank you."

"Didn't want *you*?"

"But I had to stay. Where else could I go? And Brandon caught me grocery shopping."

"He came here?"

"Brandon chased me at the store, and then to Lena's, but we locked him out, so he yelled and banged on her windows and doors until after dark. Finally the police heard him and sent him away."

Joe stared at her. "What did he want?"

"Me—I guess. But Lena wasn't scared when Brandon banged on her windows and doors. She called him 'Peeping Tom.'"

"Did he come back?"

"Brandon caught her the next morning on her front porch. She told him I wasn't home and he wasn't welcome, and he couldn't come in and wait for me because she didn't have any whiskey or gin in the house."

Joe grinned.

"She called Brandon a teen-aged, grabby kid—just a boy yet, who thinks everything he wants has his name on it, and won't grow up until he's tried every possibility. She told him he was out of the grubby age and into the grabby age, wanting everything he didn't know how to get yet, and heaven help a woman if some buster and breaker and wrecker and drinker like him goes after her. She said, 'You think everything you want has your name on it, but your name's not on my niece, thank heaven. That girl's got sense.'"

"So then she understood, and she took you in."

"No." Honor followed a crack in the windowsill with a finger. "Lena's had a long-standing grudge against my family. I knew that. My mother and father didn't help Lena at all when Lena had to take care of her mother and dad—for years. So my grandparents left Lena all their money and farms. My mother and father were bitter, and told me that Lena had wormed her way into the

115

minds of senile old people. They never spoke to her again. Lena sold her parents' house and other farms they'd bought, and went on to graduate from Wellesley, and travel in Europe…and buy this place."

"I had no idea!" Joe said. The three of them looked from the window at the empty house next door, and its overgrown back yard. "I didn't know—couldn't guess any of this. I thought you were all settled here when I found you in the garden."

"I really had no hope that day you came," Honor said. "For me, or for the baby. I was desperate…I'm so ashamed…you'll be horrified to hear how sneaking I was." She sighed. "I'd found out I was pregnant, and I had to get around Lena somehow. Talk her into letting me stay. You ought to know how I play games—you saw me at Chicago. But I didn't sneak in Chicago for anybody but myself. I've told you. It was nothing but revenge in Chicago. But with Lena I was sneaking for the two of us, Don and me."

"I wish I'd known last summer!" Joe said. "If I'd only guessed how much you needed help. But I really thought you didn't like me much the first time I came here."

"I…I'd gone through so much, and I thought you knew."

"Are the two of you getting hungry?" Lena called from the hall below. "Come on down. Supper is ready!"

Honor took Don to put him in his crib again. "I sneaked," she whispered. "I rubbed Lena the right way. She couldn't do much to help herself yet, and she needed new clothes, and her house remodeled. And who could help her but me? But I didn't have any right to work on Don's room, or mine, did I? Not when she didn't want me here. Sneaky. I'm so sneaky."

"No!" Joe said.

11

"Doctor Lombard!" Lena said as Joe came downstairs with Honor and the baby. "How proud your mother must be!"

"After two years, she probably thought I'd never get past that M.S.," Joe said. "But she's happy. Now we wonder if I can find a job."

"Come out to the side porch," Lena said. "It's such a cool night after the rain. I thought we'd eat there, if Joe will bring Don's playpen."

Children were playing tag in the park. Breeze blew through the porch. Lena had made a salad full of almonds, boiled egg and juicy chicken. Butter melted on Honor's nut bread that was warm from the oven, and real lemons were sweet in the lemonade.

Just as they finished eating, the children in the park screamed and yelled. In a moment the reason for the shouting appeared: the Good Humor Man's white truck drove with a ting-a-ling around the corner.

Joe said, "Let me get a last little snack for us." He ran out to join a line of children along the park curb, and came back to bring the ice cream bars on kitchen plates. The three of them began, like hungry children, to bite off the crackling chocolate covering, devour the vanilla ice cream, and lick the sticks afterward.

"Lena..." Joe said, collecting empty plates and sticks, "Honor showed me Don's room just now. It's big enough for a play room when he's older, but I noticed that it's got bare walls and a worn floor. I wonder..." He hesitated. "I wonder if you could use a handyman and painter, now that I'm an unemployed graduate looking for a job with room and board? I'd be glad to help you out—I've got the summer—if you decide what you'd like for Don's room. My mother and Brandon and I redecorated quite a few rooms because we moved so much, so I can hang wallpaper, spackle, paint..."

"Well..." Lena said. "I guess we could do that, if you want to come."

"It's a thought, anyway," Joe said. "You've been so hospitable. I'd be happy to pay you back a little."

"Well," Lena said again. "You could live here in my downstairs back room if you like. I've got a twin bed in the attic."

"Great! Then I can let my rented room in Iowa City go, and save money," Joe said. "I could have stayed at Berkeley to finish my dissertation, but living is cheaper here, and I wanted to be near Mom, so I came back to Iowa. I've had to be a regular miser, I'm afraid. Mother's brother, my Uncle Charley, left his money to Brandon and me for college. Brandon went through his half of it pretty fast, but I've got most of mine...if I can get a job and won't have to use it."

Joe waited for a minute and then said to Lena: "You can plan what you want for Don's room...and I wonder if you'd want to do Honor's bedroom over, too? I noticed today that you haven't been able to start on it yet. If you do two rooms at once, while I've got the time, you can probably save some money on paint, wallpaper, labor..." he laughed to show it was just a suggestion. "And we could finish off the upstairs while we're at it, too, if you have plans for your own bedroom."

118

"Well...." Lena said.

"I love the room you've given me," Honor smiled at Lena. "It looks down on gardens, and it's right next to Don's. I sit at a little table there and write sometimes."

"Have you found out that Honor's a fine poet?" Joe said to Lena. "And she's written stories, too. Maybe she'd write even better if she had a bedroom-study with bookshelves and a desk? Virginia Woolf said that every woman writer should have 'a room of her own.'"

Sitting on the dark porch, they could see fireflies now: sparks of light in the park—in the street—in Lena's garden.

"Why don't you read Joe your new poem?" Lena said to Honor. "You left it in the kitchen. Bring a candle."

"A poem!" Joe said. "Yes!"

Honor came back in a few moments with the poem, and a candle in a candlestick. The flame gilded her hair, and the shape of her breasts under thin cloth...Joe tried not to stare. "It's not a happy poem," she said, sitting down. "It's about childbirth...that's not exactly a man's subject..."

"We've all been there," Joe said.

"Yes," Honor said, and read the poem:

CHILDBIRTH
When I was everything, everything but me took
(how could I have forgotten?)
one step back and left me
newborn at the eye of death, giving
my own cry as birds do, driven from cover at
    the sound of a gun.
                That scream
Wakes me now. At the eye of a dark door
my child utters himself in terror.
(How could I have forgotten?)
Give him to me.
Milk flows for him in this enemy country.

None of them spoke for a few moments in the candlelight. Then Honor turned to Joe. "You said we'd all been there."

"And we've all forgotten," Joe said. "How could we forget? The first light in our eyes, our first gasp of that strange stuff called 'air'... the pain..."

119

"The terror," Lena said.

"I've never heard it put in words," Joe said. "Those last two lines! The mother feeding him in '*this enemy country*'! The most terrible line of all!" He stared at Honor. "You couldn't feel that! You couldn't. You mustn't! An enemy country!"

She didn't answer.

They were quiet, watching the fireflies. Don snored softly in the play pen. Finally Lena said to Joe: "What do you think of Don, now that he's turning into a little boy?"

"He's a Lombard," Joe said. "He's got the look."

"Already?" Honor said. "What look?"

"My grandfather's look," Joe said. "My father's father—my Grandpa who loved poetry. He'd sit with me on his front porch swing and recite poems by the hour. I can still remember them. They got stuck in my memory."

"You talk of your family," Honor said, "And I realize I've got this little boy and I hardly know anything about his heritage from the Lombards. Brandon never told me much about your parents or grandparents, and I've only met your mother twice."

"I've tried to persuade her to come and see you and Don," Joe said, "but she's...ashamed, I guess I'd have to say."

For a moment there was no sound but a swing creaking in the park: a young man was swinging a girl high in the air.

"I can tell you a little more about my father's father, I guess," Joe said. "Georgio Lombard. We gardened together while I was small, and he taught me so much."

"Did he ever say where his folks came from?" Lena asked.

"Italy. The area of Italy called 'Lombardy' gave us our name. My grandparents were farmers—only tenant farmers—but they couldn't make a living in Italy, so they migrated to the midwest. My mother and her two young sons—Brandon and me—lived with them when my father—their son—deserted us in California. It was hard, for her, but Brandon and I loved those Minnesota years before the old folks died." He turned to Lena. "What about your grandparents?"

"The Edwards family has been farmers for generations," Lena said. "Always living in the same place—Iowa. You mentioned the father who deserted you. What was his background?"

"Well..." Joe said, and stared into the dark garden for a moment. "I guess I'd have to say that my father came from horror."

120

"Horror!" Honor and Lena cried together.

"Not when he was a child, though the family was poor. When Dad's mother died, Grandpa Georgio married again and had another family. He was just a poor farm laborer in Minnesota when he found out that the government was asking so little for land in the west: the Homestead Act. A farm for almost nothing! Georgio couldn't imagine such a chance. His family had never owned a square foot of land."

"So he went west?" Lena asked.

"He did," Joe said. "Grandpa paid eighteen dollars for one hundred and sixty acres in Oklahoma, and brought his family there—he was one of the farmers who plowed grasslands that had existed for centuries and centuries. Grandfather said he made money for years, but the plowing, little by little, opened Oklahoma to the wind. Dust storms! The winds blew that Midwestern land all the way to New York. Coated Manhattan streets with it. You know about the Dust Bowl."

"They had to leave?" Lena asked.

"Oklahoma folks thought the rain would come," Joe said. "They used up their savings and ate their cattle and pigs and chickens and went into debt, year by year. Grandpa Georgio got tears in his eyes when he talked of it. You couldn't keep the dirt out of your barns or your house or your body—or even the coffins you buried your dead in. You put your children to bed, and when they woke, their pillows were deep in dirt, except under their heads. You shoveled that good earth out of your doors every morning, and sometimes you woke to find that there wasn't a door you could open: doors—even windows—were drifted that high. And the black clouds came up in the distance like mountain ranges. Grandfather said they called them 'The Rollers,' and when they rolled in, they turned noon to midnight. You couldn't see a foot ahead."

Honor said in a horrified voice: "How could they stand it?"

"Everything, day by day, disappeared," Joe said. "Schools, churches, towns, stores—nothing left. My father helped Grandpa Georgio load their Model T truck with all they could save, perched the young children and their mother on top of it under tarpaulins, and started west. California was supposed to be heaven in those days."

"*One truck?*" Lena said.

121

"They were lucky to have it. Lots of families crowded the whole family and belongings in one car, or used a horse and cart, or just pushed wheelbarrows."

"Where could they sleep? Where could they get food?" Honor asked

"You slept at the roadside, or fought to get a little shelter behind billboards or under railway bridges. Dad and his father weighted one edge of their tarp with stones on top of the loaded truck, then slanted the far edge down to the ground, and put more stones on it. They lived and cooked and slept under that 'tent' —the whole family."

Honor looked at Don asleep in the playpen. "How old were their children?"

"They were young—a pair of twins—all of them under ten. Andrew and Will and Sally and June, and Arthur, a new baby."

"Think of it!" Lena said. "Unbelievable."

"Some people along the road were friendly and kind and would give you something to eat if they had it, my grandfather said. Others would steal almost anything from you. Black clouds of dust made it like night on the road, even at noon."

"But your grandparents got to California?" Honor asked.

"They lost their children, one by one, to what was called 'dust pneumonia.' Only my father and his father, Grandpa Georgio, and Grandpa's second wife, lived. They buried the children along the road. And when they got to California, they were called 'Okies' or 'Arkies.' There were signs saying that they weren't welcome in stores and public places. After a while you couldn't even cross the California line if you didn't have fifty dollars."

"What could they do?" Lena said.

"Before long Grandfather's wife died of the dust too, like her children. He married again and had a son—my Uncle Charley. Charley made a fortune, and left Brandon and me the money for college. But I don't think my father ever forgot those dust-bowl years. Grandpa Georgio settled in Minnesota—his third wife inherited a farm—but my father was a drinker and a drifter. He ran away and left Mother and Brandon and me, and we've never known whether he's alive or dead."

They were quiet for a little while, listening to an owl some-where, and the chorus of insects in the dark. Fireflies rode a cool night wind.

122

Finally Joe got up and said, "I'm afraid I've stayed too long—I've got an early appointment tomorrow. Thanks for the fine food."

Lena said, "Come again soon." Honor lifted the sleeping baby from the playpen, and Joe carried the pen and chair inside.

"I'll be back before long," Joe said. As he left the house and climbed in his car, he saw Honor in Lena's front window with Don in her arms.

Joe came back with a loaded car in a few days. Lena gave him the big downstairs room at the back of her house. "Joe's study" had Lena's old dining-room table and chair, a twin bed, an easy chair, a lamp, and a fine view of her garden. Lena invited him to have his meals with them.

"We can start work on your upstairs now, can't we?" Joe said to Lena at breakfast his first morning. "Don doesn't care about where he sleeps yet, but you're in that almost bare bedroom of yours. And Honor's a poet—should we think about that? Honor tells me you're a poet too, so you can imagine the kind of workroom Honor needs. Bookshelves on every wall? A big desk in front of her bedroom window?"

"Well..." Lena said. "I've had pretty good carpenters working on my place, and a carpet store in Waterloo did a nice job on my floors..."

"And I can do the messy stuff before they come," Joe said. "Spackling walls, wall-papering, painting. Whenever you have time, we can go shopping for supplies. What colors would you like for your new bedroom?"

"Well!" Lena said. "I really hadn't thought...but maybe light blue and white? With some rose pink?"

"And how about Don's nursery, and your study?" Joe asked Honor.

"Yellow and green and white for Don!" Honor cried. "Don's sure to be a gardener—all three of us are. It must run in your family, too."

Joe turned to Lena. "Maybe we should start with your upstairs bedroom?"

Lena gave him a startled look, that was all. So they began. They made trip after trip, wheeling Don in his Taylor Tot, to choose wallpaper and paint and carpeting. They spackled the walls of Lena's bedroom, and then hung a blue, pink and green flowered wallpaper. Lena and Honor had never papered a wall, but Joe had, and could teach them to cut edges straight and match seams and not put a finger through wet paper.

Once they finished papering and painting Lena's room, the house was full of workmen again: they laid Lena's pale blue bedroom carpet, and delivered her new white furniture, and she ordered curtains and a bedspread to match her rug. When at last her bedroom was done, Lena said, "It's almost too fancy to go to bed in!"

"Now for the nursery?" Joe said, and away they went. They were a team now: there was Joe, man of all work, and Lena, very good at spackling and painting, and Honor, hard at work at any hour, and Donald Joseph, cheering them on with his first attempts at words.

Don's nursery walls had cracks, so they patched the top half, then papered that half in a green leaf pattern. Carpenters nailed wood paneling to the lower walls and built shelves for toys, and a bookcase wall. Joe, Honor and Lena painted all the wood with two coats of enamel, and workman laid the green linoleum floor. One rainy day Joe climbed a ladder with both hands full of a wallpaper border, and the nursery was finished with plump yellow bumble-bees at the ceiling to match the yellow curtains and small chairs.

One morning at breakfast Joe said, "Now for Honor's study-bedroom? We've become experts at spackling walls and spreading wallpaper paste, and she's chosen the paper she likes." So they covered Honor's study walls with a blue floral pattern to match the carpeting. Workmen built a handsome walnut desk under her big window—"My workplace in the summer light!" Honor said—and lined two walls with bookcases. When Joe brushed a last coat of varnish on the walnut, it glowed like satin, and matched Honor's new double bed, dresser and chairs.

"The two of you are spoiling me!" Honor told them when her study-bedroom was done. "How can I ever write well enough to deserve this? And my birthday present from Joe—a new typewriter!"

124

One day Honor and Lena and Don went shopping. Joe went upstairs to fasten a walnut backboard on Honor's new desk. When he finished the job, he picked up her pen lying there, then put it down. He thought he could smell he perfume she wore. She had touched the hand mirror on her dresser...

There in the empty house he felt the space Honor kept around her: a cool, quiet, private life, like a still lake, a foggy meadow, a winter snowfall.

One afternoon Joe came into Lena's kitchen waving a paper. "Good news?" Lena asked. "You're grinning like a Cheshire Cat."

Honor had Don in her arms. The baby was pink-faced from his nap; he held out his arms to Joe. "Don't worry," Honor said, as Joe took him. "I just changed him."

Don grabbed Joe's paper. Joe took it back and said, "Good news! I'll be on the Teachers College faculty next spring—right here on campus—just part-time, teaching biology."

"How wonderful!" Honor said.

"You think so?" Joe said.

"Congratulations!" Lena said.

Joe smiled at Honor: "It was the Virginia Woolf article you helped me write—that did it! After it came out, somebody showed it to Les Hawkins, head of the science department. So Hawkins called me in and hired me."

Don babbled and waved and dropped the sock monkey he was holding. Joe picked it up and gave it to him. "I'm here to ask some questions," he said, and hesitated... "What would you say to having me as your neighbor?"

"Neighbor?" Lena said.

"The house next door is for sale."

"Nobody's ever wanted it," Lena said. "It's been on the market for years. They even took the For Sale sign down last summer for a while."

"You know I'm a gardener—a Green Man for life, I expect," Joe said. "That house has your view of the park, and a big back yard with no trees. I could even build a greenhouse: there's space for one next to your lot. And there's a room off the kitchen for plant carts."

"Well!" Lena said.

"What do you folks think about having me next door?" Joe said. "Maybe you wouldn't like it? I won't buy it if you don't. You've helped me so much."

"I've never been in that house," Lena said. "It must be in poor shape. I've heard an old fellow lived alone there for years."

Joe said, "They're selling it furnished, but what's there is mostly junk. It needs work, so the price is low. I certainly won't buy it if you-two would rather have me somewhere else. But can I recommend myself a little as a neighbor, maybe? A next-door lawn-mower and snow-shoveler and painter and Christmas-tree dragger? That kind of thing?"

"Man around the house," Lena said.

"Something like that."

"Babysitter," Lena said.

"Absolutely!" Joe lifted Don high and grinned. "How do the two of you feel about this idea?"

"I'm delighted!" Lena said, and turned to Honor. "A good neighbor for us!"

"I'm sure we'd be glad to have you next door," Honor said. "It's so...unexpected...and that house is probably so..."

"It's only a few blocks from my work!" Joe said. "On the park! And it's well-built, like this one. Big. Solid. I've got until I go to work next January to fix it up...some."

It was almost dark when Joe knocked on his mother's apartment door and called, "Mom!"

"Joe!" Emily cried. He put the sacks he was carrying on her kitchen table and gave her a hug and kiss.

"Couldn't get here any earlier. Sorry," he said. "But I knew it was your afternoon off, so I've brought some steaks, and they don't take long to broil. And salad stuff. Ice cream. I'll get the table and folding chairs." He set them on grass near her door. The narrow strip of green along the parking lot could never be called a park, but birds were settling for the night there: a flutter of wings in a few trees and bushes.

Emily's little charcoal broiler, set on the grass, was big enough for the two steaks. Emily made some salads; Joe started the meat broiling. They sat together in the parking lot light. "How nice you've come for a picnic," Emily said. "Have the three of you finally finished Lena's house?"

126

"Just about. And I've got news."

"Not bad news about Brandon, I hope," Emily said. "I haven't seen him since April."

"You can imagine he's busy—new wife, new job." Joe took some pictures out of his shirt pocket. "Here's a picture of Don I took last week. Just picked up the prints."

Emily held the snapshot in the parking lot light while Joe turned the steaks over. "I'm absolutely sure of it now—Don looks like you," she said. "You were so much like Grandpa Lombard, and Don's got those same dark eyes. Pretty eyes."

"I wish you'd go see him."

She handed the picture back. "You said you had good news."

"I got the job at ISTC."

"Right in Cedar Falls!"

"Just a part-time biology instructor, but it pays. I start early next year."

"Joe! Oh, Joe! Good for you!" she cried, clapping her hands. "And you'll be so close!"

"That Woolf article helped. The head of the science department says my position might be a full-time one before long."

"You don't seem very happy," Emily said. "I'd think you'd be so relieved." He didn't answer. "Isn't this just what you want?"

"It was," he said. "But now I think I've made a mistake."

"A mistake? Taking the job?"

"No. I've bought a house. In Cedar Falls, near the campus."

"A house!" Emily cried, and listened while he talked of the garden, the big rooms, the low price...

"Next to Lena's house," he said at last.

She put down her knife and fork and looked at him. "Next to Honor? And Don?"

"I talked to Lena and Honor, and they didn't object. And I want you to live with me there, Mom," he said. "Not in this tiny apartment. Not carrying trays all day. Next door to your grandson." He took the steaks off the broiler and put them on plates before her.

"Joe!" she said. "Do you know what you're doing, at all?"

"I sign the papers next week, and move in. No. I don't."

"You're still trying."

"Yes."

They were quiet for a while, eating their steak. Finally Emily said, "You've told Honor?"

"Yes."

"She hasn't said anything?"

"No. How can she? She has to have a husband. The two of us have to keep house. She doesn't have a choice. We're fake—just two actors on a stage."

12

E mily Lombard worried about Joe, even in her sleep. She worried about him while she waited tables the next day. The Hungry Chef wasn't very busy late in the afternoon, but there were five customers at her Table 15. She was carrying a loaded tray when somebody yelled, "Mom!"

Brandon was in the doorway. The waiters and diners stared, because Brandon had a big silver bundle in his arms, and the bundle was screaming.

"Mabel," Emily said to another waitress, "Can you serve these dinners to Table 15?"

Mabel was an old friend of Emily's. She said, "Sure," and took the tray.

"And sub for me until I get back, will you?" Emily said, hurrying to get Brandon and his screaming bundle out the door and around the restaurant corner to her apartment.

"I brought him!" Brandon said as she unlocked her door. He put his bundle in her arms the minute they were inside. "Here's my boy—here's Don!"

Emily said, "Oh!" and then "Oh, my!" and sat on her sofa bed to rock a big silver bundle with a small, angry face in it. She'd never seen that face, but she recognized it...he was one of her boys come back, little and close and howling in her arms.

Don's yells filled the room. Brandon had to shout: "Isn't he a fine one, though? Your first grandchild. But I thought I'd go crazy—he kept howling, all the way from Cedar Falls. I had to hold him on my lap, and he's pretty good at wetting right through your pants to the car seat."

"That's why he's crying," Emily yelled over the screams. "There's probably more than *that* wrong. He smells—"

"I took him into a filling station!" Brandon shouted. "I tried to clean his diaper off and then I filled it with paper towels, but I couldn't figure out how to put it on again and he kept kicking it off, so I had to wrap him up in that blanket."

"He's probably hungry!" Emily yelled back. "Where's the milk for him—in your car? Go out and get it. And diapers. And Honor must have sent some shirts...let's unwrap this poor baby, and let me see if I can get him clean in the sink." Brandon took him, and Emily spread a towel on her small kitchen counter, unwound smelly Don from his cocoon, and put him there.

"Go on," she said to Brandon. She began to take off the baby's knitted outfit and a diaper full of paper towels. "Get the milk, and his diapers and clothes."

Brandon took a step or two toward the door and stopped. "There...aren't any."

"Aren't any?" Emily stared at him, holding the smelly baby tight.

"No."

"Honor didn't send...what do you mean: *there aren't any?*"

"There aren't any, that's what."

"Nothing? No milk? No diapers? Clothes?"

"Just him. I took him. I thought you ought to see him, after all this time."

"You took him?" Emily cried. "Took him? Just took him?"

Don didn't like to be naked, wet and dirty. He whined and

sobbed, working up to an outraged yell. They hardly noticed—
they were yelling themselves.

"Yes I did!" Brandon shouted.

"Does Honor know?"

"I guess she knows by now, but he's mine,"

"*Kidnapped* him?" Emily was horrified.

"You can't kidnap a baby that's yours," Brandon said.

"The police!" she cried. "The police are probably looking for
him—how did you get him?"

"Took him out of his buggy in the park when the babysitter
wasn't looking. I wanted to see him. I wanted *you* to see him.
He's all right. He just needs a cleanup and some milk, and you
know how to do that. I'll go out and buy milk. And diapers..." he
started out her door.

"Wait!" Emily cried. "We haven't called Honor! Or Lena!
Think how they're feeling! I'll bet Honor's on her way here, but
Lena might still be in Cedar Falls., and they've probably called
the police. There's the phone." She nodded to the shelf behind
her—she had Don in both hands. "Tell her Don's all right, and ask
if we can feed him. Let me talk to her."

Brandon dialed. The moment he said, "Hello...Lena?" Emily
could hear the telephone's answering stream of exasperated
words.

"Yes," Brandon said. "Yes... I did...well, I didn't..."

Words poured from the telephone again.

"I know," Brandon said when Lena must have stopped for
breath. "I just wanted to see Don and show him to my mother—"

"Tell her I want to talk to her," Emily said.

Brandon held out the phone, but Emily had both hands full of
a dirty, slippery, naked and screaming baby. "Take him," she said,
and handed him to Brandon, washed her hands, and grabbed the
phone, while Brandon held Don at arm's length and said, "Ugh!"

"Lena?" Emily said. "It's Emily. Joe and Brandon's mother.
We've got the baby here...Donald Joseph...our baby, I should say,
I guess—he belongs to all of us. He's fine and I'll give him a bath,
but he's hungry, and we don't know what to feed him. Is Honor
there?...Gone?... Honor breast-feeds him?... Maybe some warm
water?"

In a few minutes Emily told Lena goodbye, and said to
Brandon: "Honor and Joe left just a few minutes after you did, so

131

they ought to be here soon. They're bringing Don's diapers and clothes. Honor's still breast-feeding him, so all we can do is give him a drink of warm water and wait."

"Here," Brandon said, holding out a messy and sobbing baby. "They won't make it as fast I did, not with Joe's old car, unless they took Lena's!" He shouted his last words, because Don was yelling.

Emily ran warm water in her little kitchen sink and eased the smelly, sobbing baby into it, dirty little penis and all. So many years since she'd felt a baby's soft skin. Her grandson. Five months old. How lovely he was.

She crooned soft, silly words to him as she soaped him with a clean dishcloth. Don seemed to like warm water; he stopped whining and slapped at it with the miracles of his small, perfect hands. His ten perfect toes splashed in bubbles. She pulled the plug and ran clean rinse water. Not a thing wrong with him. That small, dark, curly head…just like babies she'd kissed and hugged not so long ago, when all she had were two little boys and no money.

Don liked to be clean and warm, pinned into a dishtowel diaper and wrapped in a flannel blanket. Someone was making soft noises and rocking him, and he liked that too. But when Emily tried to put him on her sofa bed beside Brandon, he yelled, so she picked him up and sang little songs she couldn't believe she still remembered. When the bottle of water was ready, Brandon took him.

"Stealing a baby," Emily said. "What did you think you were doing?"

"I just wanted to see him…hold him." Brandon sat beside her looking at Don. "I never have, not once. And I wanted you to see him."

"You just left your new job and came all that way? Does Mr. Bushnell know you've run off like this? Don't you think *at all*? Don't you *ever* think? Can't you even imagine what Honor's going through right now?"

"He's *mine*," Brandon said in a sulky voice: "She knows I'd take him if I could."

"You're not some kidnapper? How does she know it?" Emily said. "I bet she called the police. And you stole him without a single diaper or bottle of milk?"

"I figured I could get him here fast."

"He's on Honor's breast milk! He's not even six months old. Didn't you know?"

"How could I know?"

"He's your baby."

"Honor won't talk to me. She won't tell me anything! Never did. When I finally found her in a store in Cedar Falls last June, all she did was throw my engagement ring in my face and hit me with a package of meat—how can you ask a woman like that any questions?"

"You should have asked her the right questions before that."

"What questions?"

"Simple questions like: *Shall I?...Would you mind if I?...Do you want to...*"

Brandon wouldn't look at her. Finally he said, "There's been quite a bit going on since I called you last."

"You and Katie are still talking about a divorce?"

"Off and on. She's got a big bunch of friends, and plenty of guys to dance and beach-party and go to shows with, I guess. Katie claims she's tried marriage once and didn't like it—I don't know what she'll do."

"Your father-in-law—what does he say?"

"Bushnell can't do much about any of his daughters. Or wife. They rule his roost. And I can't try to get Honor and Don back and marry her until I know whether Bushnell will keep me on after the divorce. If he fires me, I'll need another job."

"Honor probably doesn't want to marry anyone," Emily said. "I don't know what arrangements she's made with her aunt... whether she'll stay with her until Don's old enough for her to have a home and job..."

"Joe's just her stand-in husband and father," Brandon said. "All he's got is a rat's-nest of a house next door." Don was pushing the nipple out of his mouth with his tongue. "Looks like this guy's had enough," Brandon said. "What do we do now?"

Emily handed him a dishtowel. "Here—put this on your shoulder, put his face on it, and pat his back."

"What'll he do?" Brandon held the baby aloft and eyed him. "He'll get rid of the water all over me? He's already done that once today. Right through my pants to the new car seat."

"You've got to burp him. He's swallowed air," Emily said. Brandon arranged Don on his shoulder, gingerly, and patted his back. Don obligingly burped, then began to yell.

133

They heard a car stop in the restaurant lot. Car doors slammed. Brandon cried, "There they are!" and jumped up with Don.

Emily took the crying baby. "Now, Brandon, just listen to me. You've done something pretty awful, and you're going to have to tell them both how sorry you are."

Emily opened her door and waved. "Don's here and he's safe," she called.

Joe and Honor came in. Emily's place was crowded: four people and a wailing baby. "Don!" Honor said, and took him from Emily to look him all over, crooning "Don....Don..." She sat with him on the sofa bed, unbuttoned her shirt, and began to nurse him.

The three others had no choice but to stand very close to her and each other in the small space, listening to the steady, contented sucking of a hungry baby. Brandon, after one look, backed behind Joe and Emily into the kitchen corner. Emily said, "We've called Lena. Told her Don was here and safe, and asked her what to do. I bathed him, and we gave him a drink of water."

"Get out." Joe glared at Brandon.

"He's mine." Brandon took a step toward him.

"Out," Joe said. "Go on home."

"Joe..." Emily said.

"Do you know what you've done?" Joe yelled at Brandon. "Scared Honor almost to death!"

"I just wanted—"

"*Wanted?*" Joe said. "You've got no right to want anything. Get out." He shoved his brother.

"At least I've held my own son." Brandon shoved Joe back. "At least Mom saw him. He's not yours. He's mine."

He yanked the door open with a last furious look at Joe. Rain had begun to fall. They heard him slam his car door and drive away.

"I'll call Lena," Joe said. "Tell her everything's all right."

When Lena answered, the others could hear her far away, relieved voice.

"How did Brandon get Don?" Emily asked when he hung up.

"Lena and I went shopping," Honor said. "We left Don with a neighbor—Amy Jackson—she often babysits for us. When we came home, Joe was there, and Amy was in hysterics. We finally calmed her down enough to hear that 'a man' had taken Don just a few minutes before."

Joe said, "It was wild, Mom. We kept asking: What man? Where? Amy finally calmed down enough to tell us that she'd taken her little girl to the park, with Don in his buggy. She said the park was almost empty except for a man sitting on a bench reading a newspaper. He evidently was hiding behind it, but she couldn't know that. Amy parked the buggy in the shade just as her little girl ran to the swings in the middle of the park and shouted, 'Push, Mommy! Push!' So Amy left Don to push her daughter, but when she looked back, a man was running away with Don. She chased him, but he raced to his parked car with Don and got away."

"Amy said the man looked like Joe," Honor said, "and she finally remembered the car was a fancy red Corvette. So we told her we wouldn't call the police, because we were pretty sure who'd taken Don."

"We thought Brandon wouldn't take a baby all the way to Illinois. And he's always wanted to show Don to you," Joe said. "So Lena helped pack up Don's things in about three minutes and Honor and I hurried here."

Don was still nursing, but he was slowing down, and his eyes were closed.

"You must have been terribly frightened," Emily said, sitting beside Honor. "I'm so sorry for the two of you, and your aunt. For everything. Everything."

"Nothing is your fault," Honor said. "I'm wearing your rings, and I'm so grateful for them—you got my note?" Emily smiled and nodded. "Thanks so much for taking care of Don, and letting us know where he was."

"He reminds me so much of my boys," Emily said. "The minute I held him, I felt twenty years old again, with a baby Joe in my arms."

Honor bent over her baby to kiss Emily's cheek, and Emily

kissed her back. "Come see us," Honor said. "Any time. Joe will be glad to bring you to Cedar Falls. So would I. You'll like my Aunt Lena. We have a bedroom for you whenever you can take time from your job."

"Won't you three stay for supper?" Emily said.

"You've worked hard all day, and certainly don't need to feed more people," Honor said.

"I'm always allowed to bring friends to the restaurant," Emily said. "Don's having his dinner, but the two of you can't drive all the way back to Cedar Falls hungry."

So they called Lena again to tell her they were having supper. When Don was full and fast asleep, Joe carried him into the restaurant.

They had hardly settled at a table when the staff of The Hungry Chef found a way, one by one, to come to them. Mabel was first, bringing a bassinet for Don, and took their orders. "Emily's grandson!" she said to Joe. "A beautiful little boy—looks just like his daddy—and such a lovely mother, too!"

Joe and Honor smiled at her and thanked her. When she left, Honor said to Emily: "I've met you just twice—when Brandon and I visited you... and at his wedding. I wrote you to say how sorry I was that I came to Chicago. I never imagined I'd make such trouble."

"You shouldn't be sorry. I admired you." Emily patted Honor's ringed hand. "Brandon called me not long ago, and said he has an apartment in Rockford, Illinois now. He's in charge of a new office that the Bushnell company just opened. Katie isn't there with him. She didn't want to leave all her friends in Chicago."

Barbara came to their table to fill water glasses and said, "Oh, Emily—you've got such a lovely grandson there." Kenny followed Barbara with their dinner plates, and clapped Joe on the shoulder. "Gonna have a quarterback there in twenty years?" he said, grinning.

Emily couldn't look at Joe. Congratulated as a father—Joe!—when everyone at the table knew it wasn't true. How could Joe stand it—pretending to be the father? Pretending to be a husband?

"Mom has always wanted to see Don—so much," Joe said to Honor. "If Brandon stole Don and frightened all of you, at least I think that was Brandon's reason: to show him to Mother. I keep telling Mom that all our trouble isn't her fault, and she tells me it's not mine." Joe's look was intense and fixed on Honor. "Mom knows I tried to help you at that graduation party when Brandon was so drunk."

"Everybody there was drunk," Honor said in a bitter voice. "You too, probably. You must not remember much."

"I don't drink," Joe said. "So I remember you wore a beautiful blue dress with sequins, and the silver necklace Brandon gave you. And a jeweled barrette in your hair."

Honor stopped eating to stare at him. " I saw you running away from the party. Running down the hall..."

"I came late and there was a crowd, but I looked for you. I saw you ducking behind the bar, and you looked so unhappy. When you left I went to find you, hunted all over that hotel—"

"You came in just as I left?" Honor said, staring at him. "You didn't see Brandon put an engagement ring on my finger in front of everybody, and parade me around with a plastic wedding cake in his other hand, shouting, 'Soon to be Mr. and Mrs. Brandon Lombard!'"

"He did that?" Joe said.

Honor said to Emily: "You knew Brandon and I hoped to marry, but weeks before our graduation I told him I couldn't marry him. And yet Brandon told everybody at that party that we were engaged..."

"He was drunk," Joe said.

"You never went back to the party?" Honor stared at him.

"No. I left when you did. I wanted to know that you were all right. I arrived late, just as I saw you leave. And I found you in the rain, and took you home."

"You never spoke to Brandon that night?" Honor asked in a severe voice.

"No. I just came and left, didn't say anything to anybody. You stared right at me as you went out the door—don't you remember?"

Honor shook her head.

"You looked so...lost. So scared," Joe said. "I wondered why you were running away from the party without Brandon—I thought you might need help. Where did you go? I went up and down the halls, looked all over the hotel. In a while, I found you and took you home, remember? I parked outside your place for a while, but there wasn't any light in your room, and I didn't want to wake you."

Honor had been staring at him. Now she gave a sudden, half-strangled laugh. "I sneaked out of that party and hid in a hotel broom closet, hiding from Brandon." She pressed her hands to her eyes for a moment, her rings sparkling in the restaurant lights. "In a broom closet. I should have stayed there."

13

Honor and Joe drove back to Cedar Falls with a sleeping baby. Joe had borrowed sheets from Lena for the old double bed in his upstairs bedroom, and he told Lena and Honor goodnight, and spent his first night in his own house.

When he woke in the morning, he was...where was he? In an old, worn-out dump. He dressed and went downstairs to a kitchen whose linoleum was black squares scuffed to gray, and white squares stained brown. The stove had four burners he lit with a match. A nearly naked girl hugging a dog smirked at him from a 1945 calendar nailed on a wall.

The first thing he wanted was a cup of coffee. The last thing he wanted was a doorbell ringing. But the worst thing of all was Brandon standing at his door.

Brandon came in and stared at Joe's junk-filled living room. "I called Mom. She said you've got a job at ISTC next spring, and you bought this old place? You're crazy."

"I like it," Joe said.

"Like what? Let me guess. Being next to Honor and Don? You're practically living with Don now, but I can't see him."

"That's right."

"So that's why I took him, took him to Mom. I'm his father."

"It's Honor's call. She's Don's mother."

"And you actually *bought* this place?"

"I didn't marry a rich girl," Joe said. "Sorry."

"Well, I did," Brandon said. "I can give Don everything."

"Except his mother," Joe said.

"Honor could! She could give our baby his own father, but she doesn't care if my boy doesn't have any," Brandon said. "And did you think I couldn't find out that your 'marriage' is common law? I hired a detective. He couldn't find a real marriage for the two of you—it doesn't exist. Honor's married name's a fake, even if Mom's diamonds aren't."

"Honor deserves everything I could give her, and everything she's willing to take," Joe said. "Don's my nephew. She could have aborted him, or abandoned him. You'd never have known. Lots of women take that way out, but Honor wouldn't. She saved him. She wanted him. Honor's got first rights. As far as I can see, she's got all the rights there are."

"He's mine. He's a Lombard. Doesn't that mean anything to you?"

"She's his mother, and she didn't mean anything to you."

"We were getting *married*." Brandon paced around the room, looked out the window at the front porch and the park, and came back to face Joe.

"Did she cry?" Joe said. "Beg?"

Brandon opened his mouth, then shut it. He had been glaring at Joe; now he looked at the floor. "She just didn't under—"

"She didn't *understand* what you were doing? That's your *excuse*?"

Brandon came a little closer to Joe. "Well, she hasn't married you, has she? All you've got is no woman and a fake marriage. You think she doesn't know what you called her behind her back?" Brandon laughed in Joe's face. He ran through the old screened porch and down the front stairs, and drove away with a squeal of tires.

J oe sat on a sagging couch for a long time, staring at the floor, until he heard a howl. A loud, despairing kind of howl.
A cat was pawing at the front door screen.

Joe opened the door, and the cat dragged himself into the living room and lay at Joe's feet.

A huge, magnificent cat: a Maine Coon. His big black ruff was crowned with tufted-white ears, and his snowy nose, chin and front drifted down to white paws. The rest of him was black, and his immense black tail, finished off with a white tassel of fur, trailed behind him.

"Are you hungry?" Joe asked. The cat laid his nose on his paws and closed his eyes.

Joe brought a bowl of water and the cat drank. When Joe gave him a bowl of canned tuna fish, he ate it all. Joe sat on the couch and watched. The cat seemed to grow larger as he ate; he licked the bowls bare, then began to give himself an all-over scrub with his tongue.

"Welcome, Gentleman from Maine," Joe said. "Welcome to my old excuse for a home." The Maine Coon, eyes tightly shut, finished his bath and licked his chops.

"You're certainly dressed for dinner," Joe said to him. "A tuxedo, no less. White gloves. But not white shoes for formal wear, big fella. Won't do. Not the style. Is that your name? Tux?"

Tux gave a last lick to his white shirt front and jumped beside Joe on the couch. A white nose with a faint scent of tuna explored Joe delicately, while a huge tail filled the rest of the couch like a second visitor.

"Tux?" Joe said to the big yellow eyes staring into his. "Are you in need of shelter? Come on. I'll give you a tour of the only home I've got. Be my guest."

The Maine Coon was beside Joe before he took a step upstairs, and climbed with him to a dim hallway where a dusty mirror leaned its shoulder against a wall. Man and cat looked at themselves. Joe drew an X on his mirrored face with his fist.

The window of a back room looked down on Lena's summer flowers. Honor had looked down at them from the house next door and said: *Lena didn't want me. She didn't offer me anything. She had a long-standing grudge.*

A long-standing grudge.

"You think Honor doesn't know what you called her behind her back?"

He went into his front bedroom, Tux at his heels, to look at the park, then kicked piles of newspapers into a corner beside the old double bed. In another room a cobwebbed sheet was draped against a wall like a ghost. When he yanked it away, he found a walnut dresser stacked with empty whiskey bottles and old magazines.

Back and forth the two of them went through rooms with bare floors, or ancient linoleum that buckled underfoot. Windows stuck. The bathtub was scoured down to rusted metal.

Joe didn't know where to begin. He didn't care whether he began or not.

But Tux set up housekeeping with bowls in a kitchen corner, and condescended to use a wooden orange-crate of sand by the garden door. One morning the prowling cat found Joe on the sway-backed living-room couch, his head in his hands.

"I should never have bought this place," Joe told Tux. "She doesn't want me anywhere near. She thinks I called her names. Nasty names."

Tux scrubbed a white nose with a white paw, then sneezed.

"Yes," Joe said. "Really nasty. No wonder she doesn't want me to live next door. So what business do I have, buying this dump, fixing it up?"

Tux came to sit between Joe's feet, and was as straight-backed and yellow-eyed as if he were waiting for orders. Even his fine, tufted ears said so, pointed expectantly.

"All right," Joe said. "If you insist."

He drove into town to rent a sander—it didn't cost much—and began to sand his living-room floor not a hundred feet from Lena's house, and Honor.

Tux did not approve of loud machines. He ate the cat food Joe bought, then retreated to the tops of doors: their lintels were just deep enough to hold four hairy paws in a line. He balanced, glaring at the racket below in the dining room...the halls... the "master bedroom" upstairs.

Joe rented a steamer next, and stripped off wallpaper that had been—incredibly—pasted horizontally around and around the high-ceilinged rooms: never-ending beige roses and blue leaves, faded into a gravy-brown.

Lena came over one morning to see Joe yanking wallpaper off the walls in a fog of steam, while a large cat contrived, with four furry paws in a row, to balance on top of a door lintel.

"A cat!" Lena said.

"He's a Maine Coon who just dropped in," Joe said. "His name is Tux, thanks to that monkey suit he's wearing."

"Huge," Lena said. "Well dressed."

"And very polite," Joe said. "I've asked folks in the neighborhood, and they say he's at their back doors sometimes, but seems to be homeless. He follows me around like Mary's little lamb, except when I use loud machines—then he takes to the air up there."

"Might be somebody's abandoned pet," Lena said. "From the college dorms. I've heard students hide their cats and dogs in their rooms, then leave them on the street when spring classes are over, if you can imagine being that cruel." She watched Joe rip a shabby rose garden off the walls. "Ugh!" she said. "Brown!" And then she said, "Could you use a little help?"

Joe unstuck a sticky brown strip from his shoulder. "Thanks! I sure can," he said. So Lena followed him along the walls, yanking paper loose, watching him steam off faded roses like a man on a hard road with not much hope at the end of it, and nothing to do but work, early and late.

The next morning Honor knocked on Joe's side door, just as he carried a sack of groceries into his kitchen.

"Come in. Come right in," Joe said, opening his door. "This isn't a house, I hope you understand—it's a work in progress." He backed against the door to let her in, and she followed him to his kitchen to watch him unload cans, bottles and boxes with a Maine Coon at his heels.

"Nice," Honor said, looking around the room. "Big." The stove and refrigerator and cabinets were as old and worn as Lena's had been. "And a very nice cat. Big. You're sure he's not a dog? Lena says he's a fellow from Maine who's adopted you." She bent down to pat the cat's ruff-fringed head.

"I call him 'Tux' because of that tuxedo he's wearing," Joe said. "I thought of naming him 'Woolf,' with two o's...for the Virginia Woolf paper you helped me write...the one that gave me my job... naming him for my blessing, you might say. But he's too polite for a wolf—a real gentleman in evening dress."

143

For a moment they stood still, smiling at each other, while Tux twined around their ankles.

Then Joe said, "Look here." He opened a door to a back room about half the size of his kitchen. "This room's a bonus! I suppose this was the 'pantry' once, with all these cupboards and shelves, but now it's my 'potting room.'" He opened another door to a backyard view of bushes and weedy grass. "And here's a door right out to the garden. Tux has his box of sand here, and I can come in from back-yard work and get rid of my muddy boots. Look at this big sink and built-in counter!"

"You've bought a gardener's house," Honor said.

"And that's not all," Joe said, going through the kitchen to open another door for her. "This back room's big enough for some light carts, and I can start seeds on them for the back garden, a couple dozen light tables. When I put four big shelves on each of them, I'll have my winter garden."

Honor followed him back to the kitchen, and helped him unload his groceries. "Your own house," Honor said, "waiting for you to find it."

Joe heard the longing in her voice and turned to her, his arms full of cans and boxes. "I have great hopes for it," he said, his own longing running through his words.

"A work in progress," Honor said.

Joe could pick up meanings as well as she could. He gave her a single intense look, then smiled at his armload of cans and boxes as if he had found a treasure.

He finished stocking the cupboard. Honor said, "I've come uninvited, but do you have time to show me the rest of your house?"

"Come and see," Joe said, and they walked, trailed by Tux, through the sunny dining room. They passed the stairs, and stood at the living-room door.

"So much work to be done," Honor said.

"Do you like white walls for the downstairs?" Joe asked.

"I really do," she said. "Lena wanted white, but you know she had to paper some rooms, thanks to all the cracks. Looks like you've got some cracks here."

"I'll use spackle, and then paint," Joe said. "I've got money enough to buy some furniture second hand, if you and Lena will help me choose. Come and see what the second floor looks like."

144

They climbed the stairs. "There's nice woodwork here," Joe said.

"Look at the carving on that bannister," Honor said. Joe opened a door, and she looked in. "A nice master bedroom with a view of the park."

"Most of the floors will be fine when I finish them," Joe said. "There's not much of the old furniture I can use." He ran his hand over the headboard of a battered double bed. "I'll refinish a few bedroom pieces when I have a chance—this one's solid walnut."

Other rooms stood empty, echoing their footsteps.

Joe took the stairs down two at a time. He stopped at the bottom, smiling up at her, Tux at his feet. Honor smiled back.

The next morning Honor and Lena came over with Don. "You've got a team," Lena said.

"You'll help me?" Joe said. They could see how happy he was.

Don sat on a blanket and watched as they filled cracks in the living-room walls. The moment Tux saw the baby, he sniffed delicately at him, and Don reached for the interesting furry toy that sat at attention beside him, like a sentinel in fur.

"Tux has decided he's going to guard Don," Joe said.

"Don's yanking that cat's mane!" Lena said, looking up from her spackling.

"And his ear," Honor said as Don grabbed for a furry, twitching plaything.

"Look at that. Tux just pretends not to notice," Lena said. As they watched, the tomcat's huge tail rose from the floor like a hairy snake, and Don grabbed it. Tux simply twitched it away and yawned.

145

When the wall patches had dried, they sanded the living-room walls, and rolled on white paint. The fireplace was a fine one, built of local stone, and polishing brought out the gray and black veining in its marble hearth. Joe ordered a fake fire like Lena's, and said: "I'll have a nice fire for you folks to sit *by*, even if there's nothing to sit *on*."

The three of them called themselves experts now at wallpapering, sanding, painting...they joked together and climbed and crawled and grunted, while Don watched them, the Maine Coon always at his side. "This is a well-built house," Honor said. "Nothing rotted or out of plumb."

After a long day of work, Honor and Lena relaxed on Lena's porch, and women from the park joined them. They laughed to see a babysitter in a tuxedo standing guard beside Don.

"That young man's certainly going to look just like his daddy," they said.

"I've got something here for you folks to see," Lena said. "Honor—you show them what it is." She handed Honor an open magazine.

Amy leaned to look. "It's *The Nation*." She looked at the page. "It's a poem." She looked closer. "A poem by Honor Lombard!"

The women came to look. "*Hackberry*!" they said. "By *Honor Lombard*!"

"You write *poetry*?" Rafaela asked Honor.

"She's had about a dozen poems published so far," Lena said.

"We read that magazine in our 'contempt-lit.' class!" Charlotte said. "Wait till I tell them the author of that poem lives right here!"

They passed *The Nation* from hand to hand.

Amy said, "Thousands of people will see it!"

"Read it to us!" Barb said, giving *The Nation* to Honor.

When Honor finished the poem, they sat looking at Honor and each other, until Lena said, "That's my tree in that poem. Right out in my back yard."

"In your yard?" Barb said. "Have I ever noticed it? I'm going to look."

Barb started down the porch steps and the rest followed. They clustered at the garden gate to look up. Higher than Lena's house, the hackberry spread a green roof against the sky. "He rubs against your roof?" Raphaela asked Lena.

"When the wind blows."

146

"He's alive," Charlotte said.

A leaf settled on Barb's shoulder, and she swatted it away. "He's awake!"

"And he's sucking water up under the grass," Charlotte said, and took a step backward, looking up. "Wrinkled old man!"

They started back to the porch. "But how did you know that?" Barb said to Honor. "About a hackberry tree."

"That's...sort of my job," Honor said, smiling a little. "If I'm going to write poems. And Lena gave me the idea. Don't expect me to get in a national magazine again, not for years. But I send poems to a monthly competition—the Young Poets Forum."

"She's won first prizes," Lena said.

Honor brought the mail in one September afternoon, and looked at Lena and Joe with a shocked expression on her face.

Lena said, "Poem money? Maybe a kind note from an editor? Contest results?"

"The Young Poets Forum!" Honor cried. "They're giving me their Best Poem of the Year Award!"

"I'm not surprised," Lena said. "You've won a lot of their contests."

Honor turned the letter over. "My prize is a hundred dollars, and I'm invited to their Poetry Gala—a dinner in Chicago in early October."

"Good for you!" Joe said.

"It's called a 'Formal Occasion.'" Honor said. "I'll be the only one to read a poem. They ask me to sit on the dais with the mayor of Chicago. I'm allowed to bring a guest, but the guest 'will be seated elsewhere at dinner.'" Honor took a deep breath. "Oh, my."

"They must have some well-heeled sponsors to throw a party like that," Lena said. "They'll put that Gala in the newspapers— lots of publicity. And there are some first-rate presses in Chicago. An editor or two might want to meet you. 'Formal' means a long dress, so you'll have to go shopping."

"But I can't go!" Honor cried. "Leave Don?"

"I'm his great aunt," Lena said. "He's almost seven months old. Weaned. Don't you trust me to babysit? I'm even an adequate cat-sitter."

"It would only take a day or two." Honor read through the rest of the letter. "They want a short summary of my background and 'professional experience'—Ha!—and my picture, and how long I'll be there. They'll publish all that in the paper 'for the convenience of editors and agents,' they say."

"Of course!" Lena said. "They're putting you in the limelight." She turned to Joe. "Can't you go with her? Your college classes don't start until the new year. Fly there a day early so you can settle in. Stay for a while, you two. You've brought a couple of old houses into the twentieth century—you need a rest. See all the sights." She laughed and clapped her hands. "And let me finance the whole thing! Can't I? In honor of my poet niece I'm so proud of?"

Lena was determined. Joe was willing. Honor didn't want to go.

"I'm only twenty-two!" she said. "I'm just beginning to have poems published. They ought to give the prize to somebody older...somebody well-known..."

"They won't get anybody as beautiful," Joe said. "And it's for 'Young Poets.' They want to encourage someone who's on the way up."

"On the first rung of the ladder," Honor said.

"Then climb!" Lena said.

Honor thought about it.

"I don't think so," she said every now and then. She taped the letter to the bulletin board in her room. When she found herself looking at it every hour or so, she turned the letter over, blank side out, but she knew it by heart by then.

Tux sat watching her one day. "Or do I think I should?" she asked a pair of large yellow eyes. " With Joe? What if he... All by ourselves. How can I? Chicago?"

Tux waved his immense tail listlessly back and forth, as if a trip to Chicago was the most boring thing he'd ever heard of, then turned his back and went downstairs.

Honor opened her closet door and saw nothing that could be called "formal dress" except, maybe, a wedding gown hidden in the corner. Stand on a platform with the mayor of Chicago? The very thought made her lie on her bed and shut her eyes, sighing.

Suddenly she heard a scream and shouts in Joe's backyard. One look out the window and Honor took the stairs down two at a time, ran through the house and garage, and found Joe in his back yard hugging Don tight, and Tux at his feet, looking twice his usual size, and growling.

"What happened?" Honor asked.

"A dog!" Joe said. "Never saw him before—a big one, sneaked out of the alley! I turned my back and there he was, ready to grab Don sitting on the blanket there. I've got to get a fence put up out here! Tomorrow!"

"Oh!" Honor cried, running to take Don, looking him all over. "Is he hurt?"

"That dog didn't have a chance!" Joe said. "In a second Tux's fur was all on end—he was twice his size and making for that dog with a scream they probably heard downtown. He landed on that dog with all four of his feet and his teeth, too, and when the dog ran away, he chased him all the way down the alley to the street."

"Oh, Tux!" Honor said to the cat. "You're a watch-cat, aren't you?"

Tux's winter fur was growing, he was enjoying two meals a day, and he was taking on a most regal luster. He rubbed his glossy shoulder against Joe's jeans and stared at Honor as if to say, "Nobody messes with me."

14

A few days later Joe came to Lena's house to borrow her long ladder, and found the two women in the living room. "Honor's just had more wonderful news!" Lena told him. "One of her poems—accepted by *The Atlantic*! Think of it!"

"Congratulations," Joe said to Honor. "Lena and I aren't surprised at all."

"Read it to us," Lena said.

Honor brought her notebook and said, "This poem is Lena's fault. She gave me the idea for my Hackberry poem, and this one, too."

"Me?" Lena said.

"Didn't you tell me how you thought you'd die when you were on a double-decked bus on an English road?"

"I did," Lena said. "And nobody else on the bus noticed any danger at all."

"What?" Joe said.

Honor laughed at him. "Do you remember somebody who constantly warned people, but nobody believed her...way back in ancient Greece?"

"Cassandra?" Joe said.

"Cursed by Apollo."

"She wouldn't sleep with him," Lena said.

"So here's your poem about it," Honor said to Lena. "It's called: 'Cassandra and the Double-decked Doom.'"

"Oh, my," was all Lena could say.

Cassandra and the Double-decked Doom

My first English morning, too young to die,
I rocketed down the wrong side of the road
in a bus as red as blood and twice as high
as a scream—there was another swaying load
of *Times* readers hurtling down on us
from the wrong side of the road, too,
                              hell-for-leather.
"Fares!" called the conductor. Bus met bus,
missing by inches. Reading tomorrow's weather,
my seatmate nodded. Snored. As usual,
I was cursed with a day-long view of doom dawning
double-decked over the next hill,
and the rest of the world yawning.

All three laughed together. "Yes!" Lena cried. "You've got it exactly!"

"It's an amazing poem. No wonder they wanted to print it," Joe said.

Honor said: "Can you imagine being Cassandra—warning, warning, warning that someone will die...some catastrophe will happen tomorrow—and having no one believe you, and say you're insane?"

"I can't claim an iota of credit for that poem, but think of it in *The Atlantic*," Lena said. "We'll frame it!"

The next day Honor said to Joe and Lena: "I don't know whether to go to Chicago or not...I don't know... I really don't know..."

"Your poems—accepted by top-ranking magazines!" Lena said. "*The Nation*, and now *The Atlantic*. You can go to that Gala and look any poet in the eye."

"I'm just starting..."

"Take Joe and go!" Lena said. "Men are so handy! They have pockets all over their coats and pants and shirts to keep tips and tickets and cab fares and hotel keys in—they open doors and carry your umbrella and pull your chair out so you don't wrinkle your dress. And a husband will certainly keep other men at least a few feet away—if you don't like any of them, of course."

Honor couldn't help but laugh. She looked at Joe, who was laughing, too, and said, "In that case, I'll be glad to have Joe."

Lena helped them plan. She rented a tuxedo for Joe. "You've got to look at least as good as Tux does," she told him, and insisted that he go along when they shopped for Honor's new clothes, because "she wanted a man's opinion." But Joe soon found out that what Lena really wanted was to get him into the men's wear departments.

"Do you have any nice suits at all?" she asked him.

Joe had to admit that he'd been a poor graduate student for so long that his old suit—he just had one—didn't fit.

Lena said she was horrified. How could he think of taking a beautiful poet to Chicago in jeans? And hadn't he worked for an old lady for months with no pay to speak of? So she bought Joe two expensive suits. "Wear them in Chicago," she said. "Do it for Honor and me. And wear them to teach your first classes...take your first step up the faculty ladder."

Lena wanted to buy them plane tickets, but they said Chicago wasn't far: they'd drive. So she loaned them her car.

Lena had booked hotel rooms for them. In a few weeks they drove her car to Chicago, and found their hotel in the middle of town, only a short taxi trip from the Poetry Gala. They were registered, they discovered, as "Dr. and Mrs. Joseph Lombard."

"Oh, look at this!" Honor said when Joe unlocked their hotel door. "A three-room suite."

Their bedrooms had fresh flowers on the dressers. The living room had that modern piece of furniture: a television set, watched by two plump recliners. "What would Lena think if she saw that tv?" Honor said, and they laughed, because Lena had often declared that she'd never put a blatting television in *her* living room—might as well have some tobacco auctioneer gabbling "Sold American!" every five minutes.

Their laughter made it seem easier to look around the rooms they were going to live in as man and wife. "Choose which bedroom you want, and we can unpack," Joe said. Honor chose one.

In a little while she held up a long black and white dress for him to see.

"I'm not dressing for revenge this time," she said, smiling at him as she hung it in the closet. "How could I ever have dared to fly away alone last December, so scared, so pregnant, so angry? Go down to Brandon's wedding party alone, parade down that reception line, watch Brandon on his back on that dance floor?"

"Brandon had it coming," Joe said. "And you were so calm, so sure of yourself, so…beautiful."

She didn't answer.

"We've been sitting most of today—should we walk a bit, and then have dinner? It's after seven," Joe asked.

So they went down to Chicago streets, and strolled in the shadows of tall buildings and the honk and roar of traffic. Now and then a chic woman passed with the crowd, her eyes traveling over Joe, and plenty of male eyes followed Honor. Joe took her hand once when people pressed close. In a moment Honor took her hand away.

They found a restaurant that was candlelit and quiet. Joe pulled out Honor's chair so she didn't wrinkle her dress, just as Lena had said he should. The waiter brought menus.

In a moment or two, Honor said, "Your hands. Your poor hands."

Joe looked at his hands holding his menu. "A gardener's hands," he said. They were big and scarred and stained dark brown at every knuckle.

"A botanist's hands?" Honor said. "A naturalist's hands? I've seen you go to Hartman Reserve over and over, and out in the fields. You bought that old treadle sewing machine to make mesh bags, you told us, and I saw you take them with you."

"I'm looking for caterpillars. Or butterfly and moth eggs," Joe said. "Then I bag them on their food plants, and they're safer from birds and bugs and beasts. But you have to move the caterpillars in their bags to fresh branches often, or they'll run out of leaves and starve, so I have to walk miles. I've done that since I was a kid."

Honor smiled. "Remember when you brought me a glass jar with an orange and black butterfly clinging to a leaf inside? You told me she'd just emerged, and she was colored like a Monarch butterfly so nobody would eat her, but she was really a Viceroy."

"I remember."

"And you opened the jar and reached in, and she hugged your finger with those delicate black legs? And before she flew away, she fanned her wings in your hand like the steady beat of a heart?"

"Only a poet would say that," Joe said. "Or see that." He put his hands in his lap. "Iowa dirt's a wonderful blessing, but it stains. It'll wear off by winter."

They ordered their dinners. Honor said, "Do you notice that the waiters in good restaurants never break into your conversation to ask, 'Are you enjoying your dinner? Everything all right?' They just watch, and when you look at them, they come."

"Yes," Joe said.

Neither of them could think of anything more to say. They ate and drank with hardly a word, like married people who had said the important things to each other years before. Their waiter—bringing their desserts, bringing the bill—watched a beautiful young woman who hardly looked at the man across the table, while the handsome fellow seemed to see nothing but her. "May you have a *very* fine evening," he said as he showed them out to a smoky Chicago street.

The city gleamed and shimmered. They walked for an hour or so, as the crowds thinned. They passed couples holding hands, or strolling arm-in-arm.

When they reached their hotel, Joe held the hotel door for her, as Lena had said a man should. They rode the elevator without a word. Joe took the key from his pocket, true to Lena, and unlocked the door. He turned on a living room lamp.

Honor went to the door of her room. "Good night," she said. "Thank you for coming with me!"

He didn't answer. She softened her voice: "I'm so tired, and

tomorrow will be a hard day. I think I'll go to bed...I'm sorry."
She went into her room and closed her door.

In a little while he heard her taking a shower. He showered too, and went to bed, telling himself he had Honor all to himself... all to himself...

There Honor was the next morning, beautiful in the gown and negligee Lena had bought her. They ordered breakfasts delivered to their door, and asked questions while they ate: *Did you sleep well? What should we do before tonight and the Gala?"*

"We have until about four o'clock, I suppose," Joe said. "Then we'll have to dress and take a taxi. What do you want to see in the Windy City?"

"The Art Institute?" Honor said. "But you've seen big museums, haven't you?"

"Only in London," Joe said. "Let's go."

So they went to the huge stone casket of priceless things. They spent hours with men in armor, saints in haloes, Egyptians on their thrones, angels on the wing...and always the portraits of beautiful women, long dead but captured in gilded frames.

"Women on every wall," Joe said. "How the painters love them."

"Naked women," Honor said, stopping before a luscious Renoir. "Posing for men—rich men—men who'll buy them, and pretend that they own these painted bodies, I suppose."

They roamed from room to room. Joe watched Honor: her profile...her dark hair falling over the shoulder of her dress...the passing men who stared at her.

At one o'clock Honor stopped at the head of a long stairway and sighed. "Tired?" Joe asked.

"Hungry," she said.

155

So they lunched at an outdoor table, with a busy sidewalk a foot away, and pigeons waddling among the waiters.

"Maybe a carriage ride?" Joe asked her after lunch. "Let the horse take a walk, not us?" So the uniformed driver helped them climb into a high, black, leather-seated carriage, and they rode away.

But the damn carriage was designed, Joe thought, for lovers. Hardly room enough for two on the jiggling seat. How many lovers had twined together there? And how many, without a word, had sat as far away from each other as possible, watching couples kissing on the park's browning grass?

Brandon had sat in his office that morning, reading the paper while Trisha pounded away on her typewriter. "Look here!" he said, pointing to an article. "My brother's wife!" he said. "Coming to read a poem of hers at some fancy dinner with the mayor of Chicago—tonight! Let's get tickets and go."

Trisha looked at Honor's picture. "She's pretty." She took the paper to read it. "It's a 'formal evening'? I could wear my new dress—but we were going to the beach this weekend..."

"We will. We'll get a Chicago hotel, go to the dinner, stay the night, then drive to the beach the next day."

So they packed, and Brandon rented a tuxedo. He picked up Trisha at her place for the drive to Chicago.

Trisha was waiting for him at the street door. "You've got to come up and meet my sister Audrey," she said. "There's plenty of time. She'll be here any minute—coming from Stockton. She called a half hour ago, and she's going home tomorrow. Never told me she was coming."

They climbed to Trisha's place. Just as Trisha unlocked her door, a tall, skinny, scowling woman came upstairs, and Trisha cried, "Audrey! You're here. Come on in."

Audrey went in and looked around. "This is an apartment?" she said. "It's a closet."

"Audrey, here's Brandon," Trisha said. "I've told you about him. He can't stay long—we're going to a party. Sorry about that. You didn't give me any warning at all that you were coming. We're going to a formal Poetry Gala dinner in Chicago, and we'll stay there tonight. Then Brandon's taking me to Lovers Beach on Lake Michigan tomorrow—I've got three days off from work."

"I come here and you're leaving?" Audrey yelled. "Now?" She stared at Brandon from his dark hair to his gleaming shoes.

"You can stay here," Trisha said. "Make yourself at home. Here's the key. Give it to the manager downstairs when you go."

"My bus home leaves early tomorrow, and you're not going anywhere!" Audrey said, planting herself in the doorway. "We got to talk. Make plans. I've got to tell you why I came—rode that damn stinking bus here."

"I have no idea," Trisha said.

"You've got no idea because you keep hanging up on me when I try to tell you what's going on, that's why!"

"So what's going on?" Trisha said.

"Hell. Hell is what's going on. You don't know—you're free as a damn bird," Audrey said. "Try having a lazy husband and three little kids, like me. And no money, of course."

"So?"

"So you won't listen. You're so happy with your boyfriend here, and your parties and beaches—haven't you even read my letters?"

"So?"

"Mom's blind now. Stuck in bed! And there's no money to put her somewhere. Somebody's got to take her in."

"Hey!" Trisha yelled. "Me? No way! I've done my turn for this family! Brought home a paycheck to feed us...went to business school nights. Now it's your turn. *You* take care of her!"

"In a two-bedroom apartment? She can sleep under our kitchen table, maybe? And who's got the money to feed her? We're on hot dogs and rice, you know?"

"She's dying?"

"Not yet. She can still swear. Scream. The kids are scared of her."

"I can't do it," Trisha said. "It's not fair. I've got a job—"

"You've got a job! Right! So you can get a job in Stockton! You can live at her place and take care of her in your free time! You're not married! You got no kids!"

It looked like a big fight was just starting. Brandon took Trisha's arm and said. "It's been nice to meet you, Audrey."

"You stay here!" Audrey crowded after them down the narrow stairs, yelling every two or three steps: "You hear me? Don't you dare go—I rode that damn bus—" Brandon kept between Audrey

157

and Trisha as they reached the street, and got Trisha into his car. "Have a good trip home," he yelled, and left shrieking Audrey on the curb.

Trisha hardly said a word all the way to their Chicago hotel. Brandon guessed she was pretty upset. He just kept quiet. But after they checked in and she started to put on her fancy dress and her makeup, she began to talk a little. "How do I look?" she asked when he was in his tuxedo and they were ready to go.

"You're gorgeous," Brandon told her as they hailed a taxi. He saw men give her the once-over when they got to the Poetry Gala.

The big banquet hall was filling with a crowd in fancy clothes. Brandon steered Trisha to a corner table about as far as they could get from the platform, and sat with his back to it.

Honor and Joe wouldn't notice him.

They'd never seen Trisha.

Hundreds of chattering people were settling at tables. Just as Brandon ordered a drink, Joe and Honor came in. Honor was in black and white, and Joe wore a tux. People were looking at the black and white pair as they waited in the doorway.

"There they are," Brandon told Trisha.

"Where?"

"The two in black and white. Walking behind the usher up to the front."

"She's a lot prettier than her picture in the paper," Trisha said. "And your brother's big and handsome...but not as handsome as you."

Honor climbed to the platform, high above the crowd. When she was seated between two middle-aged men, she smiled from one to the other and answered questions as dinner was served, but she was watching Joe. He was the only man at his table below the dais; he smiled and talked and laughed and ate his dinner, while pretty girls bent toward him over their wine glasses and plates. But Honor noticed what Joe was doing, even while he talked. No matter when she looked down at him, it seemed, he was looking at her. Not an ordinary look; it came with a slight smile, and deepened just a fraction of a second too long.

She recognized that look—the one he had given her over a wine glass once at a wedding. A gift.

Yes, she thought. And now she could give her "husband" something, at least.

The after-dinner speeches droned on and on, but Honor said to herself, over and over: *I can give Joe some honor of his own.*

At last the mayor of Chicago was saying her name: Honor Lombard. She joined him and said, "Will you introduce my husband, too? Dr. Joseph Lombard, a college professor. He's the one man at that table of women just below us."

So Joe had to stand up and be introduced.

Honor's husband. Dr. Joseph Lombard. While hundreds of people applauded, Joe bowed to Honor above him, and she curtsied a little to him...saw the look he gave her...felt a shock. Did he know she was making a promise to him? Silently, she was saying to him: *You've given me back my pride. I am so grateful, so grateful. Now I want you to be honored, and be proud of me. See? I am beginning now.*

The mayor sat down, and Honor stood alone, her hands at her sides, and recited her poem in a clear voice. Only fourteen lines. She had inked the first word of each line on the palm of one of her long white gloves.

Then a room full of people clapped and cheered as she bowed... cheered and clapped, wall to wall. As the audience began to leave the tables, many came to the edge of the platform. Honor held out her arms to Joe; he climbed the stairs to stand beside her. Flash bulbs flared.

"Here," Brandon said, giving Trisha a twenty-dollar bill. "Take a taxi to the hotel. I've got to talk to Joe."

Trisha scowled at him. "Don't want him to see me?" She left with the crowd at the door.

When Honor and Joe left the platform, a crowd surrounded them. They made their way to the door, smiling, thanking, smiling, thanking...

And there was Brandon in the doorway.

Joe put his arm around Honor.

"Just thought I'd congratulate you," Brandon said. "Good poem. Good dinner. How long are you here for?"

"Just a few days."

"Driving?"

"Yes."

Brandon said to Honor: "Let's the two of us go to the bar and have a chat."

"Honor's tired," Joe said.

"Saw your picture in the paper," Brandon said, and took her hand. "Come on."

She said, "I don't—" but she saw people from the platform passing by, smiling at her. She said, "All right."

Brandon walked Honor to the elevator, and Joe could only follow. They rode downstairs without a word. "I've got something to say to Honor," Brandon told Joe at the bar door. "Go sit in the lobby."

"No," Honor said to Joe. "You stay."

The bar wasn't full yet. Brandon pulled Honor down on a couch. "We've got Don! We're a family! You're not married. I can get a divorce!"

A short, fat little man had come to the bar doorway and was watching them. He took a few steps toward them. "Mrs. Lombard?" he asked.

"It's so simple!" Brandon cried. "We just have to forget—"

"Yes?" Honor said to the little man, getting up.

"Honor!" Brandon yelled, trying to take one of her hands. She snatched it away.

Joe grabbed Brandon's arm and dragged him toward the door. "I love you!" Brandon shouted, trying to break away.

"You wanted to see me?" Honor asked the fat little man. She smiled at him.

He said: "I'm Jensen Avery, editor-in-chief of Craven-McMann. Perhaps you remember me? I introduced myself to you and your husband after your reading?"

"Honor!" Brandon got away from Joe and started for Honor. Joe caught him.

"Do come and sit down," Honor said to Avery. She patted the seat beside her, but Avery was looking at the wrestling match at the door.

"Honor!" Brandon yelled. Joe grabbed Brandon by both arms—Joe was bigger and taller and hadn't had a lot of drinks— and dragged Brandon down the hall and through the lobby to the street.

"Honor's got an editor talking to her!" Joe said, strong-arming

160

Brandon to the curb. "Leave her alone!"

"Who says?" Brandon yelled. "You says? Maybe I'm not her husband, but neither are you! You're just some body that's handy— her escort? Haven't got near her? Well, I have, real near!"

Joe flagged a taxi, opened the door and shoved Brandon in. "*Real* near!" Brandon shouted, but Joe slammed the door and the taxi drove off.

The taxi got Brandon to the hotel. He found his room and took off the monkey suit and tight shoes, put on a shirt and jeans and boots. Trisha was asleep in her twin bed, or was pretending to be. He packed his suitcase and drank some more.

He was going to do something important. What was it? While he'd been shoved into a taxi, a plan had gone off in his brain like a bomb.

He rubbed his foggy head. What bomb? Honor up there on the platform. Trisha's dirty look. Joe shoving him into the taxi—

Now he remembered! He laughed into his pillow, then got up and sneaked out the door. Trisha was snoring, and she was a late sleeper. He'd have plenty to do in the few hours before she woke up.

When Joe and Brandon's angry voices faded down the hall, Honor took a deep breath, rearranged her expression into a smile, and said to Avery, "That man's just a relative who's had too much to drink, I'm afraid. My husband will take care of him. Tell me about your press," she said.

Avery sat down with her and talked, and Honor was grateful. He gave her his card—while her wits returned and her pulse slowed— and said that he'd left information about his press at the hotel desk for her. He wrote down her address and phone number and described the aims of the press, the classes of books they were inter- ested in publishing, the increase in book-buying after the war...

At last Joe came back, alone. He sat down just as Honor said to Avery: "A novel! It seems to me that the gains we've made as American women need to be strengthened by a sense of past struggle—a novel of women's lives before the second world war. Many novel readers are still young, and remember how their mothers lived."

"A very interesting premise," Avery said.

161

"How housebound so many American women have been, for so long!" Honor said. "Waving goodbye on the shore, while men sailed through the world!"

"Do you have a title?" Avery asked.

"I might call my novel *An Accomplished Woman*," Honor said, "from lines in a book by the great Mary Wolstonecraft in the eighteenth century. She said: *Abject as this picture appears, it is the portrait of an accomplished woman.* The model of a successful woman in Wolstonecraft's time was an abject female, all right, but how much better is our American model all those generations later?"

"Do you have a general sense of where your story might go?" Avery said.

"*An Accomplished Woman* begins with the car wreck of a rich nineteen-twenties couple in England." Honor smiled at Avery. "The mother of a baby girl is killed, along with her husband, but the baby survives, and the mother's lover is the child's guardian. He's promised to raise the baby as her mother wished—a girl growing up to become an absolutely free human being that no one can imagine. So that is what the dead woman's lover does: he takes the baby to America and raises her to be neither a man nor a woman. I mean to make it imaginative and funny and sad."

"Intriguing," Avery said. "When do you expect to have a first draft?"

"My time is my own, except that we do have a baby boy," Honor said. "But we have a live-in babysitter, and Don is a very good baby, as my husband will agree."

Joe agreed.

"Would you be willing to sign a statement that you'll give my press first rights to *An Accomplished Woman*?" Avery asked Honor.

She put on a grave look. "I...haven't spoken to other editors yet, you see. We came to Chicago hoping to make appointments."

"Of course you intend to talk to other publishing houses," Avery said. "May I suggest that you consider finding an agent? Most publishers prefer that an author have one."

"My husband and I are investigating agents," Honor said.

"When you contact an agent, you might mention that our press is interested in your book," Avery said. "We're well-known." He stood up to leave. "I certainly hope that Craven-McMann will bring your first novel to the reading public."

Joe and Honor watched him leave.

She smiled at Joe. "A novel."

"You've never said a word about a novel!" Joe said.

"Because I thought the novel I dreamed of was only a dream—until Avery asked me if I had one," Honor said. "And out it came."

"It certainly did. He's already planning to publish it," Joe said. "May I ask how my clever wife has managed to plan a novel, and have a dozen poems accepted for publication this year, and star at a Poetry Gala, *and* have a baby?"

"I hope all those poems will be published," Honor said. "And the Gala and the baby certainly are real. But if there's a novel at all, it's nothing but wisps and dreams and wishful thinking."

"*And* an interested editor," he said.

They left the hotel and found a crowded street, a traffic jam, and a line of taxis. They found one for hire and climbed in.

The driver said over his shoulder: "Not going anywhere." He sat back and sighed. Honor saw him watching them in his rearview mirror.

"Go on, man," the taxi driver said after a while. "Kiss her. You're both as good-looking as they get. Go on. We're stuck in traffic. Make hay while the sun don't shine, man."

Joe and Honor laughed.

"Thank you," Honor whispered to Joe in a few moments. "Thank you for getting rid of Brandon—and for everything you've ever done for me."

"Nobody's going to hurt you," Joe said. "Ever. Not if I can help it."

The taxi driver said, "Where's that kiss? The two of you—staring out windows like you was just dropped from space and wondering was this Chicago or Mars! Chicago's out there all right. Half of the population is honking horns."

Honor whispered to Joe: "You were there. It was so easy for me to read my poem to you, and forget that anyone else was listening. You were *there* with me—just like you were at Brandon's wedding. I wasn't alone."

"Hey, that's better," the taxi driver said. "At least the two of you are looking at each other. C'mon, guy, what are you waiting for? Kiss her. Come on."

"I'm available for listening any time," Joe said.

The driver rubbed the back of his neck, his eyes on the mirror. "Hey, folks," he said, "You got the rest of your lives to talk, and let me tell you—in a year or two, the wife'll say: 'Did you take out the trash?' and Hubby will say 'No, but how about a little fun in bed tonight?' and she'll say, 'Just take out the trash.' Oh, man, I can tell you how it'll be."

He rolled down his window and yelled at the cars: "That's right, you idiots out there. Honk those horns. When idiots are stuck in a jam, what do they do? They honk. Horns'll get the traffic moving, right?" He snorted. "People!"

At last the cars around them started to creep ahead, and they nosed their way into the line. When they pulled up in front of their hotel and Joe paid him, the taxi driver shook his head as they walked away.

15

"Brandon can't let go," Honor said as Joe unlocked the door of their suite.

"No," Joe said. "Neither could I, in his place." He turned on a living-room lamp and said, "You were the loveliest woman there. And your poem—beautiful. I was so proud to stand up there with you."

"Thank you," Honor said.

"Are you too tired…" Joe hesitated. "Too tired to stand there and say your poem again, just for me? So I can remember?"

"I will." Honor stood with her back against her bedroom door.

"Two Voices and a Moon," she said, and turned this way and that as she had done on the platform, pretending to speak to an invisible face:

> *"Summer nights have no ear for music. Lieder*
> *leave the moon alone, and the night trees."*

She turned the other way.

> *"But who seems sobbing in slow water*
> *tide beat?"*

She turned back.

> *"Even on nights like these*
> *the moon is only a stone. Trees are planted*
> *deep and deaf. See how the ocean sleeps*
> *through music. This is the truth, granted?"*

She turned.

> *"But what trick keeps*
> *night coupled with music? Waves are breaking,*
> *pulled by that full song. What rises there*
> *white with grief?"*

She turned back.

> *"Only a voice taking*
> *cloud by cloud the path of an old air."*

They were still for a moment. Then Joe said, "Thank you."

"Now it's your turn," Honor said. "Tell me what you heard."

Joe took the program out of his tuxedo pocket and read the poem again, then stood still for a while, looking at the floor.

Finally he said, "Two voices. They're talking as the tide on a beach comes in, and someone is singing a sad song—a German art song, a 'lied.' And the first voice states a fact as a truth: the natural world pays no attention to music."

"Yes," Honor said.

"But then it sounds as if the second voice objects, and says that waves on the shore seem to be sobbing."

Joe looked at the poem again. "Of course waves don't sob (the first voice argues)—and the moon is just a stone, and trees can't hear. The ocean doesn't listen: it sleeps." This first voice is very sure of itself. 'Granted,' it says, as if there can't be any doubt."

Honor waited. Lamplight made Joe's white shirt whiter; his black tuxedo was as dark as his dark hair and serious eyes. Joe scowled, thinking. "And then the first voice doesn't give up, because—it says—some trick's being played. The night *is* 'coupled with music.' The trick and the reality both exist, but differently.

The trick may be against all reason, but you can feel it being played on you, and it's beautiful. It's there. Waves *are* pulled by the music. And something lonely *is* rising in the sky, so sad. Sad as the sad song."

He smiled. "The first voice loses. The voice of reason! That's what's so amazing! *Reason loses out*, and it's because of the moon. The reasonable person suddenly feels there's a sad *song* climbing the sky—and hears the night moon, for that enchanted moment, *singing*!"

Joe stared at the poem as if he had to be right...exact. "The moon is 'taking, cloud by cloud, the path of an old air.' 'Air' can mean the atmosphere the moon seems to rise through, cloud by cloud. 'This is the truth, granted?' But 'air' means a song, too. So, for a second, the reasonable friend *hears the moon* taking the path of an old song!"

He looked from the poem to Honor and back again. "It's as if we are feeling that magical trick— for a moment— because nature seems to be sharing what we feel...perhaps the poem's two voices are in love?"

"That might be the poem's 'trick,'" Honor said.

"How did you ever get that last, absolutely magical line?"

"It was a gift," Honor said.

"A gift."

She smiled. "Like you."

Neither of them moved. Joe said, "And you're going to keep me?"

"Yes," Honor said. "I think I am."

"Honor..." Joe said, and Honor took two steps to press her face against his black tuxedo jacket. He held her so close that she could feel his breath rise and fall under the cloth.

Then he let her go, and his big hands carefully unhooked one of her diamond earrings, and then the other. The diamonds dangled and chimed softly like broken glass. He laid them on a table.

She closed her eyes as his hands ran up her back to find the clasp of her necklace, feeling for the big ring locked through the small one. When he found it, suddenly a handful of diamonds cascaded as she leaned back, and tumbled into the low neckline of her dress.

"Oh!" she said, and they both laughed as his hands went down for the diamonds.

Joe said, "I've never seen diamonds in such a beautiful setting," and put the necklace away with the earrings, then cupped her face in his hands. "Are you still afraid?"

"I wasn't afraid," Honor said. "Not even standing up there, reading my poem!"

"I never thought you were," he said, his mouth almost on hers. "Please. Don't be afraid. Don't ever be afraid of me," and he kissed her, a long kiss, and hungrier than he wanted it to be, for he suddenly broke away. "I'm not drunk," he said. "But you've been so badly hurt…"

"Yes," Honor said, and felt tears in her eyes. She hid her face against his black wool jacket again.

"Do you want me to leave?" he asked. "Honor?"

She didn't answer. He rocked her a little in his arms. "You're so brave," he whispered. "Go ahead and cry. Never mind Brandon. What an evening! What a triumph!"

When she raised her head to look at him, he wiped her wet cheeks with his hand. "Are you so tired?" he said. "Would you like me to go?"

She blinked at him and shook her head.

"Well then," Joe said. Holding her close, he led her to her bed, sat down on it with her, and snapped on a bedside lamp. "Where should we begin, do you think?" He kissed her.

Honor put her arms around his neck, long white gloves and all.

"Take it very, very slowly?" he asked. "With the very, very basics? Should we start with 'truth' and see if we can make that 'trick' your poem is about? If we suppose that what we have… is love?"

She nodded.

"Truth. The basics," Joe said. "Well…let's see…have you ever seen a naked man?"

"No!" Honor looked so embarrassed that Joe laughed and said, "Never?"

"I've seen Don. And statues. Paintings."

"But you've never seen a real, grown, human one?"

"Most of one. In Lena's garden. All summer."

"That's a good place to start," Joe said, "but there's more to me than that." He stood up and shrugged off his tuxedo jacket, jerked off his bow tie, unbuttoned his shirt, and dropped them all on a chair. He sat beside her again to take off his shoes and socks, then stood up to step out of his satin-striped tuxedo trousers, and then his shorts.

"There," he said, standing before her. "I know it's not pretty, but this is the way men have always looked...more hair, maybe...less chin...knuckles dragging on the ground. Not all curvy and soft and delicious, like you. It's my opinion that the human male has always been one of the ugliest animals on earth. What do you think?"

She was trying not to look, but she did. "Go ahead and laugh," Joe said. "It's me. It's all I've got."

Honor rubbed her eyes and took another look. "Couldn't you have managed to tan yourself all over?" she said in a critical tone. There was still a trace of sobs in her voice. She hiccuped and said, "Now you're half chocolate and half vanilla."

"Sorry," Joe said. "I didn't think I should shock my next-door neighbors."

"You...look like a model for Michelangelo," Honor said, and put out a tentative hand...

"No you don't!" Joe said, snatching up his shirt. "No touching until it's mutual! Fair is fair!"

Honor stood up, still sniffling, and said, "I guess."

Joe handed her a tissue from a box by the bed.

"Oh!" she wailed. "I've had too much wine!" She stripped off her long white gloves, took the tissue, blew her nose and said, turning around, "Unzip my back zipper, please."

Joe unzipped an inch, stopped for a kiss on her bare back, started again, stopped for a kiss...at last he came to the end of the zipper and felt her shiver as her dress dropped to her feet.

"Lacy pink!" Joe cried. A naked man stepped back to admire pink lace. "If I'm vanilla and chocolate, you're strawberry!" He lifted her lacy pink slip over her head and off, and unhooked a lacy pink bra. Big, dirt-stained hands turned her around to him. "Strawberries—and cream!" he said, laughing. "I bet Don remembers that!"

"You're a very poetical creature!" She threw her bra on the rug, kicked off her shoes, and rolled panties and garters and hose down and away.

"I'm in very close proximity to a poet," Joe said. "It rubs off."

He pulled back the spread and sheet to the other side of the bed. "Now lie face down. I'm going to rub you all over. Lie down and close your eyes."

Honor crawled on the bed and lay on her stomach. "Oh...." she said in a delighted breath as big, warm hands began to knead her tight shoulders. They rubbed her rigid back, found stiff muscles in her thighs...and there were kisses here...there... After a while all the strain of that evening was gone.

Then Joe turned her over for a last kiss. He murmured, "Go to sleep now," snatched up his clothes, and closed her door behind him.

Morning sunlight was in her room when Honor sat up in bed, wide awake. The past day ran through her head like a runaway movie—museum—park—hundreds of faces looking at her—Brandon—Joe. *Don't ever be afraid of me.*

She wasn't wearing her nightgown! She slid under the sheet again and covered her head. *His hands on her. Are you going to keep me?*

Joe knocked. She called, "Come in!" and he came, wearing a robe, and said, "Hungry?"

Honor discovered she was. "Yes!"

He came to grab her, sheet and all. She kissed him and rumpled his hair; it felt the way she'd always thought it would: springy and thick. His face was scratchy.

"First things first," Joe said as he left. "Showers? Breakfast? I'll call room service."

She got up and looked in a mirror. Her last night's makeup was a mess...all smeared with tears and kisses. She took a quick shower and shampoo, then put on fresh makeup and the beautiful pale green nightgown and negligee Lena had bought her. She braided her hair around her head to dry, and thought of Brandon yelling...fighting with Joe... Brandon played in her memory for a moment, like an actor shouting on a tiny television set, his eyes wild, but so far away: *Can't we start over? We're a family—*

But Joe was close—and freshly shaved and showered. He came in his pajamas to kiss her, and admire her gown and negligee, and

170

settled her on his bed with pillows behind her. How hungry they were when a waiter brought two loaded trays to their door. Joe put them on a bedside table, filled plates, and crawled on his bed with her. He ate half of his scrambled eggs and bacon before he said, "Is today Library Day? At a grand, big-city library? We can look up names of literary agents, and meet at least one or two of them before we leave, maybe."

"But now...I'm having some doubts," Honor said, spreading strawberry jam on a croissant. "Avery gave me his card last night, and said he'll leave more information about his press at the hotel desk for me. But I wonder if it isn't pretty silly to peddle a novel around to agents and editors when you haven't written a single word. Right? What I need to do is to chain myself to that beautiful desk you designed for me, and write it."

"And we're in Chicago!" he said. "We've hardly seen this town." He put his arms around her and said, "You've got strawberry jam on your chin." Before she could wipe it off, he kissed it off, said, "M-m-m-delicious," then kissed her some more. Finally he stopped to take a breath. "You said last night that you were keeping me," he said.

"That wonderful massage of yours!" She leaned back in his arms to look at him. "Heavenly! Men may come... men may go— but a woman keeps a man *forever* who can massage like that! You put me to sleep!"

"Not exactly what I have in mind for tonight," Joe said.

Honor blushed as red as the strawberry jam, and Joe chuckled and said, "But we do have to make some plans, I think."

"About where we'll live while you're working on your house?" Honor asked.

"A bit more pressing. What about babies?"

"Babies!"

"Do you want more? Now? Later? Never? Your choice."

Both of their faces were suddenly grave. "I don't know..." Honor said, then cried: "Oh, I do know—I do! I want your babies...want our own family, yours and mine! How could I not want that? But Don's only seven months old..."

"Too soon, I think."

"I think so, too," Honor said. "I want to be settled in our house—with you in your new job, not worried about a pregnant wife, or walking the floor with a crying baby."

171

"Then we'll wait. I came prepared," Joe said. "Always the optimist—"

"Oh!" Honor yelled, throwing a pillow at him. Joe caught it, laughed, and tossed it back.

Chicago traffic crept along crowded streets as they took a taxi to the Field Museum.

Honor kept glancing at Joe. She knew how all of him looked now: head to foot. Was that the reason he was setting off alarms— alarms like sparks sizzling along her skin—making her quiver at nothing but a touch, a look, a certain nuzzling depth in his voice? She wanted to ski her fingers along the muscles cording his arms and legs, or unbutton his shirt to look at that amazing fur on his chest. If he were a bagel covered with strawberry jam, she'd want to take a bite.

And what would it be like to make love with him? She asked herself that, of course—over and over. They went to the Field Museum and gazed up at massive prehistoric creatures who had, somehow, reproduced. How did dinosaurs twine their knife-edged tails around each other, or run their bony muzzles under each other's chins? Great stuffed lions and tigers were easier to imagine making love, all downy and velvety as they were, gold and orange and black and brown, pressing close to each other with purring growls.

After lunch the two found the gardens and the botanical collections (of course) where Honor had the undivided attention of a guest lecturer of the first order, who explained and described… and kissed her whenever the room was empty, and sometimes even when it wasn't. If people saw them and smiled, they smiled back.

They went to a ballet after dinner: a display of almost naked ladies, all legs, and men who showed almost everything, too, leaping aloft. Joe looked at Honor and Honor looked at Joe, while everyone else was watching two ballet lovers twine and untwine in their *pas de deux*. Honor and Joe held hands while muscle-bound men (and women stabbing the stage with their thumping toes) were delicately touching fingertips.

"Our last Chicago night," Joe said, when they came back to their hotel suite. "We've got our fancy clothes from your Gala—why don't we go dancing? The hotel has a dance

172

floor and a band, and I can have my arms around you in front of everybody."

"A rehearsal?" she said, and was delighted when he turned red.

So she put on her lovely dress with its white bodice that was hardly either here or there...and a long black skirt, yards-wide, that swirled...and, of course, the diamonds. No stage fright this time, as she pulled the long dress over her. No terror at the thought of walking down a wedding line. Only a handsome man in a tuxedo running his hands over her...kissing her again and again...telling her how much he loved her, and how lovely, lovely, lovely she was, and taking her down to dance.

One step on the dance floor and it was obvious (Honor thought) that the man in a tuxedo and the woman in a formal gown were a true pair of lovers, not sweating lovers in a ballet pretending eternal passion. Eyes followed them. Other dancers gave them plenty of room—and indulgent smiles. The band seemed to favor love songs.

They sat at a table in the red and gold room to drink wine. "I remember the first time I saw you in a tuxedo," Honor said.

"At Brandon's wedding dinner," Joe said. "You were so pale that I thought you might faint."

"I was terrified," Honor said. "Going down that wedding line. And then you came to my table. You looked like a very hungry wolf, I thought, but the filet mignon came just in time."

"It didn't help," Joe said. "All I wanted was you." He took her hands and kissed her left one with its glittering rings. "I think we're on show here tonight, formal as we are. Lovers. Have you noticed?" he said. "We seem to be as obvious as a couple on a wedding cake."

A wedding cake. A plastic wedding cake on a bar. Honor said the first thing she thought of: "Everyone loves a lover."

"Every man loves you."

"But look around," Honor said. "There's one man in this room that every woman is watching."

They finished their wine. The band was beating and blaring out hot jazz. "Dance with me again?" Joe asked.

They went into each other's arms on the shining floor, and began to match their steps to the band's furious beat. But after a minute they stopped to laugh and look embarrassed: the band had halted in mid-thump and toot and begun a love song, grinning at them. What could Honor and Joe do but revolve languidly, Honor's head on Joe's shoulder and most of her pressed as close to him as possible?

It was delicious. But they had been on their feet all day. "Had enough?" Joe whispered against her cheek after a while.

"I'm afraid so," Honor said. She looked sidewise at him. "Of this, anyway."

He laughed, his dark eyes glittering, and twirled her to the lilt of a Strauss waltz until they reached the door. They stopped there to laugh, because the band was already deserting the Vienna Woods for drum-beat and a wailing sax.

They kissed in empty hallways, kissed at their door as Joe unlocked it, kissed in their dark suite. Honor felt him unfasten her necklace and unhook her earrings with a practiced hand. He knew exactly how her bra unhooked, and where her high heels unbuckled. Then it was her turn, more difficult because she hadn't practiced. But he helped her with a "Here," and "At the back of my neck," and stood patiently until they were skin to skin.

He was moving so gently, touching her with such care. She knew who he was trying to make her forget; she shivered and sighed. "What you need is a warm shower and another of those rub-downs you like," he said.

In a few moments two naked lovers were soaping and rinsing and kissing each other in a downpour of warm water, washing away a long day. Laughing and dripping, they toweled each other, head to foot, and ran to his big bed. He lifted Honor to lay her face-down, and began to rub the tight muscles in her shoulders... in her back... slowly she relaxed until she seemed to melt in his arms. He gathered her close.

He was waiting. A big shoulder was under her head. A muscled arm held her tight. It seemed to her that he was saying, with every move he made, *I am Joseph Lombard.*

Honor lifted his arm from her, sat up, turned on a bedside light and looked at him: his long black eyelashes, black hair, and a young man's body sprawled and warm. But the man himself, like no other man she knew, was suddenly so clear to her that she simply stared at him.

My heart is ever at thy service. Had Shakespeare known a lover who had put himself to just that kind of service? Joe Lombard had watched her from his first sight of her. What did she want?

174

What did she need? And now he was asking: how could he love her without hurting her? He would draw back forever, for her sake. He was doing it.

"Joe!" she cried.

He looked at her, and everything he felt was in his eyes.

"I've wanted you for so long," Joe said without moving, his eyes never leaving hers. "Can you ever want me? Are you still so hurt? So afraid?"

"No!" Honor cried. "I've loved you so long! Ever since you stood at Lena's garden gate and said, *I'll be back*. And you came back, always giving, always loving, and I love you! I do! I didn't know it, but I always have! Try me and see!"

So Joe began to try. He tried so well that in a few hours they were almost too happy and exhausted to kiss once more.

"We'll make us legal when we get home," Joe said in a drowsy voice. "At the courthouse, my beautiful, beautiful wife."

It was late that morning when Honor and Joe opened their eyes to find themselves cocooned together in rustling sheets.

They were too hungry to let each other go...not even long enough to have breakfast in bed. They lay, skin to warm skin, to call Lena, and told her, between kisses, that they were leaving for home. Don was fine, Lena said, and she'd have supper waiting for them.

Finally they dressed, and strolled under cloudy skies to have dinner in a restaurant high over the city.

"What a wonderful trip we've had," Honor said as they drove out of town. "And to think I was so scared—"

"*Scared!*" Joe said.

Honor saw the concerned look on his face. "Of being on that *platform*! Reading my poem to *famous poets*!"

They both began to laugh.

"Then maybe you wouldn't want to come back to Chicago every year," Joe asked. Same time, same place, to celebrate?"

"How romantic," Honor said. "Let's!" and kissed him, and kept kissing him, since they were on an almost-empty highway.

"We've got our whole life to plan now," Joe said after a while. "You'll have Don, and rooms of your own to write in. And we have two professors from the college as near neighbors—we'll invite them to dinner when we have a decent dining room, if they

175

don't invite us first. And there's a 'New Faculty Wives' group you'll be a member of…"

"And Lena and Emily!" Honor said, "and neighbors and friends from the park, and the college…the library and stores only a few blocks away… a campus school Don can walk to…"

When they stopped for a red light in a small town, Joe kissed her. The driver in the car beside them honked. Then a car at the curb honked. The drivers grinned at Joe and Honor, so the two lovers grinned back, and kissed again. The drivers honked again. All of them were laughing as the light turned green.

16

T he morning after the Poetry Gala, Brandon woke
Trisha. "You're dressed already?" she said.
"C'mon. Breakfast."

She sat up and moaned, "Dead. I'm dead. Too many drinks at
your boring, boring Gala."

"You can sleep all the way to Lovers Beach," Brandon said.

"Oh..." Trisha wailed. "My head! I'm totally out." She crawled
from bed to dress and pack her suitcase, groaning.

They had breakfast. Trisha said she was the walking dead. She
didn't notice how totally-out Brandon was: too much whisky and
no sleep.

Brandon loaded their suitcases in the car, hurrying before
Trisha could see what he had in the trunk. Trisha got in the back

seat, stretched out and said: "Wake me up for lunch, or before you see Lake Michigan, whichever comes first. I've got to get enough sleep to put on my swimsuit and sit on a beach."

"Okay," Brandon said, and couldn't believe his luck.

Trisha was asleep before they were halfway out of Chicago; they made good time before the traffic got heavy. Once on the highway, Brandon drove fast, and didn't slow down except to get a few shots from the bottle under his seat.

A couple of hours and a lot of miles later, Brandon heard Trisha sneeze. He looked in the mirror and saw her sitting up.

"Where are we now?" she said.

"I don't know," Brandon told her. "I'm just taking the main drag. Don't need a map."

Trisha gave a little sigh, lay down, and went to sleep again.

Honor and Joe...Brandon scowled at a small town he was driving through. Those two were seeing the Chicago sights today, probably. Wining and dining. That bald Chicago mayor gave them plenty of publicity, so there'd probably be pictures in the Chicago papers—Honor wearing diamonds. Joe in his rented tux.

He drove fast. What luck—Trisha might sleep the whole way. Brandon opened the front windows. The day was heating up.

A Poetry Gala. Where'd the money come from for a party like that? Hundreds of people, and Joe on the platform with Honor, grinning and bowing and pretending he was Husband of the Poet.

After a while, Trisha was snoring in the back seat. They were making good time, but he hadn't really planned what he'd tell Trisha, when he had to.

Maybe he shouldn't have brought her, but she was wearing the nice clothes he'd paid for. She spoke decent English. Presentable. That's what she was. His secretary. They were just traveling through on business.

Another hour.

After another hour, he reached under his seat for a bottle, took a slug from it for the road, and saw Trisha was awake and watching him in the mirror. "Go easy on that," she said.

"We're low on gas," Brandon said, and turned into a small-town filling station. They went to the rest rooms while one of the men sitting on a front bench went to the pump. The other three got up to stroll around and around Brandon's red and white Corvette.

Brandon came back to his car. The men walked back to their bench. Trisha ran out, slamming the station's old screen door behind her, and grabbed Brandon by his shirt front. "We're in *Iowa!*" she yelled.

"We are?" Brandon said, and the row of locals laughed.

"No! You've flown to the moon on that fancy set of wheels, lady!" an old fellow said. "Your pretty legs are *way out!*"

"*Iowa!*" Trisha shouted, giving the old guy a dirty look. "Look at that sign!"

Brandon looked. The big signboard across the road said: "Best Fried Chicken In Iowa Five Miles Ahead."

"Yeah," Brandon said.

"*Yeah?*" she yelled. Brandon got away from her and started to climb in his car, but Trisha grabbed him by the collar this time. "You didn't just drive west by accident?" she shouted. "Hundreds of miles in the wrong direction? Drunk? On purpose? Where's Michigan? Where's Lovers Beach?"

Brandon tried to get away and crawl behind the wheel, but he had a new shirt on, and it felt like she was going to rip it off.

"Get in!" he shouted back at her. "Get in! Let's go!" There he was, half in and half out of his car, with everybody on that station bench enjoying the view, because Trisha's skirt was real short, and she was bending over to grab him.

He got his shirt away from her and slid behind the wheel. She was still yelling, but she finally got in the passenger seat, slammed the door, and they were off in the heat and dust.

Neither of them said anything for a couple of miles. Finally Trisha snarled, "You're taking us somewhere? *Not* the lake? *Not* the beach? We're in *Iowa?* Going to visit your *mother?* Is that the idea? Old Home Week? And what's she going to think? I'm your girlfriend? When you're already married?"

"You're my secretary," Brandon said. "We're traveling on business. We check into a fancy Waterloo hotel, and you can swim in the pool and dance at night—what difference does it make if you're not in Michigan?"

"Just stop this car!" Trisha yelled. "Stop it! Right now! I'm getting out! You're a liar, and I'm getting out, and I'll go back home and never see you again, ever, ever, ever!"

Brandon wasn't going to stop the car. "You're enjoying a plenty easy job at Bushnell Kitchenmaster, Inc.," he said. "You going

179

to give it up? Get fired? Just because we're going to Iowa for a while, not Michigan?"

"Beaches!" Trisha wailed. "You said we'd have beaches, and I got my new swimsuit—what in the hell are you doing?"

"Listen," Brandon said. "Just listen. Can't I give you a lot of vacations? We can go to Key West at Christmas, while all your secretary friends are stuck in Chicago snow. Maybe we can even go to Paris! Just listen. You got to do a little job for me first. That's all."

"You've been into that bottle you've got under that seat!" Trisha said. "Ever since we left Chicago. Why should I believe anything a drunk says?"

They drove quite a while without a word. Finally Trisha said, "Can we just see your mother and then drive back to Michigan?"

"We can try," Brandon said.

They got to Cedar Falls. Brandon kept out of sight of Lena's house; he parked around the corner. Trisha squinted in the car mirror to check her make-up. "Now listen," he said.

"You think she'll give us some lunch?" Trisha said. "I'm starving."

"We've got to do this right," Brandon said. "I want to surprise her. See that big old white house in the middle of the block? That's hers. I want you to walk across the park and stand across the street from her. She's never seen you. And I'm going to go up her back alley and around the side of her house and hide in the bushes under her front porch railing. When you see me under the railing, you cross the street and ring her doorbell. If she comes to the door and opens it, you go right in—don't wait for her to invite you, or she might shut the door. *Don't let her close it.* Just shove right in and keep it open, and I'll be right behind you."

"Shove right into her house like that? Scare her?"

"Once she shuts the door on you, she won't open it again," Brandon said. "She's got this thing about being robbed. If she doesn't answer the door, I'll sneak back the way I came, and you go back to the car, and we'll try again later. But don't worry. She'll like being surprised, and she's a good cook—she'll give us lunch."

Trisha started across the park, and Brandon sneaked around the block and along Lena's alley, reminding himself that the house next door to Lena's was empty, and Joe and Honor were in Chicago. All he had to worry about was taking Lena by surprise.

He ducked under Lena's side windows, and crept along under her front porch railing. Trisha saw him. She crossed the street, came up to Lena's front door, and rang the bell.

Lena answered it! Brandon heard Trisha say, "Mrs. Lombard?" as he raced up the stairs and through the door behind her.

"Brandon!" Lena yelled. "Get out of here! Get right out of here! Now! I'll call the police!"

A huge black and white cat was twining around their legs. Trisha, Lena, Brandon and the cat were jammed together in Lena's little front hall. "Just let me explain!" Brandon cried. "Just let me—"

"Who's this woman?" Lena shouted. "Get her out of here! Both of you get out!"

"Mrs. Lombard?" Trisha said, staring into Lena's face a few inches from hers.

"Get out!" Lena said to her. "If you're a friend of his, you're no friend of mine! Out!"

"Oh no," Brandon said. He was bigger than both of them together, and he backed them against the front door. "Oh no. Not until I see Don."

"Brandon!" Trisha said, wild-eyed. "What's going on? Who's Don? If this is your mother—"

"Mother?" Lena said. "Mother? I'm not this man's mother, not on your life! I wouldn't have given birth to him if you wrapped him in hundred-dollar bills and said pretty-please! He's a half-baked adolescent and a full-time drunk. If he's yours, take him back to wherever you came from. And if he isn't yours, you're the luckiest woman who ever dodged an awful lot of trouble!"

Lena and Trisha were eye to eye. Brandon dashed for the stairs. The two women and the cat were right behind him, but Don was babbling, so Brandon heard him, found the right room,

181

and grabbed the baby out of his crib. "Don!" Brandon yelled. "How you've grown! What a big boy!" Trisha and Lena rushed in, and Brandon said, "See? He's my very own son! Looks like me! Named after me, even—Don, from Bran-don!"

What could the women do? Grab Don away from Brandon? He hugged Don tight, sat down in a chair, and looked his very own son over. The huge cat leaped to the bed beside him, braced to pounce, and looked him in the eye.

"Well!" Trisha said to Lena, "Could you explain a few things to me, if you don't mind? I'm Trisha Boyle, Mr. Lombard's secretary. And you are not Mrs. Lombard, his mother? He told me you were."

"I'm no relation to him," Lena said. "I'm Honor Lombard's aunt, Lena Townsend. She's married to Brandon's brother Joe. And I don't need to tell you, I guess, that Brandon Lombard's a liar. And a thief. Kidnapper. He stole this baby once, ran out of town with him, caused his mother all kinds of pain—starting from the first time she ever laid eyes on him. Now I think he's going to try to do it again. But the police will be right behind him this time."

"Don't listen to her," Brandon said to Trisha. "She's crazy in the head. I have a perfect right to see my own son, don't I? You can't kidnap your own son! But they won't let me see him! I haven't seen him since I took him away from here months ago!"

"Where's his mother?" Trisha asked. "She lives here?"

"She lives with me," Lena said. "But she's in Chicago with this crazy man's brother for a few days," Lena said. "Reading her poem at a big poetry party."

Trisha put her hands on her hips and stared at Brandon. "So!" she said. "I think I've finally got you pretty well figured out. You've seen your kid, and he's Honor Lombard's—the poet at that fancy party? So now you've seen him. If you don't want to sober up at police headquarters, put that baby down. Let's go have lunch. I'm starving."

"You better do the driving," Lena said to Trisha. "He's got more booze in him than he ever had sense. How many bottles has he had today?"

"Too many," Trisha said. "His usual number."

And then Brandon took off with Don—pounded downstairs, across Lena's porch and took her steps to the street two at a time... to the park bank and around the corner to his car.

Trisha raced after Brandon, yelling. A streak of cat shot from the house to the park bank to Brandon's pant leg, and hung on it with four feet full of claws and a mouth full of teeth. Brandon slid into his car, dumped Don on the seat beside him and beat the big cat with both fists, while Trisha jumped into the back seat, still yelling. When Brandon hit the gas, she almost fell out trying to shut the door.

Brandon kept one hand on Don as he took side streets fast, while Tux gnawed and clawed at his leg. Just before the highway, Bandon pulled to a curb and grabbed the monster cat with both hands around its neck, strangling it until it finally let go. He threw it out the window.

His leg was bleeding all over the place, but the highway was just ahead—and he had his boy! He had Don! Trisha was yelling from the back seat, but who cared? If he had Don, he could get Honor. She wouldn't give Don up, so she'd come, and they'd be a family! He had his Rockford apartment—plenty of room for Honor and Don there.

Trisha kept yelling. He drove fast. Finally she gave up. Don wasn't yelling; he was kicking his feet in their blue socks and watching blue skies going by his window.

Brandon grinned down at his boy. He was a Lombard kid all right—he liked traveling fast. "Fella," Brandon said to him, "wait until you and I get on our Harleys."

"Harleys!" Trisha yelled from the back seat. "There aren't any of those in jail, and that's where you'll be!"

"I'll buy you a little Harley," Brandon told Don.

"Wait till that Lena of yours calls the police—you'll need your Harleys!" Trisha shouted.

"But kiddie-cars first, I guess," Brandon said, smiling down at Don.

"You're a kidnapper!"

"And then three-wheel wheelies?"

"What about his mother!"

"And then those fancy bicycles...bet you'll do tricks with one of them."

Don seemed to like that idea: he kicked even faster.

"How do you think his mother's going to feel?"

"Boots," Brandon said. "We'll take to the road in big boots."

Brandon drove fast for a while, just to be safe. Trisha stopped yelling. Finally he pulled into a restaurant along the highway near

Dyersville...the middle of nowhere—just what he wanted. He'd been watching for police cars, and he'd seen Trisha looking out the back window all the time. "Hungry?" he asked her.

She wouldn't answer. When he parked at the back of a lot between two big trucks, she got out of the car and marched into the place. Brandon limped inside with Don, and a waitress brought a highchair. They ordered big dinners.

At first Trisha wouldn't talk to anybody but the waitress, but after the food came, she seemed to loosen up a bit. "I'm sorry," she said to Brandon after a while. "I didn't know you had a baby boy. I didn't know they wouldn't let you see him." She gave him a sad look. "It must be hard."

"Yeah," Brandon said.

"A lot of men never care if they have a child somewhere in the world."

"Well, I do."

"He looks a lot like you."

"He's mine."

"Wouldn't your wife be willing to take him?"

"Katie? She's not even twenty. She's out for a good time, not babies."

Trisha sighed. "I've been sorry for you, stuck away in Rockford while Katie has all the fun."

"Yeah." Brandon gave his steak a vicious knife-cut.

"And you have to work for her dad."

"He doesn't like me."

"So what does that matter? You could get another really good job, you know? You've been working for a first-class company. You can just tell bosses at other businesses that you have personal reasons for leaving Bushnell."

"Personal?"

"You could get a divorce. Just tell Katie goodbye. She's not even living with you. What kind of a wife is that? And how's she going to feel if you unload a baby on her that's not even hers? She'll run in the other direction."

"Katie wants a divorce." Brandon was feeling better and better, even if blood was running down his leg into his sock. He could get the wife he wanted: Honor. She'd go where her baby was, and her baby was going to be in Rockford, Illinois.

"Divorce!" Trisha said. "Divorce? That's perfect! If anybody asks why you're leaving Bushnell, you can say you're divorcing the boss's daughter," Trisha said. "That's a super-fine 'personal reason,' isn't it? They'd jump at the chance to get you. A man as good-looking as you. Young. A business degree…experience…"

"You think so?"

"I know so."

"You ought to," Brandon said. "You've had a lot of experience in business."

Trisha smiled. "I ought to know a winner when I see one. You've just had some hard knocks. You need a new beginning. Somewhere out west, maybe."

"I'll give it some thought," Brandon said. "If I could break loose from Bushnell and get ahead, I might be able to get married again. And then I could have Don."

Trisha had finished her chicken salad. Brandon had finished his French fries. Trisha knew he couldn't get enough of them. She'd saved hers, and pushed them from her plate to his. "All you have to do is get away from the drink," she said. "You need somebody to live with you, keep that hard stuff out of sight, be really interested."

Brandon was feeling better, now that he wasn't hungry and had Don. Even hopeful. Maybe the Bushnells and Lena had it in for him, but he'd divorce Katie and they couldn't stop him from making good, even if he had to find another job.

"What about Don?" Trisha said.

"We'll take him back to Rockford, and I'll make a home for him—and you. I'm his daddy." Brandon began to see his whole plan; it was opening out before him like a road map. When Honor found out he had a family with Trisha and Don, she'd come blazing into Rockford after him—she'd never stand for some floozy raising Don!

He smiled at Trisha. "What did you think I was doing? Imagine yourself! Imagine yourself with Don in my apartment—maybe even in a house! No more pounding away on typewriters for you! We'll get a babysitter and keep having fun on weekends—take vacations!"

Don was fussing in his highchair. "I'm going to have one of these," Brandon said, holding up a menu with a chocolate sundae on it and signaling to a waitress. "A chocolate sundae," he told her. "A fancy one. The works."

Don began to yell.

"He's probably wet. Or worse," Trisha said.

185

A highway patrolman came in the door. Brandon slid down in his chair a little, hunched his shoulders, and glared at Trisha. Trisha stared at her empty plate. Don yelled and banged his high chair tray up and down. Brandon glared at Don.

The patrolman bought cigarettes at the counter and left.

"Your Lena *will* call the police, you know," Trisha said.

"They can't arrest you for taking your own son." Brandon watched the waitress bring him another napkin, the sundae, and a long-handled spoon. She scowled at the screaming baby.

"He's got to be changed," Trisha said, when Don stopped howling for a minute, out of breath.

"You've had so much experience with babies," Brandon said. "Big sister to all your brothers and sisters. And hey—I'm all prepared. I filled the trunk of my car with everything for my Don—bottles, baby food, diapers, milk...did it this morning before you woke up."

"Planned this?" Trisha said.

Brandon grinned. "Told you. We're in business."

She watched him take a mouthful of ice cream, hot fudge and a cherry.

"Want a bite?" Brandon said, mumbling around his cold mouthful.

Don was screaming again.

"No thanks," Trisha said between yells. "Give me the keys and I'll get a diaper out of the car, and take him to the ladies' room while you finish your sundae."

Trisha went out to the car, and Brandon laughed to himself, eating his sundae. Trisha came back, picked up Don and carried him away. Nobody could say he hadn't planned this right. You always had to be a step ahead. "Keep the competition back there in the dust!" Bushnell always said, and said, and said.

Brandon's coffee was cold. He ordered some more, and enjoyed another little private chuckle. Trisha's plans were as clear as glass. He chuckled again. Honor wanted Don. Trisha wanted the sweet married life. Katie was history.

He finished his sundae. He was sure he could get work anywhere, with his credentials. He'd take Honor and Don to California, get a top job, buy a nice house. Honor'd be so happy. They could even have more kids.

He finished his coffee and thought: Hey, look at the worst case:

186

Honor wouldn't marry him and get a real husband—didn't want Don that much. Okay. He'd always have Trisha. She knew how to take care of a baby—she'd had all those brothers and sisters. She had a good head for business, and she sure didn't want to take care of an old mother.

He waited a few more minutes. Don probably had a mess in his pants, and she was cleaning it up.

Brandon paid the bill, and limped out to his car to wait for Trisha and Don.

The car was gone.

17

L ate sunlight fell on Seerley Park, paving the grass with
gold trails through trees. A beautiful evening, but
Lena sat on her porch with nothing on her mind but
the memory of Trisha racing after Brandon and Don up the park
bank and away, with Tux a black streak in chase, and Don's blanket
dropped behind them in the grass. She'd started for the garage
and her car to chase them, but her car was in Chicago, and she
didn't have the key to Joe's car.

Had they taken Tux, too?

She hadn't been able to eat lunch after she'd called the police,
trying not to cry as she gave them whatever facts she could think
of. All day she'd listened for the phone.

Honor and Joe...returning home so happy with their Chicago trip and the Gala—and she'd have to tell them that their Don was gone...gone with a drunk...

She hadn't called Emily. What could Emily do? And if the worst happened, Emily would at least be spared bad news for a while, or hours of worry.

Lena watched children chasing each other around the park trees. Bad news. Nobody liked somebody who brought bad news. You were somehow smeared all over with your bad news—worse than skunk spray—the minute you said, "I am so sorry to tell you, but..."

A taxi came around a park corner and stopped at her sidewalk.

Lena gasped and leaped from her chair as Brandon climbed from the taxi and paid the driver. He took Lena's stairs two at a time, but not fast enough—when he crossed the porch, she was standing inside her locked screen door, glaring at him.

"You're hiding him, aren't you?" Brandon said.

"What?" Lena said.

"And Trisha, too! You saw me coming! You're hiding them! And where's my car? Hiding it too?"

"You're drunk," Lena said. "As usual. No clue. Absolutely cross-eyed—gin-soaked—babbling. As I told you before, you're less welcome here than a case of the hives—"

"Where's my boy!"

"What did you do, leave him under a bar table somewhere?"

"Let me in!"

"The only place I'll invite you is outside. You can tell me from out there where my great nephew is—"

"You've got him! Trisha took him and you've got him!" Brandon yanked and shoved and pounded at the screen door until the hook—and the screen—fell out of it. He shoved Lena against a wall and ran inside, and she heard him hunting through every room downstairs, then running upstairs, slamming doors...with all the noise, neither of them heard a car stop outside, or footsteps on the porch.

"Joe!" Lena cried, when she saw him at the broken screen door.

"What's going on?" he said. Honor was behind him.

"Brandon took Don," Lena said. "This morning."

"Took him!" Honor and Joe said in a single breath, and climbed through the broken door.

189

"Took him," Lena said. "Right out of his crib. And now Brandon's here, and he says he doesn't know where Don is! I was all alone this morning, and a girl I'd never seen rang the doorbell. Just as I opened it, she shoved her way inside—and then Brandon sneaked in behind her!"

"A girl?" Honor said.

"She thought I was Brandon's mother," Lena said. "And she acted as if she'd never heard of Don, but she found out pretty fast when Brandon yelled about 'his boy.' She told me her name was Trisha Boyle and she was Brandon's secretary."

"Trisha!" Brandon shouted, banging doors upstairs.

Lena said, "Brandon was drunk, and he ran upstairs and stole Don from his crib, and away he went with this Trisha woman after him across the park to a red car and off! I couldn't catch them—couldn't run fast enough, but Tux could. The last time I saw Tux he had all his claws and teeth in Brandon's leg. I called the police." Lena glared at Brandon as he came downstairs. "And now here's Brandon, come back without anybody! Saying he doesn't know where Don is! Ransacking the whole house! He's crazy-drunk!"

Brandon came down the stairs two at a time, and Joe grabbed him around the neck and shook him. "Where is he? Where's Don!"

"I...don't... know..." Brandon gasped, trying to wrench Joe's hands from his neck. Joe let him go, and Brandon said, "I can't find them! This old witch is hiding them somewhere! And where's my car?"

"Your car?" Honor said. "How did you get here?"

"Hitchhiked. Took a taxi from Waterloo."

"Then Don's still in your car?" Honor asked. "With this Trisha of yours? And Joe's cat that chased you?"

"That demon cat? I threw him out the window. And my car's right *here* somewhere—Lena's hidden it! And she's hiding my son, too! And Trisha!"

Honor and Joe looked at Lena.

"Drunk," Lena said.

"Lena's hiding Don and this Trisha person?" Honor said to Brandon. "Why?"

Brandon didn't answer.

"Trisha and Don and the car aren't here, are they?" Joe asked Lena.

"Of course not!" she said.

"Then they're at your house!" Brandon shouted at Joe. Before they could stop him, he ran out the broken screen door and down the bank to Joe's house, Joe at his heels. The door was locked, so he pounded on it until Joe unlocked it.

"Feel free," Joe said, and Brandon shoved past him and ran up and down, opening doors, shouting. Finally he left the house, panting, to open Joe's garage door.

The garage was empty. Brandon raced up Lena's bank, up her steps, through her sagging screen door, and sat down in her living room.

Joe, Honor and Lena surrounded Brandon in his chair. "Where's Don?" Honor cried. "You took him—now you don't know where he is?"

"Yes, I do!" Brandon said. "Trisha drove off in my car, and she's got him, and they're here! And I'm staying right here until I see them."

There he sat. No one knew what to do. Finally Lena said, "Supper's ready. Why don't you folks wash up and have something to eat. It'll be a long night, I'm afraid."

Honor and Joe went into the kitchen with Lena. The three went into the back room, closed the door and looked at each other. Lena turned on a lamp. "Well," she said.

Joe put his arms around Honor. "We'll find Don." He kissed her, and Honor hugged him and pressed her wet face against his shoulder.

"Well!" Lena said in a very different tone. "Well!"

Joe hugged Honor close and looked at Lena. His dark eyes were full of such deep happiness that Lena stared at him with her mouth open.

"This Trisha must have Don," Honor said against Joe's shoulder. "In Brandon's car. Lena, you said you called the police, so they're looking for it."

"A new Corvette," Joe said. "A red and white corvette. There aren't many cars like that on Iowa roads. They'll find her."

"But how did she get Don?" Honor said. "And how can she feed him? And Brandon said he threw Tux out of his car!"

"And why would she take Don?" Joe said. "A secretary? Or is

191

Brandon living with her, maybe? Maybe she's his new love, and they want to start their family with Don? He told my mother he might be getting a divorce."

"Trisha didn't act like she'd been drinking when they came here, I'm glad to report," Lena said. "And she didn't seem to know what Brandon was going to do—didn't expect him to grab Don."

"She didn't?" Joe asked.

"No. She was really amazed when he ran off with Don. I saw her face. She looked appalled—she ran after them as if she didn't have any other choice."

"And she didn't know who you were," Joe said.

"I told her. I asked her how many bottles of booze Brandon had had that day, and she said, 'Too much. His usual number.' And I just remembered that Trisha did know you, Honor. She asked where Don's mother was. I told her you were at a Poetry Gala in Chicago, and Trisha said she'd seen you there."

Joe and Honor looked at each other. "Joe must have brought her to the Gala," Joe said.

"We never saw her," Honor told Lena. "But Brandon caught us afterward, and made a scene."

"Oh, my," Lena said.

"I'm just remembering…" Joe said. "After the Gala, Brandon asked me how long we were staying in Chicago."

The three looked at each other.

"He was planning right then to take Don," Honor said.

Lena sighed. "Your supper's getting cold."

Joe and Honor helped Lena bring full plates to the dining room. Lena went to Brandon in the living room and said, "Supper's ready."

"I'm not hungry," Brandon said.

Honor, Lena and Joe sat down to eat Lena's hot, golden-crusted chicken pie, a fruit salad, cinnamon rolls and coffee. Through the door they could see Brandon sitting in the dim living room. The chink of silverware on china was the only sound.

There was no baby in Don's high chair. Joe saw tears on Honor's cheek. Lena had a murderous look in her eye every time she looked at Brandon.

Just as they finished eating, the doorbell rang.

"Police!" Lena said. She answered the door, and they all yelled, for there Trisha stood with Don in her arms.

"Give him to me," Brandon yelled, yanking what was left of the screen door open.

"No!" Trisha said, and backed away. She held Don tight in her arms.

Brandon lunged for the baby, but Joe caught Brandon and dragged him into the living room.

"Come in!" Honor cried, going out to Trisha. "Oh, we're so glad to see Don!" Trisha said nothing; she put the baby in Honor's arms. "Don baby," Honor crooned to him. "Oh, Don baby."

"You took him!" Brandon glared at Trisha when she came in. "You stole him! You stole my car!" He ran to the door. "Where's my car?"

"I fed him some baby food," Trisha said to Honor. "Veal. And carrots. But he's probably hungry again. And probably wet."

"Where's my car!" Brandon ran out the door and down the steps, looking up and down the street.

"You brought him back!" Lena said to Trisha. "We're so glad. Come sit down. You must be hungry, and tired."

There was no Corvette in sight. Brandon started back to Lena's, but he was too late—Joe slammed the heavy front door and locked it, and went through the kitchen to lock the back door, while Brandon hammered on the front one.

"Don't mind Brandon," Lena told Trisha. "He's banged on my doors before, and my windows. A habit of his. A nervous tic, I suppose. We just ignore it, and after a while the police come and tell him to go away. We have very efficient police."

"Brandon's drunk," Trisha said. "He drank all the way here. That's why I ran off with the baby. I'm sorry Brandon scared you this morning, bursting into your house that way, stealing Don. It scared me, too—I had no idea he was coming here. I didn't even know he had a son."

Lena raised her voice over Brandon's pounding. "You can stay with us," she said to Trisha. "Let me take you up to your bedroom, and when you feel like some supper, you come down.

There's plenty to eat. Honor's taking care of the baby, and Joe will take care of his brother. Do you need to make any phone calls? Tell people where you are?"

"There's no one I want to tell," Trisha said. "But thanks. Thanks for the welcome."

Lena said, "I've got to call the police. Tell them Don is here and safe."

They could hear her explaining on the telephone in the quiet moments when Brandon wasn't banging on the door.

Lena came back to say: "I told the police a relative had taken the baby, and hadn't told us, but the baby was safe at home now. It was the closest I could get to the truth."

Brandon had stopped pounding, but now he began again. Joe said, "Lena—lock the front door behind me, will you? I'll go out and talk to him. Maybe I can find out where his car is, and he can go home before the police pick him up."

"Brandon's car is in Independence," Trisha said.

"Independence!" Honor said. "Why?"

"When we went running across the park with Don, I heard your aunt shout that she'd call the police and they'd find the car," Trisha told Honor. "So I was scared to drive it—such a fancy new Corvette! If they caught us, the police would think I'd kidnapped the baby."

"So you left the car at Independence? How did you get here?"

"I'd stolen Brandon's car—and Don—and was driving behind a bus on the highway, and it pulled into the bus station in Independence. I was scared the police would find us if I didn't get rid of Brandon's car, so I parked the Corvette on a side street, locked it, and Don and I rode the bus to Waterloo...and then one to Cedar Falls. A nice woman by the hotel downtown gave us a ride to your house."

"Independence," Joe said. "And you've got his car keys?"

"Here they are. The Corvette's parked around the corner from the Independence bus station." Trisha found keys in her big purse and gave them to Joe.

"Brandon's certainly not welcome here," Joe said. "I'll tell him where his car is, and call for a taxi to Waterloo."

Brandon was thumping on a living-room window now.

"He can get a bus to Independence from Waterloo," Joe said. He went out, and Lena locked the door. The three women could see the brothers clenching their fists and waving their arms on the porch.

"Come with me," Lena said to Trisha. "You must be exhausted." They went upstairs with Honor and Don. "Honor has a room here, and the baby has one next door to her." She opened a door. "Here's your room. We haven't redecorated it yet, but there's a bed made up in there. Use the washcloths and towels in the bathroom if you'd like a shower. I've got a housecoat for you. We've had our suppers, but there's a meal for you when you're ready."

Lena brought the housecoat, went downstairs, and looked through a living room window. Brandon had stopped pacing up and down on her porch and shouting. He was glaring at Joe.

"All right!" Joe said. "We've phoned the police—told them it was just a family matter, so they won't be after you. I'll call a taxi, and you can go to Waterloo and take a bus to Independence."

"Independence!" Brandon said.

"And where's our cat? Where's Tux?"

"You should see my leg!" Brandon said. "There's blood in my shoe! He's got knives, not claws."

"Trisha said you threw him out a window. Where?"

"Just before the highway out of town. Had to nearly strangle him to get him to let go. What did you train him to be, a panther?"

"He loves Don, and you ran away with him," Joe said. "Here's your car keys. The Corvette's parked around the corner from the Independence bus station. I'll go call the taxi." He stepped through the broken screen, and locked Lena's door behind him.

"You'd better call your mother," Lena said when Joe had called for a taxi.

The three women listened to Joe's calm, quiet, careful voice telling his mother what Brandon had done.

He hung up and came to sit with them by the fire. "I've told Mom what happened, and she thinks Brandon may come to her place. At least I've given her a warning."

B randon crossed the street, sat on a park bench and looked at Lena's house on its high bank. Lights shone from every window.

Somebody giggled. He turned to see a pair of lovers on another bench, hugging each other. Another pair shouted as they sailed higher and higher on the swings.

Brandon's last drink had worn off. There was more whisky in his car, miles away in Independence. He didn't feel good. He lay flat on the bench with his back to Lena's house. Honor had looked at him as if she hated him. Joe had just said she did, and told him that Honor was going to be the legal Mrs. Joseph Lombard in a few days, with a sign-on-the-dotted-line marriage.

Don would be their son. "Get over it," Joe told him. "You're married. You've got a good job. Stop making Mom worry about you every minute. Do your work and ditch the drink."

The park bench was hard. Brandon turned over and hissed under his breath: "Trisha!" She'd double-crossed him, spoiled everything! Told him how great he was, and then taken off with Don! No free trip back to Rockford for Trisha Boyle...no more beaches and dinners and movies...or mornings in the Bushnell office with nothing to do but polish her fingernails.

Honor hated him? He wasn't going to believe that. What did Joe have going for him? A job at a college, working for nothing much? And that old, rundown house?

How could Honor hate him—he was Don's father! He'd just have to wait, and get rid of Katie, find a really good job, and Honor would get tired of Joe. A family! Weren't Honor and Don his family?

Brandon heard the taxi pull up, and went across the street to get in. Joe was watching them from Lena's front window as they drove off. Brandon asked the driver how much money he'd want to drive to a liquor store, and then to Independence. The price was high, but Brandon needed his car, and a drink. He bought a bottle before they left town, had a shot from it, and watched the Iowa fields go by, square mile after square mile.

His car was parked in Independence, all right. Little kids ran up and down the sidewalk beside it while he paid the taxi driver. He opened the Corvette's trunk to get another bottle for the long trip to Chicago. A streetlight showed him his suitcase and Trisha's, with baby things crammed around them, stuff he'd bought in the middle of the night for Don—he'd filled a couple of shopping carts in an all-night superstore—baby bottles, diapers, jars of baby food, baby clothes...

He got in his car and sat there a while.

Then he had another drink and looked around him at his Corvette. A beautiful car. He'd never had anything like it. Never thought he ever would.

Somebody said, "Nice car."

A little kid was looking through the Corvette's open window.

"My boy likes it," Brandon said.

"How old is he?"

"He'll be as big as you pretty soon."

The boy ran down the block to one of the row houses facing each other. A lawn mower lay upside-down in a front yard, its row of blades glinting. Small rubber boots on a porch still showed their red. One by one, lights glimmered in windows. The darkness came early now.

Brandon took another drink, pulled away from the curb, left town.

18

W hen Trisha had finished her supper, she said, "I think I'll have a shower and go to bed, if you folks don't mind. I'm so glad to be here. Thanks so much for taking me in. I certainly didn't want to drive with Brandon."

"It's the least we could do—you probably saved Don's life," Honor said. "And Brandon's. And yours, too."

"Let me know if you need anything," Lena said to her.

"I'm sorry Brandon threw your cat out the window," Trisha said as she went upstairs. "I couldn't stop him."

Joe said, "Before it was dark, I searched for him on town streets to the highway, and both sides of the highway for a mile. No luck."

"He landed on some grass, I think," Trisha said. "That's all I saw."

"He'll come home," Joe said. "If he can. I'll look for him again when it's light tomorrow morning, and we'll put a notice in the paper, and tell the police to watch out for him."

Don had been bathed and fed and was sound asleep. When Trisha had gone to bed, Lena sat by the fire and sighed. "You two must be exhausted, but tell me a bit about the Gala."

"I wish you'd been there!" Joe said. "There were hundreds at the tables, and they had their eyes on Honor the moment she came, wearing that fine dress you gave her. My beautiful wife sat on a dais with the mayor of Chicago and a half-dozen famous poets, and she was the only one who read a poem. They stood up afterward and gave her an ovation."

Honor grinned at Joe. "I told the mayor of Chicago that I had a husband who had helped me in all my endeavors—could he give him some recognition? It *was* the truth, you know. So Joe had to stand up and bow and be applauded."

"You asked the *mayor of Chicago* to do that?" Joe said.

"I did," Honor said, laughing. "And *both* of you deserve honor— Joe's given me and my baby a name, and Lena gave us a home."

"And Lena gave us our big-city trip," Joe said. "Thanks!"

"Yes! Our hotel suite was absolutely decadent," Honor said. "We went to the Art Institute, and the Museum of Natural Science, and rode around a park in a carriage, and went to a ballet, and danced in our fancy clothes in a fancy ballroom."

The three sat smiling at each other, and then yawned and sighed. "We've had a hard day," Joe said, standing up.

"Yes," Honor said, getting up to stand beside him for a moment, a very long moment. Then Joe said, "Honor and I had better be going."

"Going? Where?" Lena said. "Your house isn't..."

"Could you and Trisha keep Don until tomorrow?" Honor said.

"Why, yes, but—"

"I've got a surprise for Honor at my place," Joe said.

"We'll be there tonight," Honor said. "Thanks so much for all you've done today."

Lena looked at Joe.

Lena looked at Honor.

"Well," Lena said. "Well...? I'll be glad to keep Don... of course...?" Her sentences went up at the end with question marks; she couldn't help it.

Honor wasn't looking at anything but the rug.

"Goodnight," Joe said to Lena, opening what was left of the front screen door. As he followed Honor out, he smiled at Lena. "We *are* married, you know," he said.

A heavy rain was falling. Lena's front porch light showed Joe and Honor the way between houses; they slid down the bank's wet grass to his side porch, hand in hand. He unlocked the door and said, "Welcome home!" Suddenly he lifted Honor off her feet, carried her in, shut the door behind them, kissed her, kissed her again on every step of his stairs, and set her down at the top. The door of the big front room had been locked for weeks; now it stood open.

Joe snapped on the light, and a deep blue room glowed: blue carpet, blue drapes, and blue velvet on a glossy walnut bed. "For you," he said. "For us—I hoped. Hoped for so long."

"Beautiful!" Honor cried. "So much work—I never knew! Blue...my favorite color...and what a fine bed...and you refinished it—and the dressing table and bench and chairs to match. When did you do it?"

"Late at night. In bits and pieces. Always thinking of you. Hoping for you."

"Here I am," Honor said, hugging him.

"Come have a shower in our new bathroom," he said, sliding a hand under her wet shirt and pulling it up and off. They hung their clothes on hooks to dry, and climbed together into a rush of warm, comforting water. "My wife," Joe murmured against Honor's wet cheek. "Our house. I can't believe such a miracle yet!" Park lights shone through wet windows in their bedroom, scattering diamonds as they burrowed under new blankets and sheets. "Welcome to our bed...welcome to my life," he said between kisses, and proceeded to make her feel very welcome indeed.

At last they were too tired and satisfied to do anything more than kiss.

Honor stared through big windows at the rain. "Brandon took Don, and he'll come again," she said. "He'll always come."

"We'll keep good watch," Joe said. "He's found his car by now, I suppose, and he's off to Rockford."

"But he'll always want Don. He'll try to make him into his kind of man—teach him to take what he wants, lock him into his kind of 'manly' life—"

200

"No," Joe said. "Don will grow up here, with us, with you."
But he remembered Brandon—his wild eyes, his shouts.

"I haven't thought enough about Brandon," Honor said. "Not
enough. Not really. I watched him today, drunk and shouting and
pleading. I don't know how to explain what I felt."

"Frightened, I should think," Joe said. "Disgusted."

"Yes," Honor said. "But while I watched him and heard him,
I felt so...disconnected. I thought: How would I describe what
he's feeling and thinking? What was he really saying? What was
he giving away? What did it really mean, all his screaming and
pounding? If he were a character in a book of mine, he'd be a flat
character—badly written! Badly written!"

"Put him in a book?"

"Not like that! He wouldn't be a good, live character, because I
can't see him clearly. Just handsome. Just a drunk."

"You're sorry for him. So am I."

"How deep would words on a page have to go to be true? What
can you write about a man who fathered a child and can't have
him? One drunken attack and he loses his son. What if I'd been
the one who made the stupid, drunken mistake and had to give
up Don forever—could never hold my own baby, feed him, help
him—never. Never. Would I pound on doors and windows?
Would I try to steal him? Would I beg and yell and chase and lie?"

Joe, holding her close, could think of nothing to say.

R ain pounded on the windows of The Hungry Chef.
　　　Emily Lombard cleaned her last restaurant table of the
day, then said goodnight to the manager, and ran out the door,
thinking of nothing but Joe's sad voice on the telephone an hour
before, saying, "I love you, Mom. Let me know if Brandon comes.
If you're in any trouble, I'll be there."

Brandon! Emily stopped before she got to her door, and ran
back through the rain, fast enough to beg the cook in the kitchen
for sweet rolls, eggs, and two pieces of apple pie.

Someone turned off the restaurant sign as she unlocked her
door. A car honked, leaving the parking lot. Emily put the food
on her table and looked at the narrow couch. She couldn't open
it to make her bed; it would block the door if Brandon came. Her
body ached from head to foot: she was getting too old for a hard
job.

"Brandon," she said. Her voice echoed in the small, dark room. "Brandon..." as if he could hear her, and remember that there was one safe place he could come and be welcome. Such a handsome man. Such a handsome boy. Such a pretty baby, like the new one. The baby that was his. Poor Brandon. Poor Joe. Poor Honor. She crawled on the couch and fell asleep.

Pounding woke her. "Mom!" Brandon was calling.

She got up and unlocked her door. Brandon came in with the smell of liquor on him. For a while they stood there, arms around each other, without a word. His coat was wet.

Then Brandon said in a muffled voice: "Joe called?" and she said, "Yes."

He let her go, took off his coat, hung it on the door hook, and sat on her couch.

"Are you hungry?" Emily asked.

"Yes."

"Here's some coffee." She filled a cup and handed it to him. "And I have some apple pie. I'll fry you some eggs."

When Emily brought the eggs and sweet rolls, Brandon said, "Thanks."

He sat at her table to eat. She brought him a piece of pie.

"Have you got some bandages?" he said, pulling up one of his pant legs. The cloth was smeared with blood, there was blood in his shoe, and long scratches ran down his shin. "Joe's cat," he said. "A huge Maine Coon. He went after me."

Emily washed his leg, put iodine on it, and covered it with a gauze pad and tape, just as she had done so many times for her two small boys. She cleaned out his shoe and dried it. "Thanks," Brandon said. He wouldn't look at her. He began to eat his pie.

"Everything isn't lost, you know," Emily said. "You haven't lost your wife—yet. You haven't lost your job, or your house, or even Don—he's not dead...you can see him now and then. You haven't lost Joe. Or me. You just have to pick up the pieces and go on... and sincerely apologize, too."

"Easy to say," he said.

"Give Honor your boy," she said. "Let him go. Have another son."

"Don's mine!" Brandon cried. "He's even got part of my name...I can't—"

"You have to," Emily said. "You made Honor give up too much.

202

Her graduation...prizes...hopes for a good job. You made her into a mother, all alone with a child to raise."

Brandon had finished his piece of pie; he put his head down on the table, hiding his face in his folded arms. "I didn't go to bed last night," he said in a muffled voice. "I was buying bottles and milk and diapers and baby food for Don. Can I just sleep here a little?" He crawled off the chair and lay on her couch, his face to the wall.

Emily cleared the table and dragged a mattress from her closet. It barely fit between the toilet and the shower. If two stayed the night, one had to sleep on the floor. She turned out the light and slept, too tired to think, still wearing her clothes.

Emily woke when her alarm rang at six. The rain had stopped. Brandon was gone.

In a few hours, morning skies were clearing over Iowa. Four hungry people and a baby were in Lena's kitchen for breakfast. Honor and Joe had gone out early to look for Tux, but couldn't find him.

"These are such beautiful homes you folks have—right on the park," Trisha said to Lena. Don was busy covering his highchair tray with crumbs of buttered toast, while the rest ate bacon and eggs, sausages, fragrant coffee, and rolls that glistened with caramel frosting.

"This house would still be an old barn if Joe and Honor hadn't come along," Lena told Trisha. "Now they're at work on their place. Have some more bacon. And won't you tell us a little about yourself?"

"There's not much to tell," Trisha said, taking another bacon strip. "I'm the oldest of six children, and we grew up in Stockton. I more or less raised my brothers and sisters while I went to secretarial school—my father was gone, and my mother was...not quite right in her mind, most of the time. Finally I got a job

203

in Rockford. I worked for Brandon at his Bushnell office in the morning, and a car sales office in the afternoon. A terribly unexciting life. But I enjoyed working for Brandon. There wasn't much to do, and he took me out sometimes. But...you know...he drinks. The Bushnells tried to get him to go to Alcoholic Anonymous. Even a psychiatrist. But he didn't think he had a problem."

"Weren't you afraid to drive with him?" Honor asked.

"Yes, but I never dreamed we were coming here! Brandon said we were going to a place called Lovers Beach on Lake Michigan, and I thought we were, so I went to sleep on his car's back seat, and woke up to find we were in Iowa!"

"How could you sleep that long?" Lena said.

Trisha looked at Joe and Honor. "I went to your Poetry Gala with Brandon, and afterward he sent me home in a taxi. But I didn't sleep all night—my sister had come to Rockford to shout at me about our mother, who's blind now. We talked the rest of the night until she had to leave. She wanted me to quit my job and come home to Stockton to work, and take Mother to live with me. I couldn't sleep. I couldn't see any way out."

"That sounds familiar," Lena said. "That's what happened to me, except that I had to take care of both my parents until they died."

"Then you know! You know!" Trisha cried. "They want you to do it, and you think you should. She's my mother. But there are six of us children, and they ought to take their turns, not load it on me every time! I worked to support the family for years!"

No one spoke for a while. What was there to say?

"So my sister yelled, and I hadn't had time to sleep the night before, getting ready to go to the beach, and had too much to drink at the Poetry Gala...so I slept all that way, until I woke up in Iowa—I couldn't believe it. I told Brandon I wanted to get out of his car and go home. He said I could, but I'd lose my job at his office."

"Threats," Honor said.

"Yes. But then he said we'd see his mother and drive back to Chicago and still go to the beach."

"So that's why you called me 'Mrs. Lombard,'" Lena said.

"And then Brandon grabbed the baby! He ran to the car and drove off so fast that I almost fell out—and he threw your cat out the window! I'm so sorry."

The four of them sat quietly for a moment, imagining the scene.

"And then Brandon started driving too fast," Trisha said. "He wasn't watching the road—he had Don lying on the seat beside him, and kept talking to the baby about buying him bicycles and motorcycles, and what fun they were going to have, and he went through stop signs! Three of them!"

"Oh!" the three of them said. "How could you stop him?" "What could you do?"

"We were hungry," Trisha said. "I guess that's what saved us. Brandon pulled into a restaurant before we got to Dyersville, and Don sat in a highchair while we had dinner."

"How could you eat anything?" Honor said. "You must have been terrified."

"Brandon ordered a steak and never stopped talking."

"About what?" Joe asked.

"He was drunk, and making plans right and left. I was so scared, but I listened to every word he said, trying to calm him down. And then a highway patrolman came into the restaurant."

"And you called to the patrolman!" Honor said. "That's how you got away!"

"I almost did," Trisha said. "You probably think I should have, and was pretty stupid not to—but we'd be arrested for kidnapping! Arrested!"

"What else could you do?" Lena asked.

"Well, I did have another plan. It was all I could think of. Maybe Brandon would be tired after the big dinner he was eating, and the hours driving all the way from Chicago. And I thought he hadn't slept at all after the Poetry Gala—said he had to go shopping—in the middle of the night? I found out later that he'd bought supplies for the baby."

"Getting ready to steal Don," Joe said.

"Yes!" Trisha said. "So maybe—I thought—Brandon would be glad to sleep in the back seat for a while, and let me drive until he sobered up. Maybe I could even go back to Cedar Falls while he slept, and give Don to you before the police caught us."

Honor, Joe and Lena stared at Trisha, too transfixed by her story to eat. Trisha looked down at her plate and sighed. "I tried to think. I was afraid the dinner was making Brandon less drunk. Would he sleep and let me drive? And then the patrolman left."

Lena, Honor and Joe stared at her. "Then how did you…" Lena began.

"It was Don," Trisha said. "He was wet, and he started to yell. The restaurant didn't like that much. Brandon was so embarrassed; people were scowling at us. So I told him I should change the baby, but how? And Brandon told me he'd loaded the trunk of his car with baby supplies."

"So Brandon had planned all of this!" Joe said. "Obviously."

"I didn't want any dessert, but Brandon had just ordered a big chocolate sundae when Don began yelling. So when that sundae came, I knew what I could do."

Nobody at the table was drinking their coffee. They stared at Trisha with a chorus of "What?"

"It was so simple," Trisha said. "Brandon didn't want to leave that chocolate sundae to get a diaper from his car. Blessed chocolate sundae. Don was yelling his head off, and Brandon had just taken his first big spoonful of chocolate and ice cream and a cherry, and I said: 'Give me your car keys and I'll get a diaper from the Corvette, and change Don in the ladies' room while you finish your dessert and coffee."

"That's how you got the keys!" Joe said.

"Thanks to Don," Trisha said.

"But Brandon didn't ask for the keys back?" Lena said.

"He just loves chocolate sundaes," Trisha said. "He sat there eating, and watched me go out to the car in the parking lot. And can you imagine how I felt when I started his car, and went back to our table with the diaper to pick up Don?"

"Brandon didn't ask for the keys back?" Honor said.

"No! He didn't think of it. He was eating his sundae," Trisha said.

"Oh!" Lena and Joe and Honor said. "Oh!"

"So I took Don out of his highchair and walked away," Trisha said. "Slowly. I carried Don so slowly through the tables and by the restaurant desk and down a hall and past the ladies' room— and then I ran around a corner, down another hall to a door, and through the parking lot to the car! I slid under the wheel, put Don beside me, and hit the gas. In less than a minute we were on the highway going west. To Cedar Falls."

Honor, Joe and Lena took deep breath.

Don banged a spoon on his high chair.

"But you didn't have Brandon's car when you got here," Joe said.

"I was too scared to drive it very far—a car like that? The police were after it, I was sure—chasing a kidnapper."

"You told us somebody dropped you off here," Honor said. "A woman."

"I got away from Brandon and was driving behind a bus, and its sign said 'Waterloo.' When it turned to drive into Independence, I followed it, parked Brandon's car around the corner from the bus station, locked it, and Don and I rode to Waterloo. A nice lady, a stranger, gave us a ride here."

No one at the table spoke for a while. Lena poured fresh coffee for them. Trisha took a sip of hers and sighed. "I'll have to leave this morning, I'm afraid. I hate to go—you've all been so good to me."

"You have to get back to your two jobs," Honor said.

"Just one. I can't work for Brandon any more. I'd be too scared. My best clothes are in a suitcase in his car, so I'll lose them. He'll come to my apartment. Can't go there. When he's drunk..." She didn't finish the sentence.

"You'll still have your other job," Lena said.

"Not a very good one," Trisha said. "Typing orders for half a day. Not enough to even pay the rent."

"You don't have a car," Joe said.

"Never did. I can hitchhike back to Chicago," Trisha said. "I've done that a lot. I hitchhiked to my classes at the secretarial school."

"You can't do that," Lena said. "It's dangerous."

"But it gets you there," Trisha said.

"Let me give you money for the trip," Lena said. "After all you've done for us. Rent money, too, and money for food, until you're safely settled with a job."

There was a chorus of "Yes!"

"But your family expects you to care for your mother?" Joe said.

"If I don't have a choice, I'll be back where I started years ago." Trisha stared at her empty plate.

"What if you don't go back at all?" Honor said.

"Where would I go?"

"Maybe you'd like to live in Iowa," Honor said. "There are jobs for secretaries in Cedar Falls and Waterloo, and you can stay with Joe and me until you're settled. You could even go to the college here. You've saved Don for us, and Brandon, too. How can we *ever* pay you back for that?"

"Yes," Joe said. "Be our guest. Your family can take their turn, and care for your mother."

"Why not live at my house?" Lena said. "You've been invited to stay next door, but Honor and Joe are trying to redecorate their place before he starts teaching at the college. You might want to stay with me for a while, and escape the clutter and noise."

"Oh!" Trisha cried, staring from one of them to another. "Do you think I could?"

"You can certainly see you're very welcome here," Honor said. "Two homes to choose from. And you're about my size. I can give you clothes. And you can pay us back by being my bridesmaid."

"What?" Trisha said. "Bridesmaid?"

Honor and Joe explained. They were married, they said, but they wanted to have a real signed-and-sealed marriage at the courthouse.

"A courthouse!" Lena cried. "Married at a courthouse! Can you imagine? I told them that was barbaric!"

Joe and Honor looked embarrassed. They needed their roof repaired, they said, not a parade down an aisle. Their basement was damp in one corner. There were bats in the attic. They needed a new front porch.

Joe saw Honor shrinking away from the very thought of a wedding. Of course. It was too late. Brandon had stolen that from her.

"Joe," Lena said. "Think of Honor in a beautiful white dress and veil."

Joe gave Honor a look that made her blush. She shut her eyes, thinking. Finally she said: "A very, *very* private affair?"

"A family picnic...a wedding picnic!" Lena said. "Let's start a tradition in my back yard. I've got a six-foot fence."

Don was banging his highchair tray up and down; Honor lifted him into her lap. "Maybe," she said.

19

"My mother hasn't called," Joe said when they finished breakfast. But as they carried dishes into the kitchen, the telephone rang. Joe answered it. After a while he returned to say: "Brandon came to Mom's place last night, had supper, said almost nothing, and went to sleep on her couch. When she woke at six this morning, he was gone."

"Back to Rockford, I suppose," Lena said. "He *has* got a job there, hasn't he? I wish him well, but I'm glad he's gone. Honor, you told me once you have a wedding dress."

"In my closet upstairs," Honor said.

"Let's see it," Lena said. "I say it's bad luck if you wear it."

"While you're looking at dresses, I'll go out looking for Tux," Joe said.

The three went upstairs, and Honor brought her wedding dress, veil and white slippers out of her closet and laid them on her new bedspread before Lena and Trisha.

"Don't even think of it!" Lena said. "What do you want—a hex on your wedded life? Joe can make caterpillar sacks out of the veil, and we'll use the dress for lining my bathroom curtains. And get rid of those shoes! Walk into your married life in those? Bad luck! Bad luck! You can fill them with dirt and grow houseplants—that's safe enough. We'll get a new bridal gown for you, and a brides-maid dress for Trisha that she can use when she goes to dances around here. We'll rent a white tuxedo for the very handsome bridegroom, and have a wedding banquet in my garden—take lots of pictures to hang on a wall so Don can see them as he grows up. Right in my back yard with the high fences! You can go to the courthouse to make it legal if you want, but let's plan a very, very private affair—just what Honor wants!"

No one knew how to argue with Lena, or the weatherman: he was promising a week of sunshine, then a week of rain. So Joe, Honor, Lena and Trisha went to the Waterloo courthouse, and Joe and Honor were a legal couple at last. Joe rented a tuxedo. Emily called to say she'd wear the formal she'd worn in Chicago. The rest of the wedding party shopped for Honor's wedding dress, veil and slippers, then bought long dresses for Lena and Trisha.

Every day before dark, Honor and Joe walked the streets looking for Tux.

"Tux!" they called every now and then, and asked everyone they met: "Have you seen a big, black and white Maine Coon cat?"

No one had.

"At least we didn't find him dead," Honor said.

"Could he have kept running after Brandon's car?" Lena asked. "How far?"

"He might have been hurt," Trisha said. "Just as we turned on the highway. He landed on grass, I think, but Brandon threw him out of the car pretty hard, he was so mad at him."

Joe went to the pound, but none of the caged cats were Tux. He put a notice in the town paper...talked to the police...even described the cat to garbage crews in the alleys. And then the day of the "wedding party" came.

Emily had asked for the day off, and Joe brought her from Des

Moines soon after breakfast. The October weather was glorious, autumn flowers were still in bloom, and the ground was dry. By one o'clock, Lena's kitchen sent the fragrance of delicious food into Lena's garden as a handsome bridegroom in a tuxedo, a bride in a cloud of white, and three ladies in long, rustling dresses brought a wedding dinner to tables in the shade.

Lena had bought an expensive camera for her foreign travel, and took pictures of everyone—pretty shots...embarrassing shots.

They were finishing the last of their ice cream and cake when Trisha, wandering along the back drive with her dish of dessert, yelled "Joe! Honor!" and ran back to the others, her spoon and dish in one hand and a cascade of pink bridesmaid skirts in the other. "Come and look! Oh!"

They ran with her to a straggling row of bushes Joe hadn't cleared yet from his garden. Under dead leaves and branches lay a black and white Maine Coon.

Joe knelt beside him, not caring for the knees of his white tuxedo. "Tux!"

The cat moaned.

"He's hurt," Joe said. "I've got to take him to the vet before the office closes!" He ran for one of his planting trays, and Honor helped him lift the big cat into it. The two of them carried him to Joe's car in the back drive, climbed in the car and drove away down the alley.

It was late afternoon, but the veterinarian still had patients in his waiting room when a bride and a groom carrying a cat on a tray burst in from the parking lot. The row of people in chairs stared, while assorted dogs growled and barked at white wool, white satin and tulle.

"We're sorry to rush in on you like this," Joe said to the vet, "but we've just found our cat, and we think he's badly hurt."

"Bring him in here," the vet said, and led the bride, groom and a cat on a tray to another room. He examined Tux for a moment, then went to the open door. "I have an emergency here," he told the waiting people and animals. "Will all of you kindly wait for a few minutes?"

"Is he badly hurt?" Honor asked, as the veterinarian came back and closed the door.

"His leg is dislocated. I'll need to work on it right away."

Tux was groaning, but a shot soon put him to sleep.

"Will he be able to walk?" Honor asked.

"He's in the prime of life," the veterinarian said. "He'll be on four legs again in a few weeks. You folks had better wait in the other room until I finish."

The bride and groom went out to sit on chairs—two embarrassed people nested in veiling. Some of the pet owners smiled at them. Joe and Honor smiled back with the sort of raised-eyebrow, rueful smile that says, "Pretty weird, isn't it?"

They carried limp Tux home and put him on his favorite rug under their old kitchen stove. He slept all night, they thought. But when they came down for breakfast, Tux had eaten everything on his saucer, and sat under the table, licking the cast on his leg as thoroughly as the rest of him.

"This is your house now," Joe told Honor, scooping fried eggs on plates. "Sad to say, it's hardly livable. Lena told me she'll lend us money so we can start work on all that still needs to be done. I'm in hopes I can spend part of each day at my office planning my classes."

"New bathrooms and kitchen as Lena's wedding present—can't believe it! " Honor said. "We've got to choose wallpaper and paint and curtains, linoleum, cabinets, furniture…thank heaven we can eat at Lena's while the work's being done."

Joe looked around the worn, shabby kitchen. "Should we start here? Do you want to have a sink where that old one is? We can have tile floors in this room, and maybe in my potting room and plant room, too—easy clean-up. Maybe a breakfast nook under the windows for a garden view? Lena put her washer and dryer in the kitchen—do you want ours here? Wood cabinets?"

212

Plumbers and carpenters arrived in a few days with room plans and catalogs. Joe and Honor trudged through second-hand furniture stores, and found an almost new sofa and matching upholstered chairs from an estate sale…dark green for their green, gold and white living room. They bought two old, handsome tables that Joe could refinish for that room, and watched a gas fire like Lena's installed in their stone and marble fireplace.

Autumn rain fell, day after day. The newly-weds—and often Trisha and Lena—filled cracks, painted and wall-papered. Workmen pounded and sawed. Rugs went down, curtains went up, ancient toilets and rusty sinks went off in a truck. Don would have a room in both houses, and they papered his second bedroom blue, white and green, with wallpaper bluebirds flying in a strip under the ceiling.

One warm afternoon the "park girls," as they called themselves, were enjoying ginger ale and cupcakes on Lena's porch with the Lombards, Lena and Trisha. "My back yard's still a wasteland," Joe said, refilling cider glasses. "It's nothing but a trash heap from our back door to the alley—a wilderness of dying bushes, and a fence half-down along Lena's back drive."

"At least there's not much hackberry shade—Lena's tree is too far away," Charlotte said, and smiled at Honor. Don sat on Honor's lap, waving his plump hands at everybody as if directing the conversation.

"I wonder…" Joe turned to Lena. "Would you care if there's no border between our lots, except your back driveway, and we treat our back yards as one yard—a clean sweep?"

"Why not?" Lena said.

"Lilacs behind our houses, a hedge to hide the alley?" Joe said as he stared down Lena's side stairs to his yard. "And wide flower-erbeds, English style—I'll raise perennials from seed on my light carts."

Sandra watched Joe go down the stairs and back to his garden. "You've got your job now," she said to Trisha. "How's your house hunt coming?"

"I've found an apartment not far from here. On Tremont, that big house on the corner with all the porches," Trisha said. "Now I'm looking for second-hand furniture. I've got a bed and a chair. I ought to be ready to start college the second semester."

Charlotte finished her cupcake and smiled at Honor. "And you've worked on your novel?"

"What's happened to Catherine?" Rafaela asked.

"Read us something!" Amy said.

Honor gave Lena the baby, went upstairs for her manuscript, and sat before a view of gold and bronze park trees. She sighed. "It's *work*. Right now, I'm trying to show how Catherine sees the girls in her high school."

"She's never been with girls her age—right?" Rafaela said. "I remember. Raised in the middle of nowhere by two men."

"Let me read this part, and see what you think," Honor said. "It's during the last war, of course, but I don't think high schools have changed that much. Catherine's living in Margie's home, and she's watching Margie and her boyfriend at school, just the way you might watch strange animals in a zoo. She hasn't been raised as a usual American girl. So what does she see? That's the hard, hard part. Here it is:"

It took Catherine quite a while to understand what Margie was doing when she talked to a boy, because it was like a dance, and complicated. First, Margie's voice changed when she saw her boyfriend Jim. She had a loud, excited way of talking to her girl-friends, or else she whispered and giggled, but when she saw Jim coming to her in the school hall, Margie's voice softened; it wasn't loud or excited. Her eyes changed, too: the eyelids drooped a little.

In fact, Margie drooped all over. She didn't hold her books and notebooks tight; she played around with them instead. She didn't stand on both feet or hold her head up. When Margie saw Jim coming, she made herself smaller—she'd slide her spine down a doorframe an inch or two. If there was nothing to lean against, she'd stand on one foot, and bend the knee that was holding her up to make herself shorter. Margie never looked straight at Jim, unless she tipped her head to one side. She didn't form words with her mouth in the same way: her lips pouted instead, and hung open a little. Her eyes went up and down his face as if it were a ladder, not staying anywhere. Most of the time she looked at the floor.

Jim was different. You could see the difference from far away, just watching the two of them in the hall. He gripped whatever he had in his hands tight, and usually stood on both feet, looking down at Margie. He didn't shout, or slap her on the back, the way he shouted and whacked his friends. He looked uncomfortable.

*When he got back to the group of boys, they hit him with their
big hands.*

The women on the porch had little smiles on their faces. "Oh,
yes," Charlotte said. "I've seen how girls act with boys. Done it
myself. I don't think boys have changed much since the 'forties,
have they?"

"There was a girl in my town who didn't act that way," Rafaela
said. "I don't know whether anybody else noticed it, but I did.
Now that I think back, I believe people *did* notice. Such little
things. She'd walk right up and stand on two feet and look boys
in the eye."

"Interesting!" Amy said. "I'm going to start watching what girls
do." She looked puzzled. "What do I do when I meet a man?"

Don slid from Lena's lap to stand for a moment. Then he
dropped to hands and knees and crawled on the porch floor from
one woman to another. Tux followed him, until Don pulled
himself up by a chair, holding Tux's tail in a firm grip.

"Don's got his daddy's eyes," Charlotte said. "He's going to
look just like Joe."

Day by day, Honor was beginning to believe that Joe's house
was her house, her son was his son, and she could step
into Joe's arms at any hour and his arms would hold her. When
their bodies touched as they worked on their house, they stopped
to kiss. While they raked leaves, happiness played over them like
the sunshine.

Honor wrote for hours her room. Sometimes her words worked,
and she threw pages in the air, amazed. Sometimes she groaned.
October gilded her typewriter with light from golden trees, and
struck rich russet veins in the wood of her desk and bookshelves.
A glance at the bed gave her memories of Joe sprawling there with
a smile, or lying asleep in her arms. Books had begun to line the
room, shelf after shelf, and she could see Joe in their garden from
the big window. Trucks brought loads of good garden soil down
the alley and, shovel by shovel-full, she helped Joe build up flower
beds, and seed new lawns.

The last day of October was warm, even when the sun was going
down. Honor left her writing, and sat holding Don on Lena's
front porch. Children were leaving the park. It was Emily's free

215

afternoon, so Trisha and Lena had driven to Des Moines to shop with her, and stay at a hotel that night.

She heard a screen door close. Joe climbed up the bank from his house, smiling at her. He was halfway up to the porcs when a car pulled up at the park curb.

"That's Carl Bushnell," Joe said. He ran downstairs, shook Carl's hand as he left his car, and the two men climbed to Lena's porch.

"Honor!" Carl said, and looked at Don in her lap. "I haven't seen you folks since last year, I'm afraid, and now you two have this young fellow!"

"He's Don," Honor said. She lifted Don to his feet, and the baby waved his arms and pushed his feet hard against her lap. "Donald Joseph Lombard."

"Congratulations!" Carl said. "We've been out of touch, I'm afraid: my company is expanding, and we're opening new offices..."

For a moment Honor thought Carl was going to touch Don's curly black hair, but Carl hesitated, then shook Don's small hand. "A fine boy," Carl said. He straightened up and looked at Joe. "Certainly looks like his dad. Definitely a Lombard. I've just come from Chicago. Is your mother here?"

Joe said, "I'm afraid not. She'll be in Des Moines with Honor's aunt and a friend until tomorrow."

Honor got up with Don and said, "Won't you come in?"

"I'm sorry to miss your mother," Carl said to Joe as they went inside. "I had a few talks with her at the wedding, and we have a lot of respect for her."

"Do sit by the fire," Honor said. "And would you like some spiced cider? Or coffee?" She put Don in his playpen.

"Coffee would be fine," Carl said. Joe lit the fire.

"And you'll stay for dinner, won't you?" Honor asked. "And for the night? We'd be pleased to have you. Joe and I live next door, so we have plenty of room in these big, old houses."

"I'm sorry," Carl said, "but I can't even stay for dinner. I'm on a tight schedule, but I had to come see you."

Honor went to the kitchen for coffee and heard Carl say, "Two houses side by side. How did you manage that?"

"Just luck," Joe said. "Ours came on the market again just as I was offered a teaching job at the teacher's college here. I start in the spring."

"Good for you," Carl said. "Congratulations." Honor came with a tray of coffee cups, cream and sugar. It seemed to her that Carl looked years older than he had at Katie's wedding.

"Your wife and your daughters are well?" she asked Carl.

"The family in Chicago is fine, thanks," Carl said. "Brandon went to work for me in Rockford, as you know."

"Mother told us Brandon was in Rockford, but we haven't heard from him for weeks," Joe said. "We have his new number, but we can't seem to reach him, and we didn't want to bother you. Early this month we missed him when he came with his secretary when we were out of town."

"He was here? When?"

"October fourth."

Carl stared at the fire for a few moments. "I'm sure you know that Brandon had problems with drink. He was struggling to handle...everything, I guess, but he wasn't making good as a traveling associate."

"I'm sorry to hear that," Joe said.

"When I first met him, I didn't know about that problem of his," Carl said, not looking at them. His eyes were on the fire. "It seemed to me for a while that Brandon was...this sounds sentimental, but it's true...it seemed to me that he might be the son I'd always wanted. He even had a degree in business. I couldn't believe my luck. Katie was so young—she might have fallen for the member of some band, or a gold-digger—she's not the steady type, like her mother."

Carl sighed. "But the marriage wasn't going well, I'm afraid. By the time Brandon left Chicago, we knew him pretty well, and Katie didn't want to go to Rockford with him. You remember what trouble he had at their wedding. We got him help after a while—Alcoholics Anonymous, psychiatrist, all that. He just wouldn't show up for appointments."

"How sad it is for all of you," Honor said.

"We've worried about him," Joe said.

"When I met Brandon, he seemed to have everything," Carl said. "The training, the youth, the energy. And he lived with us for quite a while before he married Katie—we were friends, until the booze drove us apart. I've lost more than one good Bushnell employee to drink." Carl rubbed his eyes as if they were tired. He said nothing for a while, but looked at Don. The baby had fallen

217

asleep in the playpen nearby, one arm around his toy monkey, and Tux on guard.

"I had a meeting scheduled in Rockford last week," Carl said at last. "I thought I'd check on Brandon—we hadn't been able to contact him for a while, either. We never knew that he came here to visit while you were gone."

"Did you and Brandon have time together last week in Rockford?" Honor asked.

"I never saw him," Carl said. "Couldn't find him."

"Couldn't find him!" Honor and Joe said in chorus.

"No. I went to the Bushnell office in Rockford and found nobody had been there for a while—not Brandon, not his secretary. When I checked Brandon's apartment, the manager said Brandon hadn't been there for weeks." Carl kept his eyes on the fire. "The manager mentioned that a young woman often came there with Brandon, and I found a woman's clothes in the closet."

For a moment or two Carl was silent. Then he said, "I couldn't hunt for him myself, and I began to worry. Finally I hired a detective. After a while he called to report that Brandon's car hadn't been found in Illinois. Or anywhere. He checked the police, airport records, trains, tours…"

"He just disappeared?" Honor said in a shocked voice. "When he had a job? Responsibilities?"

"Brandon might have taken a break from his job with me easily enough," Carl said. "Taken a vacation, you know. But he had a secretary, and we discovered that she hadn't shown up for weeks at a second job she had in the afternoons. We couldn't be sure, of course, that Brandon had taken someone with him, but my detective began to investigate this young woman—Patricia Boyle— and found that an agency had placed her in our Bushnell office in Rockford, and at her afternoon job, also. No one knew much about her at our Bushnell office, but the detective found a secretary who worked with Patricia in the afternoons: Sally Finley. She remembered that Patricia said a fellow was taking her to 'Lovers Beach' on Lake Michigan early this month, and she was excited about going. The detective checked, and found that 'Mr. and Mrs. Brandon Lombard' had made a reservation at that resort, but they never turned up."

"Patricia Boyle—'Trisha'—left Brandon during his trip here early this month," Joe said. "She's staying with us. But we assumed that Brandon would visit his mother when he left here, and then go back to Rockford. He was driving a red Corvette."

They sat quiet for a moment, watching the fire. Then Joe said in a low voice, "I may be wrong, Carl, but I think you know something more. This can't be easy for you, and we thank you for coming."

"You're right. That's not all I know," Carl said. "I'm not sorry, I guess, that your mother isn't here. Will the two of you tell her everything I've said?"

Joe and Honor said they would.

"Then I have to say that the detective called me yesterday," Carl said. "A farmer was doing some fall plowing in eastern Iowa near Dubuque, and he happened to see what he thought was a car half sunk in a creek about a mile from his place. There's a wide creek there, in thick woods. You couldn't see a car from the highway, though it ran pretty near. It was Brandon's car. Brandon was in it."

Carl looked at Don asleep in the playpen, his arms around his sock monkey and his small chest rising and falling with each breath. Above him, Lena's books gleamed on living-room shelves, row after row.

The fire flamed and sank, flamed again. Children shouted in the park across the street, playing games in the gathering dark.

"I'm so sorry," Carl said at last. "To have to come and tell you."

"We thank you so much," Honor said.

"Yes," Joe said. "It's a kind... and hard... thing to do."

Carl stared into the fire.

"Brandon," Joe said.

"Yes," Carl said. "He was in the new Corvette I bought him. He loved that car. You say he came here, and then left. The coroner believes he died almost instantly."

No one spoke for a while. Finally Carl said: "A strange thing. The car was smashed so that its trunk opened. There were two suitcases still in the trunk. I brought them in my car for you today, hoping you knew where this 'Trisha' was. You can give her case to her, if you will. But a load of what seemed to be baby clothes and baby food had spilled from the trunk and was sunk in creek mud. An empty baby bottle floated along the bank."

Sunset light was fading. Lights began to show in houses across the park. Children ran past, calling.

219

"I had Brandon sent to a morgue in Dubuque," Carl said. "I wanted to tell your family myself—I couldn't let you hear any other way. And you must tell me what you want me to do. For him, you know. When you and his mother have time to plan." He handed Joe his card.

"We can't thank you enough," Joe said in a low, dull voice. "All of us."

"Please tell your mother—and Honor's aunt, too—how sorry our family is," Carl said, getting up from his chair. "Will you call me when you're able to make plans? I'm afraid we've lost her son...your brother...Katie's husband."

"It was so good of you to come," Honor said. "Such a dreadful trip to make. Won't you tell your family how sorry we are?"

"I didn't want you to hear it any other way," Carl said. "I've always wanted a grandson. I suppose if Katie had had a boy, he might have looked like your son did... like a Lombard."

"We're both very grateful," Joe said, and shook Carl's hand.

Honor followed the men out on the porch. Wind rose in the dark autumn night, rustling dry leaves. Joe brought the suitcases from Carl's car. Carl drove away.

Honor said, "We couldn't tell him."

"No," Joe said.

"We could never tell him. Not any of it."

"No."

"Your mother!" Honor cried. "When we tell her, how can she bear it?"

For a moment they could do nothing but listen to the rising wind.

"It was raining that night, remember?" Joe said. "Brandon must have found his Corvette in Independence. He was drunk. Driving too fast."

Honor said, "Carl would never say so, but I'm sure he blames me for Katie's sad marriage. They couldn't have been happy—Brandon moved to Rockford without her. And if I'd married Brandon, he'd have found a job, and we'd have rented an apartment and had Don..."

"You'd have been happy?" Joe kissed her tear-wet face.

"Brandon would be *alive!*" she said. "I wouldn't have to remember how his friends tormented him because I 'left him at

220

the altar!' I threw his ring in his face...shamed him at his wedding and ruined his wedding night, hurt his wife, kept his own son from him! How would I have felt if he'd kept my own baby away from me—wouldn't even let me see him?"

"Brandon went through life like some kind of crazy rocket," Joe said. "You didn't make him that way."

"I thought I loved him," Honor said. "I really thought he loved me."

"He wouldn't look behind, or care what he'd done. Didn't look ahead, either," Joe said. "You couldn't stop him. What kind of life would he have had? Or you and Don, if you'd married him."

After a while, Honor said, "How will we ever, ever tell your mother?"

Over Joe's shoulder she saw a small glimmer coming up the street. It traveled along the park now, climbing the hill, and grew larger as she watched, then broke into glowing orange balls.

"Halloween," she said.

"Halloween?" Joe said.

Honor brought a basket from a corner of the porch. "Lena and Emily got the treats ready before they left."

Orange pumpkin lanterns bobbed along the park. Three lanterns stopped in front of Lena's house, and beggars climbed Lena's steps.

The porch light fell on them as Honor held out the basket and called, "Trick or Treat!"

A skeleton climbed the last step and reached for candy. His white skull had no neck; its broken grin hung on his shoulders, and its gap-toothed jaw was too long for the huge nose hole and the even larger eye-holes, deep and empty. But the skeleton held a round cardboard head on a stick: it was a curly-headed, blank-eyed child's face like a big sucker, held cheek to cheek with a death's head.

The witch grabbed a candy bar. Her mask was as stark white as a china plate, except for the huge hook of the nose, and vacant eyes. The face was so big that it was more of a breast-plate than a face—someone else's mouthful of long fangs hanging over a child's rumpled jeans and sneakers.

The ghost dragged his sheet along behind the other two. His eyes and mouth were pulled down in agony: a silent scream.

"Take off your masks," Honor said.

Three hideous faces stared at her.

"Will you?" she said. "Each of you can have *two* treats from the basket if you do."

The witch was the first to lift her fanged, blank-eyed witch face to show a small blond girl with chocolate smeared on her chin, darker than blood. She took another chocolate bar.

The skeleton raised his dead-white skull from his shoulders. The cardboard child's face on his stick wobbled beside the little boy's grim, intense eyes. He peered under his death's head, pawing in the candy, and finally chose two lemon drops.

The ghost struggled with his cocoon of sheet, until the witch helped him push his screaming mask aside. His small face was blank as he spilled candy from the basket, trying to find two chocolate kisses. He grabbed them and followed the others downstairs to the dark street.

Orange lights bobbed across the park, blinked out and were gone.

A NATURAL DEATH
by Nancy Price

This novel of the Carolinas in pre-Civil War days is beautiful, terrible, heart-breaking – A powerful evocation of what it meant to be black and a slave.   *-Publishers Weekly*

A rich first novel with a large cast of characters that movingly dramatizes culture and life in the South Carolina of the 1840s...quite remarkable.   *-Kirkus*

The author is a poet; her first novel is a rich and realistic account of vividly recalled times past.   *-Chicago Tribune*

A brilliant first novel by poet Nancy Price, deserving of respect for unerring detail, realistic treatment, and accurate reporting of rhythm and idiom. The Carolina rice-growing country in the 1850s becomes so real under Ms. Price's hand that the smells and sounds remain long after the pages are closed...A sensitive and humane writer of merit.   *-Houston Post*

An authentic and fascinating evocation of the past.
- Shirley Ann Grau
Washington Post

Mesmerizing prose...frightening, absorbing and enlightening reading.
-Cleveland Press

From the standpoint of a historian, it is a novel I could not put down, for the detail is as fascinating as it was accurate and compelling.   *-Carl Degler*

I felt as though I had been living in the terrifying world of a South Carolina slave plantation...A fascinating novel: vivid, poetic, very moving.   *-Ann Petry, author of* The Street

223

My God, what film it would make...There is nobility in these characters–and absolutely no sentimentalization. It's not just fiction: it's
Literature.   *-Mary Carter, author of* La Maestra

The novel draws the reader...we read as things happen, not as if they
once happened...as if we are watching a film. This is a sensitive,
sympathetic and historically accurate novel. And it is by far one of
the best about the antebellum South.   *-Providence Journal*

An authentic and fascinating evocation of the past.
                                               -Washington Post

Price's portrayal of both sides of the slave society is both persuasive
and saddening.   *-New York Times Book Review*

The book is saturated with that inimitable atmosphere that is South
Carolina...[a] long and absorbing novel.
                                               -Chattanooga Times

A splendid, strengthening addition to the literary voice of
the South.   *-News and Observer, Raleigh, N.C.*

AN ACCOMPLISHED WOMAN
by Nancy Price

A seductive, almost hypnotic book...so much of its intensity and suc-
cess derive from the manner of its telling ...a language...that avoids
difficulty and unreadability. I found myself racing...excited by all its
elements and by the way Price has managed to put them in sophisti-
cated and engaging relation to each other.   *-Chicago Tribune*

Elegant detail.   *-New Yorker*

Nancy Price is a very talented writer and her characters are unique,
her story line is inventive and unusual. This is a moving, even terrifying novel with rare richness, subtlety and depth.
                                               -Publishers Weekly

Strikingly illustrates the extent to which we are all products of our own and others' imagination. *-New Republic*

Price can create the essence of a scene with a few vivid words...Intense and deeply moving...a touching love story that reveals things all women should know about themselves.
-Los Angeles Times

Catherine Buckingham was reared...as a thoroughly liberalized female in an unliberalized age. Her struggles to adjust create a stunning yet tender odyssey...Readability issues effortlessly from Ms. Price's fine prose. *-Cleveland Press*

Heady and powerful. *-Booklist*

Ms. Price tells her story quietly, allowing points of understanding to make themselves unobtrusively and, therefore, indelibly...It's altogether a very neat piece of writing, and Ms. Price is a valuable artist.
-Philadelphia Bulletin

A young girl's coming of age, coming to terms, coming to grips. Prices's understatement, her very tentativeness, makes for a story that can only be described as innocently passionate and achingly erotic.
-Detroit News

A sheer pleasure to read. *-Chattanooga Times*

Finely written, whole chunks of this second novel are dedicated warmly to the proposition of indefatigable character–and that's very nourishing. *-Kirkus Reviews*

A heady, powerful novel. *-Advance Booklist*

What would happen if a girl were allowed complete freedom [in 1920-30] to explore, to experiment with life?...Nancy Price has written a fascinating novel, a brilliant and deeply disturbing study of what it means to be a woman. *-Charlotte N.C. News*

Nancy Price, novelist and poet, has blended a keen feminist sensibility with a fine poetic style in this strangely haunting story...a meaningful statement about...the unrealized potential of generations of women and the lifelong impact of an ideal love affair.

-Cleveland Plain Dealer

What unfolds *is* a kind of "love affair that never existed"...Price's stunning diction, human compassion and intellectual rigor not only portray "An Accomplished Woman"–but how women are "accomplished."

-Des Moines Register

After I'd read the last page I could only lay the book down and stare at nothing for a long time, my cheeks wet with tears...Read this book, it will change your heart, not your head.   *-Sacramento Bee*

To describe more of the story is to take away from the sheer pleasure that it is to read the whole novel. Rarely does one come across a love story such as this told with so much sensitivity.

-Chattanooga Times

Compelling and poignant...More than just an accomplished novel; it is a work of art.   *-Houston Chronicle*

SLEEPING WITH THE ENEMY
by Nancy Price
(filmed by Twentieth Century Fox and starring Julia Roberts)

A sensitive and humane writer of merit.   *-The Houston Post*

Powerful, moving and well-controlled thriller...chilling scenes of observation and pursuit, and the author...brings the novel to a triumphant conclusion.   *-Publishers Weekly*

Rich characterizations, an ability to move the reader emotionally, and a lovely sense of atmosphere...right on the money.

-San Francisco Chronicle

Absorbing...sensual...the reader roots for Sara/Laura all the way.
-*West Coast Review of Books*

The plot [is] every woman's nightmare...mesmerizing...You won't be able to put it down.
-*Houston Chronicle*

A tense, tightly woven novel...Price has managed in the writing to be absolutely faithful to the villains as well as the victims...The characters and events are so vivid that one is troubled, longs to know what becomes of these people.
-*Louise Erdrich*,
Minneapolis Star and Tribune

Terror grips like the coils of an anaconda.
-*London Observer*

NIGHT WOMAN
by Nancy Price

The tension rises almost unbearably.
-*Express-News (San Antonio)*

NIGHT WOMAN is a brilliantly disturbing study in co-dependency, but it is also a story of courage...Price is masterful in her characterizations: the characters are frighteningly real...Much as you might want to, you won't be able to put it down until you've read the last page.
-*Houston Chronicle*

Following up on her novel SLEEPING WITH THE ENEMY, Price returns with a terrific suspenser...Don't even wait for the movie.
-*Kirkus Reviews*

Highly recommended.
-*Library Journal*

Well-written and engaging...an intriguing situation. The book pulls its punches until the very last chapters...gritty, wry characterization, chilling images of insanity...long, ultimately satisfying...will keep readers flipping pages.
-*Publishers Weekly*

NIGHT WOMAN is too fine, too moving, to be labeled derivative...Highly recommended.
                                                    -Chicago Tribune

SLEEPING WITH THE ENEMY...was made into a blockbuster movie. NIGHT WOMAN could do the same...a story that is run through the crucible of seething, rampant emotion.
                                        -Macon Beacon (Georgia)

Gripping story...a nail-biter of a climax...engrossing.
                                            -Kansas City Star

NIGHT WOMAN is so well written that it raises the psychological thriller to another level.   *-The Orlando Sentinel*